HIS MOTHER'S BONES

An absolutely gripping killer thriller full of twists

STEVE PARKER

Detective Ray Paterson Book 7

JOFFE BOOKS

Joffe Books, London
www.joffebooks.com

First published in Great Britain in 2021

Cover art by Nick Castle

ISBN: 978-1-78931-889-0

For Little Star.
Welcome.

CHAPTER ONE

Sir Scott Anderson, Metropolitan Commissioner of Police, had had a rough night. His first disturbance was a telephone call from a DCI Goodwin late the previous evening, and thereafter he'd been unable to get back to sleep. DCI Goodwin had sent him a video to watch. A video of a dying police officer. A dying declaration. A dying declaration that Anderson hoped would finally end the careers and see the imprisonment of the two police officers who had plagued his short time as commissioner. Two police officers he considered to be wild, destructive and damaging to the integrity of the Metropolitan Police Service: Detective Superintendent Ray Paterson and Detective Inspector Johnny Clocks. He loathed the pair of them for their insubordination, their arrogance and their complete disinterest in following any rules. But what irked him the most was that somehow these two slippery bastards had always outfoxed him.

He pulled on his Lycra cycling shirt and adjusted it until he felt comfortable, wriggled into his leggings and shorts and picked up his shoes. Normally his driver would have picked him up and driven him to work, but he felt like he needed the exercise. He checked his appearance in the full-length mirror in his bedroom, turned sideways, tucked in his stomach and grinned to himself. More than good enough. He would change into the suit he kept in his locker when he got to Scotland Yard.

His appointment with the deputy commissioner wasn't official but, given the information he'd received the night before, he knew that he wouldn't be refused. He picked up his backpack, cast a final glance at himself in the mirror and headed downstairs to the kitchen. The smell of toast and peanut butter hung in the air.

'Morning, dear!' he called to his wife, Alice. She was seated at the kitchen table, still in her dressing gown and holding a cup of tea. In front of her was a small plate covered in crumbs with a couple of crusts of toast pushed to the side.

'Good morning. You sound cheerful.' She turned to look at him. 'Where are you off to?'

'This one mine?' He pointed to a mug of tea on the counter. His wife nodded. 'Thanks. Actually, I'm off to work this morning.'

Alice frowned. 'Work? I thought you were suspended.'

He took a quick sip of his tea. 'Not suspended, dear. On gardening leave. I did tell you that.'

'It's the same thing though, isn't it?'

'No. Let's not get into that again, please. With a bit of luck, I should be reinstated later on. I'll let you know how it goes.'

She shrugged. 'What makes you think you'll be back at work? What's happened?'

He smiled, walked across to the table and picked up his laptop, left there the previous night. 'I think I've got something on those two officers that may well see me exonerated from those ridiculous bullying allegations.'

Alice sighed and shook her head. 'You *think*?'

'I *know*.' He stuffed the laptop into his backpack and snapped the top shut. 'You're fed up with me going on about them. I'm sorry. I really am. But you have no idea what they're like. They must be brought to heel. Someone has to teach them that they're not bloody untouchable.'

'And that someone has to be you, does it?'

He looked at her and tried to stifle a feeling of contempt. 'Well, I am the commissioner so, yes, it's on me to bring these two . . . reprobates before the courts for their abominable behaviour.'

'That's a new one . . . *abominable behaviour*. Not heard you use that before. Is that a crime then, dear?'

He took a deep breath before answering. She didn't understand. Would never understand. 'Depends on the behaviour, *dear*.'

'So, what are their actual crimes? I think it's about time you told me.'

He held his cup under the running tap and wiped it around with a cloth before placing it upside down on the draining board. 'Well, let me see . . . violence . . . inciting acts of violence . . . lying under oath . . . aiding and abetting murder . . . attempted murder . . . actual murder. You name it, they'll have done it.'

'And you have evidence now? That's why you're going in, yes?'

He cleared his throat. 'I have what I believe to be compelling evidence of their involvement in a murder, yes.'

Alice nodded slowly. 'Okay. That's good. Of course it is. But . . . if this falls apart, will you please just give this up and leave it alone? Look at the trouble you're in now. Just take the money and retire. You've done your bit, for God's sake.' She pushed her cup away, reached into her dressing gown pocket and took out a pack of cigarettes.

He scowled at her. 'Not in the house please, Alice. We've spoken about this, haven't we?'

She took a deep breath then tossed the pack on the table next to the cup. 'When will your driver be here?'

'Driver? Not today. I know you don't take much notice of me anymore, but did you not spot the fact that I'm wearing cycling gear? It's a beautiful day, so I thought I'd take the bike. It's only twenty minutes or so.'

He bent down and kissed Alice on the back of the head. 'I'll call you later to let you know how it's all gone. Bye.'

Without turning she nodded. 'Okay, bye.'

* * *

She waited until she heard the front door close before breathing a sigh of relief. She reached into the other pocket of her dressing gown and pulled out a small yellow tube of antidepressants. She opened the lid, popped two tablets and washed them down with the remnants of her now lukewarm tea.

'I'm leaving you,' she said to the empty room.

CHAPTER TWO

Christine Lord became aware of a bright light behind her eyelids as she swam up from the depths of her unconsciousness. The brightness caused her to squint without opening her eyes. In that moment between sleep and wakefulness, there was a burst of confusion as she tried to hold on to the now rapidly receding dream in which she'd stood at her sink preparing the vegetables for the family's evening meal. The night's offering was to be a tasty vegetable pie with potatoes, a firm favourite with her two children, particularly her daughter, Jeanine. Children? It seemed funny to call them that now they were fully grown. Both children were at Oxford University. Jamie was studying history and Jeanine had just obtained a first in law. She was expected to go on to a successful career in law and politics, as had her father, the Right Honourable Michael Lord, QC.

Neither parent was pinning their hopes on their son Jamie amounting to much, despite his education. Even with his obvious intelligence and quick mind, there was something about him that had always relegated him to the back of the family's hopes and dreams for their children. Diagnosed as bipolar in his late teens, his occasionally violent outbursts were now largely under control, thanks to the medication he was taking. Of course, when he forgot his meds or got himself into all-night drinking parties with his uni friends, then he could be a handful, as two security guards had recently found out to their dismay.

Accused of inappropriate touching of a female student at one such party, he was approached by the two guards, intent on removing him and making arrangements for him to spend the night elsewhere. He saw them coming and, on the reasonable assumption he was about to be manhandled out of the building, chose to headbutt the younger guard, breaking the man's cheekbone. The older one he pushed backward across two tables, sending glasses and food flying in all directions. His friends had seen him like this before and took direct action, piling on top of him and holding him firm until the police arrived, when he was arrested and taken away.

It was Michael Lord's clout with the college's dean and fellows that got the incident hushed up. The girl was financially compensated and the two guards promoted to supervisor positions in exchange for their 'understanding' and silence on the matter. It was all swept under the carpet on the promise that this would be the first and only time this kind of behaviour would be tolerated.

Christine had objected to the incident being hushed up. Michael was always bailing their son out of trouble and making excuses for him. This sexual assault was the final straw for her, and she genuinely felt that prosecution was in order. Jamie had overheard the argument between them, and for the part she took, and because he felt she always preferred his sister over him, he grew to loathe her even more.

Christine opened her eyes. A sheet of opaque polythene flapped a few feet above her head. Her body felt heavy and tired, and for a moment she drifted back to sleep. She jerked awake again. Something told her she wasn't dreaming; she was in trouble. She tried to turn onto her shoulder to push herself up. She couldn't. Through her drowsiness she realised that both her arms were pinned down. Adrenaline coursed through her veins and she tried again, more urgently this time.

She squirmed, realising that her legs were also secured to the ground. She struggled harder now, panic taking over. The tape across her mouth turned her terrified cries of 'Help me! Help me!' into no more than muffled growls.

'Hello, Mother.'

She stopped wriggling instantly and turned in the direction of the voice, stricken with both fear and disbelief. *Jamie!*

'I'm sure you have questions.'

She stayed silent.

'I'll happily answer them for you, but you have to promise me something first. You have to promise me that you won't scream. Do you understand?'

She nodded her head frantically and felt cold sweat run into her eyes.

'Good.' Jamie bent over her and, none too gently, ripped back the tape from her mouth.

'Jamie! Jamie! What's going on? What are you doing? Please . . .'

Her son held a finger to his lips. 'Shh! It's okay, it's okay. Calm down.'

'I don't understand . . .'

'I'm sure you don't. I imagine this is the last place you expected to find yourself. Do you know where we are?'

She shook her head.

'We are on the roof of Southwark Crown Court. I believe you know it well, yes?'

'I . . . I . . . I don't understand . . .'

'I know. You've already said. I brought you here. *We* brought you here. To teach you something.'

A second figure stepped forward into her peripheral vision, and her pulse quickened until she could feel it throbbing in her ears. 'Who . . . ?'

'This? This is the King, Mother. This is the Lawmaker.'

The man, his pasty white face framed by his hoodie, gave her a slow nod as an acknowledgement but said nothing.

'The King? What do you mean? King of what?'

Jamie smiled. 'He is the King of all, Mother. It is he who rules and it is he who decides.'

She looked across to 'the King'. All she saw was a young man with a look of arrogance on his face and dead eyes set either side of a Roman nose. 'Decides? Decides what?'

Jamie looked across at 'the King' with an expression that bordered on reverence. 'He decides all things. He decides your punishment.'

'My punishment? What are you talking about? Punishment for what?'

'For the contempt you have shown to me all of my life. For your betrayal of me.'

'What betrayal? What are you talking about? Please, Jamie. Let me go. Please!'

Jamie chortled. 'I'm afraid that time is past, Mother. As you and Father are both judges, we thought it would be fitting to bring you here, to this place of law. A place you spent most of your time in. A place where you spent most of my childhood and a place, I suspect, that robbed you of your capacity to be kind, to show mercy and, most of all, to show compassion. That was all I ever wanted, Mother. For you to be kind to me, to show me some compassion — to spend time with me, to notice me. But all you ever had time for were two things. The law and my bloody sister. All I wanted was a sliver of the attention she—'

'I'm sorry. I'm so sorry. I didn't mean—'

'To what? To turn against me? To betray me? To give me over to the police? To put me on trial?'

Christine burned with a blend of fear, pity and perhaps remorse. 'Jamie! I didn't.'

'But you wanted to, didn't you?'

Tears filled her eyes as she gave a tiny nod of her head. 'I'm . . . I'm so—'

'So, what? Sorry? Is that what you were going to say? You're a tad too late, Mother.'

'I . . . I was going to say . . . that I felt I had no choice. You were off your meds. The poor girl you assaulted was traumatised.'

'No choice? Traumatised? Listen to yourself. You need to come down off your high horse, Mother. You should have been protecting me. *Me*, not her. Instead, you wanted Father to have me arrested. To have me put away.'

'You . . . you did wrong, Jamie. You must see that.'

'Wrong, schmong. I grabbed one tit and put my hand up her dress. Inserting one finger without permission is hardly the sex crime of the year, is it?'

'It was still a crime, Jamie. It was vile, it was degrading and it caused her great suffering.'

'Suffering? Let's talk about suffering then, shall we? She never suffered as much as I did — knowing each day that my own mother wanted me put in prison.'

'You wouldn't have gone to pris—'

'You can't know that!' She blinked as he spattered her face with spittle. 'And what hurts is that you were happy for them to take me. My own mother!'

She shook her head. 'I wasn't happy. But . . . we heard stories from other students . . . that it wasn't the first time you'd behaved that way.'

Jamie jumped up and shouted, 'Stories? Oh, stories. Well, that's okay then. Everyone loves a good fairy tale, don't they? Because that's what it was. A bloody fairy tale!'

'There were witnesses. Six of them all saw you do it.'

'Friends of hers, Mother. Of course they would say that.'

'She was with two friends, Jamie. Witness three was just at the party and the other three were your friends.'

He dropped to one knee, near to her head. 'Friends? No friends of mine, Mother. Betrayers all.'

'Let me up, Jamie. Please. We can talk about this. It's not what you think. *I'm* not what you think.'

Jamie cocked his head to one side. 'Oh, you are, Mother. You are absolutely what I think you are. Cold, unemotional, uncaring, uninterested. You're an awful woman who made my life as miserable as you could.'

'That's not true. You know that's not—'

He forced the tape back over her mouth and pushed his hand against it. The surface under her head was soft and damp — like soil, even though Jamie had said she was on a roof.

'Now it's my turn, Mother Dearest. My turn to show you what it's like to ask for something only to be met with a cold, harsh refusal. You are so going to wish you'd been a nicer person.'

Her eyes fixed on his, imploring him not to do whatever it was he had planned for her.

He stood up and a cruel smile appeared on his face. 'This has all worked out perfectly. I'm going to leave you here, Mother. Alone. Just as you left me alone, so many times. Father is off on one of his jaunts to America — a "conference", he calls it — so he won't be back for a week and we both know he won't call. Never has. Never will. And while you're here alone, you can spend the time wondering exactly what it is you did to me to warrant this. Just like I did as a child. Wondering what I'd done to upset you, to hurt you *so* badly that you didn't want to come home to me, to be with me. And then, finally, in your last act of uncaring, to try and abandon me to my fate with the courts.

'As I grew older, I realised that I hadn't done anything wrong. Not really. You were just a heartless bitch who didn't give much of a shit about me. And this, dear mother of mine, is how I feel about you. I just don't give a shit. So, I'm going to leave you here, in the cold, in the dark, and soon you'll start to feel the fingers of my punishment prod against you.'

Christine's eyes filled to the brim with tears and she let out a long, painful moan.

'I have to go now, Mother. Don't be scared. The police will come for you in a few days. By then, you'll have learned your lesson. And, before I go, I wouldn't waste your time trying to attract attention. The ceilings beneath you are solid concrete. At least two foot thick. You're in the middle of the roof — a good hundred feet or so away from either access door — and when we leave here, I'll relock the door behind me. There's no reason for anyone to come up here, and certainly not in this weather. Chilly this time of the year, isn't it? The good news is . . . the forecast is cold with bright sunshine for the next few days.'

Christine shrieked into the tape over her mouth.

'Ooh. That reminds me . . .' Jamie pulled out a piece of black duct tape from his inside pocket. The ends were stuck together and he carefully peeled them apart. As the ends fell away, Christine's eyes widened. Stuck to the tape were two ten pence pieces, an inch or so apart. 'This is to enhance the surprise you have coming, Mother. I've heard it said that when one sense closes down another opens. I'm hoping it will be the sense of touch. As she shook her head, Jamie stuck the coins over her eyes.

'Goodbye, Mother,' he said.

CHAPTER THREE

DAY 1

'Good mornin', Raymondo, me ol' cocker. 'An' 'ow you doin' this bright an' breezy mornin'?' Despite putting on a cheerful voice, Detective Inspector Johnny Clocks wasn't a fan of the wind and wet, and he huddled under a tree for some protection from the driving rain that had been falling throughout the night. With his phone pressed to one ear and a finger jammed in the other, he struggled to make himself heard against the noise of the rain beating against the tarmac path. The sound of arriving uniformed police officers slamming car doors and shouting to each other added to his growing irritation. Flashing blue lights illuminated the scene around him and intermittently lit up the dead body he was looking at.

Ray Paterson, his voice thick with sleep, mumbled into the phone. 'Clocksy? D'you know what time it is?'

''Course I do. I ain't stupid.'

'It's half five in the morning.'

'I know. I said I wasn't stupid. I can tell the time. The clue's in me name.'

'What d'you want?'

'I wondered if you wanted to come out and play.'

'What?'

'Got a cracker 'ere, Ray. This one's a beaut.'

'What?'

'Fuckin' 'ell, Ray. Wake up, son. I said, "This one's a beaut."'

'What are you talking about, John?'

'Got called out to a scene. Bloke in a park, dead as a doornail, big 'ole in 'is back an' . . . Nah. I'll wait till you get 'ere. Don't wanna spoil it for yer.'

There was silence on the line. 'Ray? Don't you go back to sleep! Get up!'

'*What?*' Paterson sounded annoyed.

'You comin' or not?'

'No. Eileen said no.' Eileen Markham, the Met Police psychiatrist assigned to Paterson and Clocks to assess their ongoing mental health, had become fascinated by them both as individuals and their work dynamic.

'Oh, fuck 'er, Ray. Don't worry about it. C'mon. Come out an' play. You know you want to.'

'I'm in enough shit as it is, John.'

'And?'

'And, what's the point of poking the bears all the time?'

'Really? I can't believe you're askin' me that. 'Cos it's a laugh — that's the point. Look, you can go back to bed an' stay on the sick if you want to, but this is a good'un, Ray, a proper good'un. An' I reckon this is just the start of things to come.'

'Why do you say that?' Paterson's voice sounded livelier.

'This ain't yer run-o'-the-mill, "'ole in the back" sort of murder. This is . . . ritualistic, I'd say. You love a ritual killin', doncha? Remember those black kids? That was ritual stuff. You loved it. You an' me both know these are never isolated, an' I need you down 'ere with me.' He paused. 'You comin' or not?'

'Yeah. I suppose so. Why not? I can hear rain. Is it raining out there?'

'If you can 'ear it, then it is, isn't it? Jesus. Yeah, it's 'ammering down. Just put yer coat on and grab yer little pink umbrella, you little Mummy's boy, you. You'll be fine.'

'Where are you?'

'Under a tree in the middle of Southwark Park. You can't miss it. It's a big green thing. Lots of trees and blue lights flashing all over the gaff. I'm near the boatin' lake.'

'On my way.'

Clocks ended the call and cursed loudly as a drop of freezing cold water dripped onto his neck and slid down inside his collar. He spotted the duty inspector's car arriving and debated leaving the shelter of his tree. He decided against it. He'd stay sheltered until the inspector left his car, wait for him to get soaked and then wander over to him. He knew his decision was right when he saw Inspector Stuart Norris get out of the car. Clocks didn't have a lot of time for 'No-Nuts' Norris — too much by the book for his taste and he wasn't known for strong decision-making when it was needed. Still, he was always good for a piss-take.

Clocks watched as Inspector Norris put on his peaked flat cap and made his way to the crime scene with a uniformed PC. They ducked under the tape and walked closer, torch beams cutting through the darkness. Clocks grinned to himself when Norris jackknifed over and threw up. The PC spun around quickly and bent double. He wasn't sick, but Clocks reckoned he was already regretting coming in for his night shift. This was a sight that would stay with him for life.

Clocks shook his collar out and pulled it closer to his throat before stepping into the downpour to make his way toward Norris, who was still bent over.

'Mornin', No-Nuts!' Clocks ducked under the tape. 'Feelin' better now you've 'ad a good 'ol clear out?' He winked at the PC, who was now standing. 'All right, son? Why don't you go an' get yerself a nice greasy fry-up while me an' yer guv'nor 'ave a chat? Do you good. Nothin' like a slippery plate of double egg 'n' sausages with a couple of fried slices floatin' around in grease when yer stomach's a bit dicky. Trust me.' The PC heaved and struggled to keep a hold of the contents of his stomach. He staggered off, leaving Clocks and Norris alone. Clocks made a bet with himself that the PC would throw up before he cleared the tape. He was right. Inspector Norris also threw up again.

'There you go. That yer Pot Noodle all gone now?'

Norris ignored him and swayed backward and forward.

'Bit rough this one, innit?' said Clocks.

Norris wiped his mouth with the back of his arm, then spat before wiping again.

'Can you stand? If you can't, siddown on the grass. You're soaked now anyway.'

Norris pulled himself up and glanced at Clocks. He shook his head. Clocks felt a bit sorry for him. Not everyone had the stomach for the job.

'Look. There's nothin' for you to do 'ere, Stu. I've got it under control with some 'elp from your lads. They're a good bunch. Got straight on it. Go back to the nick an' get yerself a cuppa tea or somethin'. Paterson's on his way. Leave it to us an' don't worry about it.'

Norris waved away the offer. 'I'm . . . okay. Just wasn't expecting . . .'

'Yeah, I know. In a way, I'm glad you weren't. I'd 'ate to think this was normal.'

Norris sucked in a deep breath as he fought to regain his composure. 'What do we know?'

'Not much. One of your boys was on 'is way back to the nick to write up a crime sheet, noticed that the chain on the gate was danglin' an' thought he'd 'ave a little look about. This is what 'e found.' Clocks nodded toward the body of a man draped on its stomach across a large ornamental rock. The head was turned away from them and the arms were secured by ropes attached to two metal spikes driven into the ground at angles.

'I've sent your boy off to 'ospital to get treated for shock. Poor little sod's only a kid. That's 'is childhood dream of bein' a copper fucked, I should imagine.'

'Mine too,' said Norris. 'No one told me there'd be nights like this when I signed up.'

'That's 'ow they get you, mate. Lies.'

Clocks saw the headlights of another car arriving. In the flashing blue lights he could see it was Paterson. He checked his watch. Twenty-five minutes.

'The guv'nor's turned up,' he said to Norris. 'You wanna stay or go? Up to you.'

'I'll stay,' said Norris.

Clocks nodded and walked off to meet Paterson, who was stepping out of his car, all suited and booted with a golfing umbrella as protection from the elements. Clocks wondered why *he* never had the sense to carry an umbrella in his car. Then he remembered he wasn't that sensible.

'John!' Paterson called out. 'This better be worth it.'

'Would I lie to you, guv?' Clocks shouted back as he closed the gap on the two of them. 'You're gonna love this. C'mon.'

CHAPTER FOUR

The two men made their way toward the crime scene with Paterson trying not to get his Gucci shoes covered in mud. 'What have we got?'

'We've got ourselves a male, getting on a bit. Someone's tied him face down across one of the ornamental rocks, right next to the play park. You know what I mean? Kiddies climb on 'em.'

'Tied him?'

'Yeah. Well, sort of. They've tied rope around 'is wrists and feet an' then pegged 'im down so 'e couldn't move about too much. Geezer's only wearing 'is strides. We found 'is jacket an' shirt lyin' next to him. Nothin' in the pockets.'

Paterson raised an eyebrow and shook his head. 'Go on.'

'Then they've cut into his back and ripped it open.'

Paterson stopped and looked at Clocks. 'Ripped it—'

'Yeah, wait a minute. Don't spoil it. I'm gettin' to the good bit. Our naughty boy's then pulled our victim's back open some'ow, severed 'is ribs then got 'old of his lungs, pulled them out and slapped 'em either side of the fuck-off big 'ole 'e's made.'

'Christ.' Paterson shook his head. He heard a retching noise. 'Is that Norris?' He kept his voice low as he nodded in the direction of the inspector.

'Yeah. One of 'is lads found our vic.'

'Has he fucked anything up yet?'

Clocks chuckled. 'Nah. I was 'ere before 'im. Got everything sealed off. Mind you, we'll 'ave to tell the forensic boys when they get 'ere to mind all the sick 'e's chucked about.'

Paterson smiled. 'Mr Norris. How are you today?'

'So-so. Thanks for asking.'

'Pleasure. Have you touched anything?'

'Of course not. I'm not stup—'

'We both know that's not true. I seem to remember you not having a house searched properly. Missed a few dead bodies, didn't you?'

Paterson couldn't resist the dig as he recalled the night he and Clocks visited the house of a woman who had just killed a burglar and a uniformed police officer. She'd also seriously wounded another. Once the woman was arrested, Norris allowed a forensic team inside without having a thorough search carried out. The house held the bodies and body parts of murdered children.

Norris ignored the jibe. 'Oh, Jesus Christ!' he muttered, turning his attention back to the mutilated man on the rocks.

Paterson walked up to the body. 'Do we know who he is yet?'

'Nah. Can't really see 'is face clearly an' I've not looked in 'is pockets yet for ID.'

Paterson recoiled when he got closer to the body. 'Jesus Christ!'

'It's not, is it?' said Clocks taking another look. 'Nah, I don't think it's 'im, Ray. 'E ain't got a beard for starters an' 'e's the wrong way round. Every picture I've ever seen 'as 'im facin' yer with those big soppy brown eyes lookin' up to 'eaven. Plus, there's a big circle of light around 'is nut. Definitely not 'im.'

'D'you know what this is?' said Paterson.

Clocks looked again. 'Yep. It's a dead body.'

'This is a Blood Eagle.'

'A what?' said Clocks.

Paterson carried on looking at the body. 'When you told me what had happened to him it was the first thing I thought of, but I had to see it to be sure. You were right, John. It's a form of ritual killing all right.'

'The fuck's a Blood Eagle, then? Never 'eard of it.'

'Not many people have. Legend has it, the Vikings used to kill people in this way. Someone who'd done them a grievous harm. Perhaps killed someone they love.' He pointed to the lungs. 'See the lungs?'

'Bit 'ard to miss, really, seein' as 'ow they're on the outside an' 'anging down.'

'The lungs are supposed to represent the wings of the eagle. The victim is always alive when they're blood eagled. The opening of the back is usually made with something like a large knife exposing the lungs then the ribs are broken away from the spine, most likely with a hand axe, and then pulled apart to make room for the lungs to be lifted out. The vic, if he hasn't already died from shock, is then left out to die slowly. Sometimes, if the poor bastard takes a while to die, birds or wild animals stop by for a feast.'

Clocks's nose wrinkled. 'Fuck me, that sounds painful.'

'You think?'

'So 'ow come you know all this?' said Clocks.

Paterson shrugged. 'I got a PhD in the historical sciences when I was at uni.'

Clocks raised his eyebrows. 'Really? I never knew that.'

'That's because I'm pulling your plonker. I watched *Vikings* on Amazon Prime.'

'Oh, you wanker! I thought you were even cleverer than you already are.'

Paterson smirked. 'So, now we've established it's not our Lord Almighty, have a quick look in his pockets for some ID.'

''Ang on.' Clocks stuck his hand in the victim's nearest trouser pocket. Nothing. He rummaged around inside another and pulled out a small black leather wallet.

Clocks stared at him. 'Oh, fuck me sideways with a baseball bat!'

'What? What is it?'

'Er . . . you're not gonna be an 'appy little bunny.'

'Why?'

'We know 'im.'

'Do we? Who is it?'

'Drum roll, please.'

'Get on with it, John.'

'All right. Just settin' the mood. It turns out our vic 'ere is none other than Sir Scott Anderson, late of the Metropolitan Police.'

Paterson froze. 'What? What'd you say? Anderson?'

Clocks held up the small wallet he'd pulled out of the body's pocket. Anderson's Silver Token, a form of warrant card held only by officers above the rank of commander.

'Jesus.'

'I bet you wish it was now, mate. The Second Comin' would be easier to explain than this.'

'Oh, fucking great. I suppose we'll get pulled in and blamed for this now.'

'Nah. Don't worry about that. We've got bigger things to worry about.'

'Like what?'

'Like the fact that if we don't get a tent over him soon that 'ole in 'is back is gonna fill up with water and he'll bleedin' drown next!'

CHAPTER FIVE

Clocks turned to Paterson. 'So, what's the plan, Stan?'

'First things, first,' he said. 'We have to make sure this is kept under wraps for as long as possible. Got to make sure nobody here leaks anything out, for starters. Get Jock Hudson out of his whisky-soaked bed and down here. I want him to see this in situ.'

'Ooh, 'e'll love you for that. Not many pisshead pathologists are in the rollin'-out-of-bed-in-the-beltin'-rain game, and least of all Jock. 'Sides, 'e's probably nursin' a king-size 'angover.'

'Not my problem. I want him here. I'll put a call in to the acting commissioner, tell him what we've got and I expect we'll have to go over and see him when we've finished here.'

Clocks pulled a face that suggested that yet another trip to the Yard was more than likely going to ruin his day.

'Round up every officer here for me, John. We have to make sure they understand the importance of discretion with this one.'

Clocks nodded, turned sharply and walked off, dodging puddles and muttering under his breath. He got to the yellow tape that sealed off one side of the crime scene and shouted. 'Oi! You lot. C'mere!' He waved the uniformed officers toward him with both hands. One or two seemed reluctant to leave their posts. It was drummed into them at training school and out on the streets that once posted at the scene of a murder, that was where you stayed until expressly relieved by a senior officer and replaced by another uniform if necessary. Clocks's instruction offered no replacement.

'C'mon. Move yerselves! I ain't standin' around in the fuckin' rain for the fun of it, am I?'

The uniforms abandoned their posts and headed toward him. Paterson joined him as the crowd of soaking wet police officers gathered around.

'Morning everybody,' said Paterson. 'For those of you who don't know me . . . us—' he nodded toward Clocks — 'I'm Detective Superintendent Paterson and this is DI Clocks. I'm the SIO in this case.'

A few of the officers nodded.

'Question . . . does anybody know who our victim is?'

Everybody shook their heads.

'Sure?'

Nobody spoke.

'Okay. Good. For your info, our victim here is a prominent person and it is vital at this stage of the investigation that nothing of this scene leaks out. Nothing. Do you all understand?'

Again, everybody nodded.

'Excellent. Again, for your info, a watch will be carried out on all social media channels, and if I discover a picture on Facebook or a tweet or any bloody mention of this crime scene at all, I swear to God the person who posted it will be out of a job so fast they won't know if it's Christmas, Easter, Eid or Hanukkah. Understand?'

Heads nodded furiously.

'So, now's the time to 'fess up. Has anyone done this?' He scanned the crowd for a guilty look. His eyes lit on a young male officer who avoided eye contact. 'What did you do?'

'Sir . . . I . . .'

'What'd you do, knob'ead?' Clocks moved toward him. The officer lifted his eyes toward Clocks.

'Facebooked a picture.'

'Of what, exactly? You show 'is face?'

'No. Just his back.'

Clocks shook his head, balled his fists and got his face within an inch of the officer's nose. 'You fuckin' arse'ole! What's the matter with you bloody kids postin' every fuckin' thing you see an' do? You're a bloody copper, son! You don't get to do this shit. Get it the fuck down, now! Do it, you arsewipe.' The officer reached into his pocket and pulled out his phone.

'Anyone else?' said Paterson to the crowd.

Silence.

'Let's hope not.' He turned to the young PC. 'When you've done that, officer, report back to the station and write out your report first. Include in it what you've done and then write out your resignation. You're done.'

The officer looked up at him. 'Sir . . . Please . . . No. It's gone. I've got rid of it.'

'And I've got rid of you. Back to the station and do as I said.' He turned his back and walked back to the crime scene. Clocks followed behind. 'Can you give Jock a bell for me, please? I'll call the office and find out who the on-call senior officer is for the area. He can call the acting commissioner when it's a more civilised hour and let him know what we've got.'

Clocks nodded. 'It's the acting commissioner 'imself, Ray. Morne, I think 'is name is.'

'Good. Then I haven't got to worry about waking him up.'

'Ray . . .'

'What?'

'Bit 'arsh on the kid, weren't you?'

'Yep. Consequences, John. People have to learn that there are consequences to the things they do. This fucking social media nonsense is getting on my nerves. He's a copper and this is a crime scene, not a bloody sideshow. I'm not having this investigation fucked up because he wants a bunch of likes from his pretend friends. He should know better. Chances are, the word's out by now and that picture will have been shared all over the place, so we're going to have trouble containing it.'

'Yeah, but they won't know it's Anderson, will they? 'E took a picture of 'is back. That's the juicy bit, innit?'

'Don't care. Consequences.' He stopped in front of Anderson's shredded body. 'He was a right prick, Clocksy, but he didn't deserve this. Nobody deserves this.'

'I make you right, guv. I make you right.'

'Has to be more than one person, you agree?'

'Yep. For now. Can't see 'ow else they would 'ave overpowered 'im or tied 'im up like this. The killin' bit was probably a doddle. Big sharp thing to cut 'is back open is easy enough, but I tell you what . . . you gotta be some kind of a sick fucker to pull 'is bleedin' lungs out and leave 'im to die.' Clocks shook his head, pulled his phone out and turned away. 'Let's give Jock an early wake-up, then.'

Paterson sighed. 'What did you do, Anderson? What . . . did . . . you . . . do?'

CHAPTER SIX

'Sir . . . Sorry to disturb you so early in the morning. It's Detective Superintendent Paterson here.'

'Sorry? Who is it?' Acting Commissioner Sam Morne was awake — just. Paterson guessed he was in no rush to get up from his chair, where he had probably been dozing. Being the on-call senior officer for the Met was presumably a pain in the arse. No doubt he figured that, given the sound of the rain hammering against his window, a cheeky little nap would be fine.

'Superintendent Paterson, sir.'

'You're off sick aren't you?'

'Just resumed. DI Clocks called me in. I'm afraid I have a nasty one that you need to know about.'

'What is it?'

'I don't want to use names over the phone, sir. Do you use Telegram?'

'Telegram? A bit like WhatsApp isn't it?'

'Yeah. WhatsApp was built off the back of Telegram. High-level end-to-end encryption with a self-destruct timer sequence built into the message service.'

'Self-destruct? Really?'

Paterson rolled his eyes. 'Really. I assume this is a job phone, and if it is, scroll through the apps until you find it. I'll wait.' The line went silent for thirty seconds.

'Got it,' said Morne.

'Hang on. Sending the name now. It'll be on your screen for five seconds.' Paterson typed in Anderson's name and pressed send.

Six seconds later Paterson heard Morne whisper, 'Oh, Christ.' He thought about telling him that he and Clocks had already ruled Christ out as the victim but decided he wouldn't appreciate the joke. Paterson started furiously tapping the virtual keys on his phone. *Need you to convene a meeting with whomever it is you deem necessary and I want you to issue a D-notice on the press. At the moment, only Clocks and I know who the victim is and we need to keep it that way.*

He sent a second message.

One of the officers on scene took photographs and posted to social media. As far as I know, it does not identify our victim. Photo has been removed. Officer will be dealt with. I'm waiting for the senior pathologist to arrive. Once that's done, will come into the Yard and meet with you. Hope to be there by midday.

'Sir,' said Paterson. 'You get all that?'

'Yes, yes. I'm on it. Thank you. I'll see you at noon.'

'Sir.'

'And Paterson . . .'

'Sir?'

'Make sure this is done by the book — to the letter.'

Paterson smiled. 'Yes, sir.' He hung up.

He turned to find Clocks walking back to him. 'Any luck with Jock?'

'Yeah. He's got the fuckin' 'ump up to 'is eyebrows. Thought I was on a wind-up for some reason.'

'Not like you'd do that, would you?'

Clocks shrugged.

'What's his ETA?'

'Reckons 'alf an hour, forty minutes.'

'Was he pissed?'

'Was the *Titanic* 'it by an ice cube?'

'It was not.'

'And 'e was not. Just don't stand too close to 'im when 'e rolls up or you'll get off yer tits. You know what a Jessie you are when it comes to alcohol.'

Paterson pulled a face.

'You speak to the big boss?' said Clocks.

'Yep. Not a happy big boss. I scheduled a meeting with him and some others at noon. I want you with me.'

'Oh, good. You know 'ow much I love a meeting.'

'Are you going to get out of your pram when we're in there?'

Clocks shrugged again. 'I'd like to think I wouldn't, but who knows? I'm cold, tired, soaked to the skin and the bloke who seemed to spend his workin' life chasin' after us is bent over a rock with 'is giblets on display. We've now gotta wait for a pissed-up, pissed-off pathologist who's gonna fuck around for the best part of an hour in a bloody monsoon and then 'e'll come to the stunning conclusion that our man is, in fact, dead. And to cap it off you're gonna drag me off to see some shiny suits in a centrally 'eated office. Me suit will start to steam up and I'll get all sweaty an' antsy when they start asking pointless fuckin' questions that we don't know the answer to, and so, yes, I probably will get out of me pram if they don't play nice.'

Paterson nodded and sniffed. 'Fair enough. Tell you what. Soon as Jock's gone, you can go to the station for a shower and a change of clothes. Splash yourself with a bit of talc. Should calm you down a bit.'

'You reckon?'

'Not for a second.'

CHAPTER SEVEN

'So, best we make ourselves busy until Jock rolls up,' said Paterson. Clocks agreed. There was no point standing guard over a dead body in the pouring rain. That's what the uniformed officers were for.

'Right. Let's take stock of what we've got.' Paterson looked around him. We're in the middle of a park. No nearby buildings. No CCTV.'

'Good bet Anderson never walked 'ere, so 'e was likely brought by a vehicle of some sort,' said Clocks.

Paterson nodded.

'I'll get it actioned. Ooh. Forgot to tell yer. We've got some new team members since you've been on the sick.'

'Any good?'

'Bloody 'ope so. Seriously, you won't believe their names.'

'Go on,' said Paterson.

'We've got a DC Thomas Gunn. I know, right? Tommy Gunn. Couldn't make it up.'

'And, who else?'

'A bird. DS Suzi . . . wait for it . . . Rocket. Suzi Rocket. 'Ow cool is that for a name?'

'Rocket and Gunn.' Paterson felt a wry grin creep to his lips. 'Sounds like a formidable pair. Do we know what they're like as coppers?'

'Seem all right so far. Came highly recommended. Both served time on other squads, burglary, drugs an' all that. They know their way around a suit. Oh, an' just so you know, the bird 'as got a couple of big ol' weapons of mass debation lurking under 'er jumper, so that's turned out right good for team morale, that 'as. Needed a bit of cheering up round the office.'

Paterson shook his head. 'You're getting married.'

'True. In a couple of weeks too. But last I heard, lookin' don't make you go blind, does it? Nothing wrong with lookin' is there? Wankin' . . . that makes you go blind, apparently.'

'Who told you that?'

'Me dad. "Blind" Brian Clocks. I know. Sounds like Brian Cox, the space geezer. It's not 'im though. 'E's not me dad. Me dad did all right out of it though. Got 'imself on the disability *and* a blue badge for his car through wankin'. Although I 'ave told 'im to stop driving now.'

'You're an idiot, Clocksy.'

'True. Now, where were we? Oh, yeah. Un'appy Anderson. So, CCTV checks of the streets. See if there's anything since the park closed last night to when it opened this mornin'.'

Paterson looked around and pointed into the distance. 'There's a block of flats over there. What's that you reckon? Twenty floors?'

Clocks followed Paterson's finger. 'Yeah, that's Maydew House but, fuck me, you'd need to be lookin' through the 'Ubble telescope to see Anderson from there. That's a non-starter, Ray.'

'Through the what?'

'The 'Ubble telescope. That big one that sees right into space.'

'I know what it does, I've just never heard it called the Ubble before. It's pronounced "Hubble". Has an aitch in it.'

Clocks pushed his shoulders back. 'Oh, oh, okay. We goin' there are we, poncey boy?'

Paterson grinned. He figured he could do with a grin.

'You 'avin' a go at me again, 'cos of the way I speak? 'Cos I don't 'ave a plum in me mouth and a silver finger up me arse.'

'Spoon. Not a finger.'

'Yeah, right. Spoon, finger, whatever. I know all about you jolly-hockey-sticks, tally-ho brigade and your strange ways with animals. I'd rather come from a council estate an' talk like this than stick me knob in a pig's 'ead like your mob do just so you can get ahead in life.'

'We don't all do that, John. That's a fallacy.'

'Is it? Is it? I don't know what "fallacy" means, but I bet it's something to do with pig sex.'

'It isn't. It really—'

'Don't interrupt me, you sanctimonious git.'

Paterson raised his eyebrows. 'Bloody hell! See? You do know some big words. There's hope for you yet.'

Clocks looked him in the eye. 'I know a few small ones too you piss-taking, silver-fingered, pig-fuckin' twat.'

Paterson burst out laughing. 'A delightful turn of phrase, John. Well done.'

'Bollocks, knob'ead.'

'Okay. Fair enough. Enough of the japes. We need to check for any local businesses that may run a night staff of some kind. Bakers, petrol garage, that sort of thing. Early morning cleaners, postmen, vagrants. Anyone who might be out and about who might have seen something out of the ordinary.'

'Yeah will do. Ray . . .'

'What?'

'Can I get under yer umbrella?'

Paterson looked at his saturated friend in his dishevelled dark suit. 'What for?'

'To try an' keep a bit of this rain off.'

'Off what? There's nothing left to get wet.'

'So, that's a no then?'

'No. You can get under it if you want. C'mon.'

Clocks stepped under it and with one hand grabbed the stem. With the other he pushed the catch upward turning it inside out.

'What the fuck?' Paterson shouted as the rain began to soak him.

Clocks gave him a big grin. 'Always lead by example, Ray. Always.'

CHAPTER EIGHT

The Home Office senior pathologist, Jock Hudson, was nursing a king-sized headache as he pulled up at Paterson's murder scene. It was no secret to anyone that his drinking had now reached a tipping point, and that, combined with his fiery Celtic temper, had put him on the path to a forced retirement. He didn't want to go. Cutting up dead bodies and figuring out what had killed their owners had been his life for the best part of forty years. In his more lucid moments, however, he knew that the job had taken its toll on him, pushing him to the bottle and now to the edge of an ignominious ending to a glorious and respected career. The bottle, in its own insidious way, had extracted its toll, destroying his liver. Hudson knew it wouldn't be too long before some youngster would be dropping what was left of it into a steel bowl the way that he had done countless times before. God, it seemed to him, loved a bit of irony. The circle of life.

He stepped out of his car and took a second to get his balance. Drink or illness. He couldn't be sure and he didn't particularly care anymore. He announced himself to the uniformed PC standing guard at the outer cordon and struggled to duck under the tape, nearly losing his footing. The uniformed officer caught his arm and steadied him.

'Sir, are you all right?'

'Aye, laddie, I'm fine. Just lost ma footing there, son. Ground's slippery.'

The PC nodded. 'Yeah, it is. Be careful.'

Hudson waved as he walked to the second cordon. He managed to negotiate this one more sure-footedly. Ahead of him, Paterson stood under an umbrella. Clocks looked saturated and wouldn't be in the best of moods. He was certain more piss-taking was coming his way. Paterson and Clocks had done nothing but make fun of him since they'd first met. Clocks he'd known for years, Paterson since the murder of his wife, Lisa. Hudson wrote up the report that exonerated Paterson from any wrongdoing when he took revenge on the man who had torn her to pieces.

Despite their constant mick-taking, he enjoyed being around them. Their joking was sorely needed in a world obsessed with political correctness. He would miss them in the months to come.

'Paterson!' he shouted, struggling to make himself overheard against the wind and rain. After a few more footsteps and a couple more shouts, Paterson turned.

'Jock!'

Clocks turned around too. 'Oi, oi, Jocky boy. 'Ow's it goin'?'

'All right boys. Who's tae be the first to start on me today, eh? Come on.'

'I'll go,' said Clocks. Paterson grinned at Clocks. Clocks peered at Hudson. 'Did you bring yer torch light nose with yer? Or are you still wearing ladies' make-up to cover it. Y'know . . . the Max Factor you 'ad on durin' the Childmaker case.'

Normally, Hudson would have felt both embarrassed and defensive about his 'drinker's nose', which was noticeable even in dim light, but this was the least of his problems today. 'Fuck off, ye heathen bastard.'

'Oh, that's nice, innit? Tellin' me to fuck off. If I didn't know any better I'd swear you were bein' racist.'

'It's not racist to tell you to fuck off, John,' said Paterson. 'God knows I've told you enough times myself.'

'Yeah, I know. But 'e's a Jock an' I'm an English, so anything we say to each other must be racist by definition on account of me *being* English and therefore institutionally racist.'

Paterson shook his head, his face a picture of bewilderment. 'What?'

Clocks shrugged. 'I don't make the rules, guv.'

'You're a wee fuckin' idiot, Clocksy,' said Hudson. 'You know that, don't ye?'

Clocks shook his head and shrugged at the same time. 'Wass 'e say, Ray? I can never understand a bleedin' word 'e says to me.' He turned to look at Hudson. 'What. Did. You. Say? Me, John. Me, English. Me, no understandee. Comprende?'

Hudson looked at Paterson, who had a grin on his face. 'Can ye no control him yet, Paterson?'

'What do you think?' said Paterson.

'Hmm. I know ye cannae.'

'What'd he call you, Ray? Sounded like cun—'

'Leave it, John.'

Hudson turned his back on Clocks. 'So, what hae we got, Paterson?'

'See for yourself.' All three walked closer to Anderson's body.

'Jesus fuckin' Christ!' Hudson stopped in his tracks, aghast at the prised-open ribs and bloodied pink lungs.

Paterson shook his head. 'It's not. We've already had that discussion.'

Clocks stood back and chuckled. 'Did you understand 'im, guv?'

'Yeah. You have to tune in, though. I've been taking Scottish lessons online too, so that helps.'

Hudson sighed. 'Will you two no' stop fuckin' around? Doin' ma heid in.'

'Fair enough,' said Paterson. 'It's actually Commissioner Anderson.' Hudson snapped his head around to look at

Paterson. 'It really is. We found his ID. And, of course, we both know him personally. It's definitely him.'

'Shit!' said Hudson.

'Shit, indeed,' said Paterson. 'So I need you to be on your "A" game for this one, Jock. You okay with this?'

'Of course, I am.

'Good. Where are your tent boys? This is taking too long. We've probably lost a fair amount of evidence by now. Washed off.'

As the words left his mouth, two white vans pulled up and the occupants climbed out to don their white suits.

'You seen anything like this before?' Paterson said.

'Christ, no. This is . . . horrible. Horrible.'

'It's a form of ritual killing called a Blood Eagle. I'll tell you all about it later. Right now I need you to get me a time of death and what it was that actually killed him, and don't say, "the bloody big hole in his back".'

'Aye, but I'll no' be able to gie ye that till I've got him back on the table, ye know that.'

'I know. Just a rough time of death, then. Soon as you can. It'll give my team some sort of time reference to start a trawl of local CCTV. Do what you can for me, eh?'

Hudson nodded. 'A rough time? I'd say that was anytime from the park closing to him being found. That rough enough?'

Paterson smiled. 'I suppose I walked into that one, didn't I?'

'Aye, laddie. That ye did.'

'Right. We're off to see the wizard, then,' said Paterson.

Hudson wrinkled his nose.

'I'm meeting with the acting commissioner and a few bigwigs at Scotland Yard. So, if you can get your photographers to send me through some pics I can show them, I'd appreciate that. Should upset their delicate little tummies nicely.' Paterson turned to Clocks. 'Ready, John?'

'Born ready, mate,' said Clocks.

'Paterson . . .' Hudson waved Paterson toward him. 'A quick word afore ye go.'

'What's up, Jock?'

'I know I've got problems wi' the drink, but dinnae ever think I dinnae bring my "A" game to the table. This man here . . . Anderson . . . I dinnae care if he's the bloody commissioner or not. He's just a sack of meat tae me now. A puzzle, and he'll get the same treatment everyone gets, okay?'

'Sure,' said Paterson, looking a little sheepish. 'I'm sorry, Jock. I didn't mean to offend you.'

Hudson smiled. 'You didnae, ye dumb bastard. But I got you there, eh? Ha! How does it feel?'

Paterson cocked his head to one side and gave him a smile that maybe supported Clocks's view that he had just got off the Sunshine Bus. 'Good one, Jock. Got me there. Savage.'

'Aye, boy. That I did. Now, you an' Princess Leia there can fuck off out of ma crime scene.'

Paterson gave him an exaggerated salute and walked off to join Clocks.

'What's 'e want?' said Clocks.

'Tried to wind me up. Fell flatter than a kipper in a trouser press. I don't know, John. I don't think he's well. Looked rough to me.'

Clocks shrugged. 'Probably the drink. Maybe it's got to 'im at last.'

CHAPTER NINE

At 11.45 a.m., Acting Commissioner (AC) Sam Morne, Deputy Assistant Commissioner (DAC) Elizabeth Boyle, Peter Stannard, the Assistant Commissioner in charge of crime (ACC), and Lee Sterling, the Borough Commander and Paterson's immediate boss, were all seated around a large oak table that sat squarely in the middle of the glass-framed office.

In front of each of them was a single sheet of A4 paper, which was to be used for note-taking purposes only and would then be collected and shredded at the end of the meeting. Nothing on paper or electronics would leave the room.

'Thank you all for coming,' said Morne. 'As I said in my call to each of you, we have a grave situation, which cannot be mentioned over the phone. One never knows who's listening these days or how they're bloody well doing it.'

'I take it that this room *is* secure then?' said Sterling.

'It should be. MI5 designed and built it on our behalf. Secure against all forms of audio and video recordings by both internal and external means.'

Sterling nodded.

'I have two things to talk to you about this morning,' said Morne. 'Earlier this morning, I received a phone call. It is with deep regret that I have to inform you that Mr Anderson was found dead this morning.' That got the room's attention. 'Unfortunately, it was not from natural causes. I don't know the full details surrounding his death as yet. The officer in charge of the case is coming in at noon, hopefully, and he will fully update us.'

'What do you know so far?' said Stannard.

'That's it. Obviously, the OIC wouldn't say much over insecure communications and I agree with his actions. I wanted to get you together first to work out a plan of action on how we deal with this.'

Everyone nodded.

'Who is the officer in the case?' asked Stannard.

Morne closed his eyes for a few seconds and shook his head. He knew they wouldn't be happy.

'And that's the other thing I wanted to talk to you about before he gets here. It's . . . er . . . Detective Superintendent Paterson. Ray Paterson.'

ACC Stannard stared at him for a second or two before speaking. 'Are you joking? Tell me you are.'

Morne met the man's gaze. 'I'm not.'

'Isn't the man on sick leave or gardening leave or something?' said Stannard.

'He was, yes. I understand he resumed work this morning. It seems that Detective Inspector Clocks, the first CID officer on scene, called him up, and he put himself back on duty. I'm not particularly happy about it, but he is, for now, the OIC.'

'Well, get him replaced,' said Boyle.

'I could do that, of course, but I'm not sure that is the best course of action.'

'Why not?'

'Because, whatever you think of him, Ray Paterson is a bloody good copper. He is liked by his team. He's professional. Those two always get results and, for some reason, the press loves them. When this gets out, the press will be onto us to know why Paterson and Clocks are not on the case. Then we'll be on the back foot to explain why.'

'I'm sorry,' said Stannard. 'Am I missing something here?'

'Like what?' said Morne. He knew where this was going straightaway.

'Are Paterson and Clocks the only two officers we have on Murder Investigation teams?'

'No, they're not.'

'I thought not. And can you explain to me why we give a fig about the press? When did they start telling us who we assign to investigate murders? Did I miss the memo?'

Morne looked down at his feet for a moment before looking back up at Stannard. 'No, Peter. There was no memo. The press do not tell us anything of the sort. However, they will know by now that there's been a murder in a public place and they'll want details. Hopefully they won't know it's Anderson, and we need to keep it that way. I would suggest we try our best to keep them onside for this one because we're going to need to keep a lid on it for a while.'

'Issue them a D-notice, then,' said Sterling. 'That'll bloody well keep them gagged.'

'I'm not sure it will. We can stop them going to press, of course. But someone will leak it, someone who'll take umbrage at being stopped by us and will turn to social media. An anonymous post, perhaps. That's all it takes these days.'

Stannard nodded. 'I see your point.'

'I thought it might be an idea if our press office contacted all of the news outlets and informed them that an exclusive will be coming their way if they play ball with us in the early stages. Every editor loves a scoop, and if they think they're the ones to get it, they'll wait.'

'Playing one off against the other,' said Boyle.

'Playing them all off against each other, Liz.'

'They won't be happy once they realise they've all been played.'

'I know.' Morne shrugged. 'I'll worry about that later. For now, I think we need to keep it quiet until we know exactly what we're dealing with.'

All heads turned at the sharp tap on the door. Morne's PA, Kelly Diamond, stood outside. Morne waved her in.

'Yes, Kelly. What is it?'

'Detectives Paterson and Clocks have arrived, sir. They're signing in downstairs.'

'Thanks, Kelly. Bring them in for me, please. There's a good girl.'

Peter Stannard frowned.

CHAPTER TEN

Kelly Diamond was all smiles as she greeted Paterson and Clocks when they stepped out of the lift.

'Greetings, gentlemen. Welcome to Scotland Yard. I'm Kelly. Acting Commissioner Morne has requested that I show you to the office for today's meeting. If you would follow me.'

Paterson and Clocks looked at each other. This was different. Normally they just got waved through to see the boss.

'Cheers, babe,' said Clocks. 'No need to do that, though. We know the way.'

Kelly smiled. 'This isn't the usual meeting room, sir. It's secure. Away from prying eyes and ears.'

Clocks frowned. 'Sounds like they're 'olding it in the bog.'

'Most definitely not there, sir.'

'Should 'old it in there, though. Shit's gonna 'it the fan one way or the other, so seems like the best place for it.'

'If you could show us to the room, Kelly, I'd be grateful,' said Paterson.

'Certainly, sir.' She flashed Paterson a smile. 'This way.' Johnny Clocks shook his head.

As they walked along the hallway, Clocks nudged Paterson a few times and pointed with his head toward Kelly. Paterson looked at him and mouthed, 'What?'

Clocks smiled and gave him the thumbs up. 'You're in there, son,' he whispered.

'Behave yourself,' Paterson whispered back.

Kelly knocked on the door to the office, opened it and announced Paterson and Clocks to the room. She stood aside as they walked past her.

'Actually,' she whispered to Paterson. 'How about we meet for a drink sometime and we'll see whether or not you're in there?'

She smiled and exited the office.

'Good morning, gentlemen. Thank you for coming.' AC Morne shook Paterson's hand. 'And you must be DI Clocks?'

'The one an' only,' said Clocks.

'Yes, of course. Pleasure to meet you.' Morne reached out to shake Clocks's hand.

Wonder how long that'll last, Paterson thought to himself. He looked around at the faces of the assembled group, recognising all three. 'Good morning,' he said.

'Good morning,' said Boyle. 'Please, sit down.'

Paterson pulled out a chair and sat opposite her. He'd known her predecessor and had got along with him, but the only thing he really knew of her was what he'd been told: a sharp intelligence, a fiery temper and she didn't suffer fools gladly. He'd seen that from watching her on TV. He'd been particularly impressed when she more than held her own in interviews with Andrew Marr and John Humphreys and put Piers Morgan in his place when he got a bit too shouty for her liking.

'Thank you,' he said to her.

'Ta.' Clocks dragged out his chair, leaving tracks in the thick carpet. 'Bit warm in 'ere, innit?'

Boyle and the others ignored him.

'I understand you're the officer in charge, Mr Paterson,' said Stannard, 'That correct?'

Paterson turned his attention to him. He'd been present at meetings with him and seen him on the television many a time. What he'd seen hadn't impressed him. Stannard was the sort who would ask a question of someone and then talk, sometimes shout, over the answer, a particular form of ignorance Paterson had no time for. He just hoped that Clocks would not get all fired up if he did it to him. 'Yes, sir. That's correct.'

'You were off sick weren't you? How did you catch this call?'

'I got a call from DI Clocks early this morning. He felt I should be there as it was a particularly nasty murder.' Stannard's eyes darted to Clocks, who threw him a wink.

Stannard turned back to Paterson. 'So, tell us what you know so far.'

Paterson cleared his throat. 'Well, sir, it seems that Mr Anderson was taken to Southwark Park sometime during the evening, secured to a large ornamental rock and tied by his wrists. Face down. Got the picture?' Everybody nodded. 'His feet were also secured to stop him moving about too much.'

Stannard raised a single eyebrow. 'And?'

'His back was opened up with some kind of sharp implement. I suspect it was a large knife, maybe a small axe.' Boyle winced at this information. Paterson caught the look. 'I'm afraid it gets worse ma'am. His ribs were severed from his spine and his lungs were pulled out through his body and placed either side of his back.'

'Jesus . . .' Boyle's face was one of horror.

Clocks couldn't help himself. 'We thought that at f—'

'John. No.' Paterson shook his head. Stannard eyed them both carefully.

'Sorry,' said Paterson. 'To continue . . . when we examined the body, we had no idea who it was at first. DI Clocks carried out a routine search to see if we could find some form of identity and we found his silver token in his back pocket.'

'You had no idea who it was? Your own commissioner?' said Stannard. His tone was accusatory, and it didn't sit well with Paterson.

'No, sir. To be fair, it was dark and raining torrentially. It was difficult to recognise him under those circumstances and our first priority was to get the scene under control and the vic . . . Mr Anderson, under cover pending the arrival of the senior forensic pathologist. There are things to do at a crime scene in an order of priority. Looking at his face wasn't a particularly high one at that point. I was just pleased he still had one.'

'And why didn't you wait for the pathologist and forensics to arrive, Paterson?' said Stannard. 'Before you went rifling through his pockets. You may have destroyed evidence.'

Clocks pulled his shoulders back and fixed his gaze on Stannard. Paterson caught the move out of the corner of his eye.

'Given the severe weather conditions, *sir*,' said Paterson, 'I formed the opinion that the vast majority of exterior contact evidence would already have been rendered unusable.'

'Would it not have been better to wait and let the professionals collect evidence?' Stannard kept his eyes firmly on Paterson.

'I wasn't collecting evidence. I was looking to identify him.'

'Don't be impertinent, Paterson,' Stannard snapped.

'Excuse me? I don't consider it impertinent to push back against criticism. I've done this more than enough times to know what I can and can't do at the scene of a crime, so don't be worrying yourself over forensic evidence, *sir*.'

Stannard bristled and drew a sharp inward breath.

'Let's not get into an argument gentleman, please,' said AC Morne. 'We have a terrible situation to deal with here and it has to be dealt with swiftly and quietly. We can't have it leaking that the most senior police officer in the country was so brutally and publicly . . .'

'The word you're lookin' for is *butchered*, guv,' said Clocks.

All eyes turned to him and nobody looked impressed.

'What? Well, 'e was. Can't beat about the bush. Someone did a right number on 'im, an' we need to get on and find out who it was a bit lively before someone else gets butchered.'

Clocks pushed his chair back and looked straight at Stannard. 'Might even be you next, guv, if this is a cop killer.'

'What are you doing, Mr Clocks?' said Morne.

'Gettin' on, guv. A bit lively.'

'Er, sit yourself back down, please. We haven't finished.' Clocks scanned the room. It was obvious they weren't about to let him or Paterson go just yet. He sat back down.

'Anything else we need to know, Mr Paterson?' said Morne.

'Couple of things, sir. DI Clocks has a point about it being a cop killer. It could very well be, which then puts us all on alert. Whoever did this started at the top. He could well be working his way down through the ranks. Just bear it in mind.'

'And the other thing?' said Morne.

'I believe this type of death is an execution method that, historically, was attributed to the Vikings of old. It's known as the Blood Eagle and is usually handed out as a form of extreme punishment for some perceived wrong. It has strong ritualistic connotations associated with it.'

Stannard's eyes narrowed. 'You seem to know an awful lot about it.'

'I'm an educated man, Mr Stannard. I studied medieval history at uni.'

'An' 'e saw it on the telly,' Clocks chimed in. '*Vikings*. Amazon Prime.'

'And I saw it on the telly. Amazon Prime,' Paterson echoed.

Stannard sat bolt upright. 'You think this is funny, do you?'

'Not in the slightest,' said Paterson. 'It was indeed on the telly, but my understanding is that there's no direct evidence they actually did carry out such barbarism. It's been handed down through spoken history. Folklore. There's no doubt in my mind that someone, for some reason, has copied this particular form of execution, and we need to find out why. If our killer is keeping true to the ritual of the execution, then we need to find out who the hell Anderson pissed off enough to go through with this.'

Stannard stared at Paterson again. The implied accusation didn't go unnoticed.

'Oh, I see. You think it's me. That makes a fucking change.'

'Language, Paterson,' Commander Sterling said.

'With respect, sir, I've been back at work less than half a day and I'm already in the frame for someone's murder. I'm getting just a little bit sick and tired of catching the blame for every police officer that dies in this job. Don't even go there, okay. You know it wasn't me.'

'Do we?' said Stannard.

Paterson whirled on him. 'You should do, *sir*. God knows you've got enough bugs and microdot CCTV scattered about my house to know what I'm up to every minute of every day. Not to mention the ones in my car.'

Boyle looked mortified. As the DAC, she had given permission for the surveillance measures to be put in place.

'What?' Paterson rounded on her. 'You think I didn't know? Did you honestly think I wouldn't have the brains to run counter-surveillance measures on a daily basis? Well, unfortunately for you, I have the brains *and* the money to have these measures carried out remotely so that you wouldn't see me wandering about the house looking for your bugs. I was going to save it as a surprise, but I have a file about three inches thick that will form part of the lawsuit I'm about to launch.'

'Yep. Me 'n' all,' said Clocks. 'Done my 'ouse an' all, ain'tcha? Hope you ain't posted up any of me and me missus gettin' our leg over. I won't be too chuffed with that, an' neither will my missus, I can tell yer. She'll go garrity. Insecure about 'er body, see?' He stared at Elizabeth Boyle. 'But, if you've got any copies floatin' about, let me 'ave a look at 'em.'

'I can assure you, Mr Paterson—'

'No you can't, ma'am. You or someone in your department would have had to authorise this, so you're not in a position to assure me of anything. Now, Anderson hated us. Fact. Was it mutual? No. To be honest, we were totally indifferent to him. He was just pissing up the wrong tree. We couldn't have cared less about his little witch hunt, and that's the truth of it. But even if we had hated his guts, this isn't on us, and your little video cams will attest to our movements. That said, I want to find out who did this. Whatever he was like as a human, he didn't deserve to die like that. Now, you can take us off the case and put us under yet another pointless investigation if you want.' Paterson shrugged. 'I don't give a fuck one way or the other. Otherwise, you do what you do and just let us get on with the investigation.'

The room stayed silent for a little too long. Paterson wasn't going to let them off the hook. Someone needed to make a decision.

AC Morne decided. 'You and Clocks will remain in charge of this investigation.' He looked around the room. 'Any objections?'

'You know my thoughts,' said Stannard.

'We do. Thank you,' said Morne. 'Okay then, we're done here for now. Thank you all for coming. Please let Mr Paterson have your phone numbers, just in case I'm not around for any reason — meetings et cetera.'

Boyle fished out a business card from the top pocket of her jacket and held it out to Paterson. 'This is my direct line and on the back is my private mobile number.'

Stannard did the same. Handing his card over, he gave Paterson a cold look. 'Make sure you don't give out my private details to anyone. Understood?'

Paterson glared at him.

'I expect you to report any developments in the case to me as soon as they happen. I don't care what time of the day or night. You keep me informed, Paterson. Understood?'

'I'll go through Mr Sterling first. He's my immediate line manager. Understood?'

'Actually,' said Morne. 'I'd like to break with protocol this time around. I want you to call me first if you get anything and I'll cascade it down the line.'

Clocks rolled his eyes. Management speak.

'Good. Then there's nothing else to be said for the time being. Mrs Boyle, I want you to go to Number 10 and inform the PM of what's happened and where we are at the moment. Stress the importance of secure communications. I have to go and inform Mr Anderson's family. It's only right it comes from me.' Everybody rose from the table as the three senior officers made their way out of the office.

Paterson and Clocks were about to leave when Morne stopped them. 'Sit back down, please, gents.'

'What is it, sir?' said Paterson. 'We're busy.'

'I know, I know. Look, I just want you both to know that I didn't believe any of Anderson's bullshit about you two. In fact, I was instrumental in standing against him and having him placed on leave.'

Paterson and Clocks sat looking at him. Both impassive.

'I know you can both go off on a tangent when you want to, but I'm okay with that. I was good friends with Wallace Young, and he had rock-solid faith in your honesty and integrity, and if he did — well, that's good enough for me. All I'm saying to you is, tread very carefully with this one. This is super sensitive.'

Clocks nodded. 'Fair enough, guv. Believe it or not, we do know 'ow to tiptoe.'

AC Morne sighed. 'If you say so, Mr Clocks.' He turned to Paterson. 'Now, I have to go and tell a wife that her husband is dead. Never a nice thing to do.'

'I'd like to come with you, sir, if I may?' said Paterson.

'Do you think that's wise, Mr Paterson? Given that Anderson wasn't your biggest fan, I would imagine he'd have made mention of it to his wife. You may not find a warm welcome there.'

'Probably not, sir, but we are going to have to speak to her at some point, so I guess now is as good a time as any. If you let me have his address, you can jump in with us if you want?'

Morne's eyes flicked to Johnny Clocks.

'Don't worry about Clocksy, sir. I have some biscuits in the car. He's much more docile when he's eaten.'

Morne smiled. 'Thank you, but no. I'll get my driver to take me there. More formal that way.'

'Understood,' said Paterson. 'See you there.'

* * *

Paterson and Clocks made their way back down the corridor toward Kelly's desk. She looked up and smiled as the two men made their way toward her. Paterson smiled back and reached into his pocket for his card. He handed it to her, told her to give him a call later that evening and turned to Clocks who was looking around at the different offices.

'John,' Paterson said.

'What?'

'Where'd that bit about killing senior policemen come from? That's new.'

Clocks chuckled. 'I know. I made it up. It just amused me to think they'll be shittin' bricks and lookin' over their shoulders until we catch whoever did this.'

'Nice one,' said Paterson.

''Ere, give us a look at that Stannard geezer's business card, will yer?'

Paterson fished it out of his pocket. 'There you go. What's the matter?'

'Nothing. He said his personal mobile numbers on it too, didn't 'e?'

'Yeah. Why . . .'

'Nothing. Didn't 'e also say to not 'and it out to anyone?'

'He did. John, what are you up to?'

'Kelly,' said Clocks. 'Where's the photocopier room, babe?'

'John. No!'

'Why not? It'll be a hoot.'

Paterson nodded. 'Yeah it would but . . . no. Just no. Give it back.'

Clocks looked at the back of it then handed it over. 'Too late, mate. I've got it now. It's in me memory bank.' He turned away and walked off. 'Kelly, you got a marker pen of some sort?'

She looked at him, bemused, then pulled out a black Sharpie from her drawer.

'Oh, an' where's the bog? I'm bustin' for a whizz. Me back teeth are floatin''

Paterson realised straight away what he was going to do. 'Clocksy! Do not write his phone number on the walls. Do not!'

'As if I would.' His face lit up. 'Oh, come on. It'll be fun. Lighten up a bit. 'E won't know we've done it.'

'Er, "we"? There's no "we" at all.'

'Look, I go in the gents' bog and write, "For a good time, call Peter. No fantasies refused. I love it." Where's the 'arm in that?'

'Where's the harm? Everywhere! He's the bloody assistant commissioner for crime, for Christ's sake.'

Kelly chuckled.

'Yeah, but the people callin' won't know that, will they? C'mon. This is too good to waste, Ray. You know it.'

CHAPTER ELEVEN

Paterson pulled the car up outside the ornamental wrought iron gates of Sir Scott Anderson's Georgian-style manor house and looked around — no sign of Acting Commissioner Morne as yet. He suspected he wouldn't be too far behind.

Clocks let out a long whistle. 'This place ain't too shabby, is it? What d'yer reckon? One, one point two mill?'

Paterson looked over at the house. 'All of that, I should think. I doubt you'd get much change out of four and a half, five million.'

'Fuck me. All right for some, ain't it? Was 'e in the same lodge as you then?'

'What lodge?'

'Oh, don't gimme that. You're a bloody Mason. Don't think I don't know.'

'A Mason?'

'Yeah. The funny 'andshake brigade. Y'know, where you all stand around with yer tits 'anging out and yer trouser legs rolled up while you kiss a chicken on the arse. I know what you get up to, you lot.'

'I'm not a Mason. Doesn't interest me.'

'What? You must be with all your money.'

'The two don't necessarily go together, y'know? It's not a binding obligation to join once you have a few pounds in the bank.'

Clocks looked suspicious. 'I dunno. Seems right up your alley that does.'

'What? Rolling up my trouser leg?'

'No. Kissing chickens on the arse. That's got your name written all over it.'

Paterson laughed as they stepped out of the car. 'Sorry to disappoint you, mate. But I'm really not. Don't have time for that, what with all the pig sex I'm having.'

A chauffeured car turned into the road and pulled up behind them. Acting Commissioner Morne stepped out in full regalia, looking every inch a senior policeman: tall, immaculately groomed and not a hair out of place. He set his peaked cap carefully on his head and spent a few seconds adjusting it. He quickly checked his reflection in the driver's window before speaking to Paterson. 'Have you seen anybody?'

'No,' said Paterson. 'Haven't been here that long ourselves. Just got out the car.'

'Okay. So, I'll introduce us and deliver the bad news. We'll have to gauge her reaction before you ask her any questions. I know you have to get on, but we need to be sensitive. You may have to come back in a day or two.'

'Let's see how it goes, shall we?' Paterson pressed the buzzer on the intercom. On the third press a tinny voice asked who it was, and five seconds later the gate swung open.

As they made their way toward the house along the gravel path, Paterson took in the surroundings. Judging by its size, he guessed the house was probably five or six bedrooms on two floors. The front entrance was flanked by two white pillars on either side, and a mock gas lamp hung down to light the entrance. Everything was kept neat and tidy in the grounds. No kiddies' playthings out front, so unlikely that Anderson had grandchildren or, if he did, they weren't allowed to play out the front of the house. Separate from the house itself was a double garage.

AC Morne climbed the steps and pressed the bell. No answer. He pressed again, longer this time. Still no answer. He looked across to Paterson, who shrugged.

Morne pressed it again. 'Want me round the back, guv?' said Clocks.

Morne shook his head. 'Hold on a moment, Mr Clocks. Let's not be hasty.'

'Fuckin' 'asty?' said Clocks under his breath. 'Been 'ere a minute already.'

The door suddenly opened and a young man peered through the opening. It was immediately apparent that he had some form of physical disability. His jaw was twisted and his right arm was pulled in against his chest.

AC Morne was taken aback. He instantly assumed the young man was Anderson's and was shocked that he was unaware that he had a disabled son. He'd never made mention of it.

'Er, yes,' said Anderson. 'I'm sorry to trouble you but could we speak to your mother, please?'

The young man shook his head. 'Mummy . . . Mummy's not here. S-s-sorry.' He grinned at Morne.

'Well, we know yer dad's not,' Clocks whispered to Paterson, who turned and glared at him.

'Can you tell me when she'll be back?

'S-s-sorry. I don't . . . know.'

Morne nodded. 'Okay. Not to worry. Is there anyone else we can talk with? It's quite important.'

'No. S-so . . . sorry. My s-sister's out . . . as . . . well.'

'That's quite all right. Do you have a phone number for either of them, please?'

The young man shook his head.

'Okay. What's your name, please?' said Morne.

'Fane,' the boy said.

Paterson wasn't sure he'd heard him correctly. 'Vane, did you say?'

He shook his head. 'No. No. Fane. F. A . . . N. E. Fane.'

'Okay, fellah,' said Paterson. 'Got it now, thanks. Can I ask, do your mum and sister often go out together?'

Fane nodded. 'To the shops.'

'All right. That's fine. Would you mind if we came in and took a look around?'

Fane's eyes widened and he pushed the door. Paterson stopped it with his hand. 'It's okay, son. I didn't mean to upset you. I'm sorry, okay?'

Fane looked at him through the gap. 'Mummy says . . . n-not to let anyone, not anyone . . . into the h-house.'

'That's fine. I understand,' said Paterson. 'Listen, when your mum comes home, can you tell her the police called and we need to speak to her please? It is very important.' He held out his business card and pushed it through the crack. The boy reached out with his good hand and took the card. He didn't bother to read it.

'Thank y-y-youuuuu.' He closed the door, leaving three bewildered policemen standing on the porch.

'Well, that was unexpected,' said Morne. 'I had no idea.'

'About what?' said Paterson.

'That he had a disabled son.'

Paterson shrugged. 'Maybe it wasn't something he felt he needed to share.'

Morne nodded. 'Perhaps. Rather leaves us in a situation, doesn't it? Do you have any suggestions?'

'Got one for you, guv,' said Clocks. Both men turned to look at him. 'Given the kid's one of the broken toys, I reckon 'e's gonna need a bit of care. Maybe full-time.'

'He's what?' said Morne.

'One of the broken toys.'

'Whoa!' said Paterson. 'Bloody hell, John. Behave yourself. Don't say that about him. You can't say things like that that anymore.'

'What? Not even if he's broken?'

'No. It's offensive.'

'Fuck me. What isn't offensive these days?'

'He's not broken.'

'Well, 'is hand is. Tell yer the truth, I wouldn't trust him to make a cuppa tea on 'is own.'

AC Morne shook his head.

Clocks carried on. 'So, if no one's at 'ome with 'im then either Mum or Sis is comin' back soon or — an' 'ere's the worryin' bit — they've both been swagged off too.'

'Swagged?' said Morne.

Clocks rolled his eyes and sighed. 'Right, 'ow would you smart people say it? Swagged. It means taken. Captured, kidnapped. Swagged. Goddit now?'

'Yes, thank you. I've got it now.' Morne looked across at Paterson.

'It's a possibility we have to consider, sir,' he said.

'Agreed. What do you think is a reasonable amount of time to give it?'

'Really, sir? I'd say none. We have the commissioner of police murdered and his wife and daughter possibly missing. I'll get one of my team to sit on the house in case anyone shows up. But in the meantime we pull out all the stops. We need as much information about these two as possible. We need neighbours spoken to, local shops visited, train station and petrol garage CCTV checked within a five-mile radius. We need a check done with missing persons to see if any bodies matching their descriptions have turned up within the last twenty-four hours. We need to find out if there are any relatives we can contact. They may have gone visiting but, whatever the reason, we need them found.'

Morne looked quite shocked. He knew he should have thought of that. 'Er, yes, yes. Quite right. I'm sorry. I wasn't thinking. Still in a bit of shock, I suppose.'

'You'll get the 'ang of it, guv,' said Clocks. 'Knock about with us long enough and nothing'll shock you anymore.'

'Sir,' said Paterson, 'can I ask you to take care of the missing persons aspect of this for us, please? With your clout, things will move an awful lot quicker.'

'Yes, yes. Of course. Leave it with me.'

The three headed back to their respective cars. Paterson opened his door then stopped, closed his eyes and breathed in the damp morning air.

'You all right, Ray? What you doin'?' said Clocks.

'Clearing my head.'

Clocks clicked his seatbelt in place. 'That ain't gonna take too long, is it? Fuck all rattlin' around up there to block it up.'

Paterson got in and closed the door, ignoring Clocks's comment. 'So, now we could be looking at another two victims. Bloody great.'

'We don't know that yet,' said Clocks.

'I know. But it was a good point you had out there.'

'I know. I always 'ave a point. Can't do anything about it yet, though. So, we'll 'ang on 'ere for a while. I'll call up the local nick an' get a uniform out to replace us. I'm not wasting one of our firm sitting on a door all mornin'. We'll 'ead back to the Bat Cave so you can meet the new bods. But first stop . . . Rosie's café for an FBB.'

'A what?' Paterson said.

'An FBB. A fuckin' big breakfast. Bloody 'ell, Ray. I thought you knew that. How long have we been together? It's like you don't listen to me.'

Paterson looked across at him, aghast. 'You want breakfast?'

'Yeah. What's wrong with that?'

'A few hours ago we were looking inside Anderson's back. We saw his lungs hanging out.'

'And your point is?'

'Jesus. Doesn't it upset you?'

'Doesn't what upset me? The fact that a man's dead or that 'is giblets were 'anging out?'

'Both.'

'Nope. Shit 'appens an' I want me breakfast. Two sausages, egg, chips, fried slice, baked beans and a cuppa should go down a treat about now, so pull yerself together, you big Nancy, and let's go.'

Paterson shook his head. 'You'll have to wait until a local gets here to replace us, and that might be a while. So, make the call.'

'Aye, aye, skipper!' Clocks pulled out his phone. 'I wonder if there's a local café nearby that does a bit of the ol' Deliveroo? I'll ask. D'you want anything or not?'

Paterson sighed. 'Yeah. Go on then. I'll have an avocado and chickpea sandwich on rye bread.'

Clocks sniffed. 'Ray, I'm phoning a café not Nigella bleedin' Lawson. They won't 'ave any of that ol' bollocks, an' you know it.'

'Ask them for me.'

'No. They'll think there's something wrong with me.'

'Leave it, then. It's not important.'

'Why can't you just 'ave a sausage, egg an' bacon sandwich like me? Like normal people?'

'It's not healthy.'

Clocks opened up the Deliveroo app on his phone. 'Sausage, egg an' bacon sandwich for one, then.'

CHAPTER TWELVE

Replaced on the door of Anderson's house by a uniformed constable and with Clocks's urge for a greasy breakfast now satisfied, they walked into the main office of Tower Bridge police station. Paterson was greeted by warm smiles, pats on the back and a little bit of ribbing from the established members of the team. All of them wanted to know if he was feeling better and all of them said that, no, thanks to his newly grown stubble, they could barely see the scar left along the entire length of his jawline. The scar served as a reminder of his encounter with one of three seriously deranged people involved in the murder and dismemberment of children in the vain hope of 'building' a child to replace their own that died. Welcomes over, Paterson's priority was to gather the team, speak to the new members, assign tasks, set up a murder board and hold a briefing on the morning's events. First priority for Clocks was a cup of tea.

'Right. Good afternoon, ladies!' Clocks shouted as he walked toward the back of the room. All heads turned toward him. 'Which one of you lot wants to make your favourite DI a cup of Rosy Lee?'

There was no response.

'C'mon then. Any takers? None of you? No? Well, I ain't doin' it meself. Got things to do. Miss Rocket. You're on tea duty. Two sugars in mine. Make it lively.'

DS Suzi Rocket pulled herself up to her full five foot five and frowned. 'Why me?'

Clocks sighed. 'Because you're a lady and therefore an excellent maker of tea.' Her frown grew deeper. 'An' I'll 'ave a couple of digestives while you're out there. Off you go.'

'John,' said Paterson, 'remember what we said. We had that little chat, remember?'

Clocks looked at him then nodded. 'I do. Yeah. Sorry.' He turned to DS Rocket. 'Sorry, Suzi. That was very sexist of me. Please, forget the biscuits. I'll get them meself. You 'ave a rest, love.' He turned back to Paterson, a big grin plastered all over his face. 'Better?'

Paterson shook his head. 'Introduce me, John.'

'Oh, shit! Yeah. Nearly forgot. Sorry. Suzi, 'ang fire with the tea, love. Come an' say 'ello to the guv'nor.' He waved her over. 'C'mon.'

She made her way over to Paterson, who beamed his best smile at her and held out his hand. 'Good morning. I'm Detective Superintendent Paterson. Pleased to meet you.'

She took his hand and shook it firmly. 'Good morning, sir. Pleased to meet you.'

'Please, don't take any notice of DI Clocks. I'm sure you've already worked out that he can be a bit of an arse at the best of times. Quite frankly, he doesn't quite grasp that the world has somehow managed to move on without his help and we're no longer in the seventies. He also likes to play to the crowds.'

DS Rocket smiled at him. 'Thank you, sir. I appreciate that. I've already got his measure. Got that in the first two minutes when he couldn't take his eyes off of my chest.'

Paterson grimaced. 'As I said, stuck in the past. I've sent him on courses, but it hasn't done any good. Three instructors went home in tears and one of them was a man. He was trying to teach him about racial sensitivity but . . .' He turned to look at Clocks and shook his head. 'It didn't seem to go too well. Anyway . . .' He turned back to DS Rocket. 'Glad to have you aboard and I'll have a proper chat with you as soon as I can. But, as you've no doubt gathered, it's going to be a busy week.'

DS Rocket smiled and nodded. 'Well, whatever you want me to do, let me know.'

'I still want you to make me a cup of tea,' said Clocks. 'We'll see where we go from there. I've let you off gettin' the biscuits, haven't I?'

DS Rocket gave him the finger.

'Charmin',' Clocks said. 'No one's got any respect these days.' He called over DC Tommy Gunn.

'This is Tommy, sir. Tommy Gunn. His last posting was on the Child Sexual Offences team.'

The two men shook hands.

'A pleasure to meet you, sir,' said Gunn.

'You too. How are you finding us so far?'

'Yeah, it's interesting, and of course, now we have this case . . . I'm very much looking forward to being part of the team.'

'Any problems?'

Gunn shook his head. 'None at all. Get the odd bit of ribbing about my name, but I'm well used to that. Water off a duck's back to me.'

'Just as well then,' said Paterson. 'What names has DI Clocks come up with for you?'

'Well,' Clocks said, 'I was thinking Machine Gun or Bullet or maybe Shotgun. Not settled on one yet, but I will. Ooh! Popgun! Yeah, that'll do it. Popgun.'

Half turning, Gunn stopped. 'Nice one with the Childmaker, sir. It sounds like that was some crazy shit.'

Paterson gave a curt nod. 'Yes, it certainly was. Thank you. John . . . office.'

Paterson sat down at his desk and opened the bottom drawer. He rummaged around for a few seconds then looked up at Clocks, who was lowering himself into a seat opposite him. 'Where's that bottle of gin gone?'

'Gin?' said Clocks.

'Yes. Gin. I had a full bottle in here before I went off sick. Where is it?

'Dunno. Must 'ave fallen out.'

'Out of a desk drawer?'

'Must 'ave. Can't think of any other reason it's not there.'

Paterson grinned. 'No, me neither.' He pushed the drawer shut and sat back in the chair. 'We need to talk, mate.'

'What about? Am I in the shit again?'

'No. Not yet, but we both know it won't be long before you are — before *we* are. We need to take a breather and see where we are with this case. Goes without saying we've to get on top of this fast. We're going to have to interview a number of Anderson's high-ranking mates up at the Yard, and that includes the three we met this morning. They won't like it, but . . . tough. I want as much background info on Anderson as we can get. Even if you take the ritual element out of this killing, it's still bloody barbaric, and we need to find out who hated him enough to risk doing this in a public place.'

'It was dark, Ray. Mitigates a bit of risk.'

'A bit, but not much. Think of what it took to get him there, John. Let's assume that he was unconscious when he was tied to the rock. We need to know how that happened. How was he transported there and was there more than one person involved?'

'I reckon so. An unconscious man's an 'eavy ol' lump. Even a weedy little knob like him.'

Paterson nodded. 'And then there's the time it took to perform the Blood Eagle.'

'You reckon it took a while, then?'

'Dunno. But given his back was hacked open, his ribs separated from his spine and his lungs pulled out you have to wonder how long something like that *does* take.'

'If you know what you're doin' I don't suppose it'd take too long. A few good slices with a decent sharp knife to open up his back, less than a minute maybe. Another six to eight whacks with an axe to do 'is ribs, another minute p'rhaps and then a few seconds pulling out 'is giblets. Not long at all, I should think. Mind you, I should think all that stuff was a bit on the slippery side, so that might 'ave added a minute or two tryin' to get 'old of 'em.'

Paterson sighed. 'You said, "if you know what you're doing". You don't think this is a layman?'

Clocks shrugged. 'Doubt it. Whoever did this isn't squeamish, are they? This ain't gonna be the work of someone who wigged out an' lost 'is top an' decided to do . . . that . . . to 'im. This is planned out all proper, like. I reckon whoever did this knew 'im.'

'Why d'you say that?'

'Anderson was a cop, albeit a shiny-arsed pen-pusher. He would have had his head screwed on, particularly if he thought we were after him.'

Paterson did a quick double take. 'Us? Why would he think that?'

'Not sayin' 'e did. But given 'ow much 'e despises . . . sorry, *despised* us, an' that 'e tried to 'ang every crime from the last fifty years on us, 'e might 'ave thought we'd try an 'ave a pop at 'im. Revenge? I dunno. Don't matter. All I'm sayin' is, I'd think he'll 'ave been wide awake and careful.'

Paterson nodded slowly. 'Okay. I can see that. If he was on high alert then he would have been extremely wary of strangers approaching him. So, what are you thinking?'

'Hear me out. Three theories. First one . . . a butcher.'

'What? A butcher? Where's that idea come from?'

'Well, they're pretty good with knives an' choppers an' axes. Separating meat from ribs would be easy for them. Plus, they're not the squeamish kind.'

'Maybe. But I can't see Anderson knocking around with butchers as mates, can you?'

'No, to be honest. An' I can't see 'im 'avin' one as an enemy either. I mean, who 'as a butcher as an enemy? Gotta be stupid to piss one of them off. Once they've chopped you up, it's in the mincer for you. Sausages all round. Not gonna 'ave butchers in the family either are they? Anderson an' 'is lot don't strike me as the kind to 'ave a workin' man sittin' next to 'em at weddin's an' funerals so . . . theory number two.'

'And that is?'

'A Viking and 'is mates.'

'Don't be stupid.'

'Fair enough. Moving on to theory number three . . . Maybe it was the missus an' the daughter who did 'im in an' they're off on their toes.'

Paterson thought about it for a second. 'Can't see that either.'

'Why?'

'It just seems too . . . too extreme. It doesn't feel right.'

'There you go with that *feelings* bollocks again. You need to forget about all that and look at the evidence.'

'Which is?'

Clocks fidgeted. 'All right. Not much, I'll give yer that, but you know what I mean.'

'It's not them. It makes way more sense to assume they've been snatched by the person who did this or someone he's working with. We need to make sure that the search for them is ramped up if we don't get anything useful in the next eight hours.'

CHAPTER THIRTEEN

DAY 2

Ray Paterson was second into the office and took a minute to just enjoy the silence. Whenever he could, he would always get in an hour or two earlier than everybody else. It was just his way. With a million things to do, he knew the day ahead was going to be long and arduous. In the back of his head, he was waiting for the call to the next murder. Johnny Clocks was right: a murder as grotesque as yesterday's was just a calling card, a precursor of more to come.

He checked the bottom drawer of his desk again and was disappointed to see that Clocks hadn't replaced the bottle of gin that he'd nicked while he was off on sick leave. It was too early for a drink anyway. He sat back in his chair and ran his mind over the events of yesterday from the morning to the evening. The late-night team debrief had brought out nothing of any use. A dozen CCTV recordings had been collected from various offices, petrol stations and street cams, but these had so far shown nothing. The monotonous slog of more viewings would have to be continued today. Door knocking had yielded a negative result; no one had come forward to say they had seen anything strange. There was no update on Mrs

Anderson or her daughter. The senior management team at Scotland Yard was giving consideration to putting that aspect out to the press.

The press had gotten wind of the case now and had immediately been slapped with a D-notice that prevented them from printing anything in the papers that may give away Anderson's identity, at least until such time as his family could be contacted. Paterson thought that it was a dumb move telling the press that Anderson was the victim because, until that point, they didn't have a clue who the victim was anyway. But somehow, they had a picture, albeit not a very clear one. He knew it was just a matter of time now until everything leaked out.

His desk phone rang, startling him. 'Hello?'

It was a female voice. 'Mr Paterson, it's PC Hay from the front desk. I've got an Inspector Lawton from Thames Wapping on the phone. They want to speak to someone from the murder squad. Shall I put him through?'

'Yes, of course.' The phone went dead for a second.

'Morning,' said a gruff voice.

'Good morning. Detective Superintendent Paterson here. How can I help?'

'Got one for you, sir. A strange one, too. We got an email come in to us about forty-five minutes ago telling us to go to a specific spot on the river where a boat called *Rose* was moored and we'd find something of interest. A bag. We thought it odd, but I jumped on one of our patrol boats and had a look at where they said. We found a bag dangling off the side of a boat. Most of it was submerged in the water. We pulled it up — heavy it was. Opened it and found a man's body inside.'

Paterson's mind raced. Could this have anything to do with Anderson's murder? Could it be the same killer again? But a body in a bag wasn't exactly in the same league as a Blood Eagle.

Inspector Lawton's voice brought him out of his thoughts. 'And this is where it gets weird . . .'

'Go on,' said Paterson.

'Well, inside the bag were two dogs, five snakes and, believe it or not, a small monkey. I'm guessing that when the bag went into the water everything inside was alive.'

'Why'd you say that, Inspector?'

'Well, the victim was torn to shreds. My thinking is that the animals knew they were in trouble and freaked out, desperate to get out of the bag. Our man is riddled with bite wounds, as are the dogs and the monkey. I get the impression it was carnage in that bag for a fair old while. Our victim has lost an eye, most of his throat and a large part of his stomach. He's got bite and scratch marks on his shoulders, neck, head and face. All over, in fact. Did I mention he was naked?'

'No.'

'Sorry. He was naked. Terrible mess.'

'Where's the body now?'

'We've got him in our morgue. We'll keep him here until you arrive.'

'Do you know who owns the boat?'

'Not yet, but we're on it. Shouldn't take too long.'

'Okay. I'll be on my way shortly. Have to wake up a few people first.' Paterson glanced at his watch. 'Gimme an hour.'

'No rush,' said Lawton. 'Not like he's going anywhere.'

Paterson hung up and made another call.

'The fuck . . .' said a fuzzy John Clocks.

'Morning, Johnny boy. My turn to wake you nice and early. Get yourself into the nick a bit lively, mate. Thames Wapping have got one for us, and it sounds like it could be our boy's work again.'

Clocks's voice was instantly more alert. 'Where?'

'The river boys have fished him out and got him on their slab. Got a tip-off about it. Get yourself in and I'll tell you all about it when you're a bit more with it. They're expecting us within an hour.'

'An hour?'

'Yep. An hour.'

'Fuck me, Ray. I'll 'ave to skip me shower.'

'Like that's a thing.'

'Fuck off.'

'Oh, John . . .'

'What?'

'Seeing as you're dodging the shower, do a quick detour and pick me up a coffee will you?'

The phone went dead.

'Good man,' Paterson said into the dead receiver.

CHAPTER FOURTEEN

Fifty-five minutes after Paterson woke him from his slumbers, Clocks burst into the building with two styrofoam cups in a cardboard tray. Suzi Rocket and Tommy Gunn were at their desks, working away. He acknowledged them with a nod of the head then strolled into Paterson's office.

'Mornin',' he said.

Paterson looked up from the notes on his desk. 'Don't sit down, John. We're going to be late.'

'What? Can't I even have me coffee? Five minutes is all.'

Paterson nodded. 'Five minutes. What did you get me?'

'Your favourite. A whatthefuckalatte.'

'Low-fat oat milk latte with a shot of vanilla? A wisp of cinnamon and a secondary wisp of chocolate?'

Clocks looked at him. 'Yeah, that's the one.'

'It's not is it?'

'No, course it's not. I've told you before I'm not standing there makin' a lemon of meself asking for all that poncey bollocks you like. You've got a bog-standard latte an' that's it. If it bleedin' kills me I'll make a man of you yet. Now, what we got?'

Paterson recounted the conversation he'd had with Inspector Lawton, stopping to check the notes he'd made when the call ended.

'Sounds a bit gruesome, dunnit?'

'Well, we're going to take a look in a minute.'

'Fair enough.' Clocks swigged at his coffee and grimaced. 'This is nearly bleedin' cold. I asked 'er for extra 'ot.'

'How can you have *extra* hot? Hot's hot, isn't it?'

'Apparently not. I was in a queue once when I 'eard some bird asking for extra 'ot. So I did the same.'

'And was it?'

'Nope. At least I don't think so. I still burned me lips on it though.' Clocks downed the last of his drink. 'I think the soppy cow who served me this mornin' must 'ave 'ad 'er deaf ears on. That wasn't 'ot in the slightest.'

Paterson left his cup unopened. 'Come on. Time to go.'

CHAPTER FIFTEEN

Paterson stared down at the body the river police had fished out of the water: a male, late fifties, naked. His body was covered in bite marks and scratches, just as Inspector Lawton had said. The man's hands were tied behind him and there was duct tape over his mouth.

'We've called the pathologist in. Should be here soon, sir,' said Inspector Lawton.

'Is it Mr Hudson?' said Paterson.

'I believe so. Do you know him?'

'Yeah. He's a good man.'

'I hear he has a problem. Not so hot these days. Likes a drop of the old sauce.'

Paterson looked up from the dead man and glared at the inspector. 'I don't appreciate gossip, Mr Lawton. Keep that to yourself.'

Lawton's face flushed. 'Yes, sir. Sorry.'

'Tell me about this email. Who's it from?'

Lawton fished around inside his jacket and unfolded a printout of the email. He handed it to Paterson.

'*Police. We have shown ourselves vengeful. Proceed to the south side of these waters. There, upon the fair maiden* Rose, *awaits him that hath done wrong. T.*'

'What's "the fair maiden *Rose*" when it's at 'ome?' said Clocks.

'Initially we had no idea, but one of the crew remembered there was a small boat anchored up. It had the name *Rose*. We checked there first, and sure enough we found him. Could just about make out the top of a bag. Strangely, it was sewn up. We pulled it up, cut it open and . . .'

'Any idea how long he'd been in the water?' said Paterson.

'It would be a guess.'

'Guess then, guv,' said Clocks.

'I'd say about eight to ten hours but, to be honest, it's not that easy to tell given the state of the body and the fact that it was sealed inside a leather bag.'

'Leather?' said Paterson.

Lawton pointed to a large leather bag, big enough for a human and some animals, lying on a nearby metal examination table. It was dark from the water that seeped onto the table and dribbled through the drain hole. 'Yeah. Sorry. I didn't mention that did I? No idea why leather was chosen.'

A uniformed PC poked his head into the room. 'Sir . . . the pathologist is here.'

'Show him in, Godstone.'

PC Godstone stepped aside to let Jock pass him.

'Inspector Lawton,' he said. 'And you two fuckers.'

'Jocky Boy!' said Clocks. ''Ow the devil are you, you ol' reprobate?'

'Wonderful. Nae fuckin' aboot, mind. What we got here?'

'Some bloke done up like a ready meal. 'E was in a bag with a bunch of live animals. Looks like they chowed down on 'im before they all drowned.'

'Succinct, Clocksy,' said Paterson. 'But you'll need to write the report up a bit better than that.'

Jock made his way over to the body and took a good look up and down the torso. 'Definitely alive when he went in,' he said. 'Nasty stuff.'

'Can we leave you to it, Jock? We've got to try and figure out where an email come from.'

'Email?' Jock started looking the body over.

'It was sent to here telling Mr Lawton's team where to find him. Looks like it could be same person who did the park killing.'

Jock nodded. 'Away wi' ye then, laddie.'

'Ta-ta, Jock,' said Clocks. 'Keep us posted.'

Jock waved his hand, dismissing them from the room.

The three policemen left the morgue.

'He's a bit abrupt, isn't he?' said Lawton when they were out of earshot.

'Jock? It's just 'is way, mate,' said Clocks. 'Takes it all very seriously. No bad thing.'

'Can you get your full report over to me as soon as, please?' said Paterson. He handed Inspector Lawson his card. 'And of course, any on-scene pictures you've got.'

'Certainly, sir. You'll have them within the hour.'

They thanked him and headed back to their car.

'D'you reckon this type of killing might 'ave some sort of fancy name like Anderson's Blood Eagle?'

'I don't know, John. We'll need to get some proper help from someone. Someone who might know what this is all about, because I'm sure I bloody well don't.'

'We could call 'im Ready Meal Man or Mr Big Sack, couldn't we?'

'I don't think so, mate. Bit disrespectful.'

'I s'pose. Still, 'ave a little think about it. One of 'em might grow on yer.'

CHAPTER SIXTEEN

'Well, that was different.' Paterson slid into the driver's seat.

'Somewhat. So, we're goin' with the theory that this was done by the same one who did Anderson in, yes?' said Clocks.

Paterson shrugged. 'For now. Seems reasonable at this stage to look at them together, given the unusual nature of both killings and their relative proximity to each other. Both on our side of the river. Seems to me to be a racing certainty. What are the chances of two gruesome murders taking place so close together geographically and time-wise?' He started up the car and pulled away.

'Yeah. I'm with you. So, back to square one with the questions, but we need to figure out why this is 'appening. D'you reckon that the two murders are a particular form of message, then? You said the Blood Eagle was a method carried out in . . . What was it? Roman times?'

'The Dark Ages. A bit later than Roman times.'

'Right. Dark Ages, then. So that's historical. Jock's never seen anything like it an' 'e was probably around in the Dark Ages. So someone somewhere would appear to 'ave a bloody good knowledge of this sort of killing.'

'Or they saw it on the telly. *Vikings*, remember?'

'Yep. But this bloke in the leaky ark—'

'Ark?'

'Bag. Ark. Same thing . . .'

Paterson shook his head. 'Not really, is it?'

'Well, no. Not exactly. But to be fair, it was an enclosed space and involved animals chucked in with a human, so . . . close enough.'

'If you say so.'

'I do. Ooh! We could call our victim Noah.'

Paterson shook his head.

'So, I think we need to find out if this is some sort of Dark Ages type of murder too. We might be able to pick up on a link of some kind an' get ourselves ahead of the game.'

'Sounds like a plan. What's the rest of it?'

Clocks looked over at Paterson.

'That's it?'

'That's it. That's all I've got. You're the boss. You get paid the big bucks. Over to you.'

Paterson pulled up at a set of lights. On the inside, a cyclist waited with them.

'I'm thinking perhaps a historian of some sort. Someone with a specialist knowledge of the Dark Ages.'

'Crackin' idea, Ray. You 'appen to know of any 'istorians? Anyone knockin' about in yer little black book under aitch for 'istorian?'

Paterson shook his head.

''Ang on a minute. I'll ask this bloke 'ere.' Clocks dropped his window. ''Scuse me mate.'

The cyclist looked over at him. Paterson rolled his eyes.

'Sorry to trouble yer. I can see you're busy, but I was just wondering, would you 'appen to know any 'istorians by any chance? Preferably a specialist in the Dark Ages. An' it would 'elp if they knew summin' about torture and execution. Anyone? No?'

The cyclist gave Clocks a look that suggested he wasn't sure if it was a wind-up or not. 'Nah, sorry mate. I'm just on my way to work.'

'Yeah, all right. No worries.' Clocks closed the window and turned to Paterson. 'Bloody stupid answer that was, weren't it? *I'm on me way to work.* What's that gotta do with anythin'? Twat!'

'Very funny, John. We'll have to go find one, won't we?'

'Where from?'

The lights changed and Paterson pulled away. 'Dunno. A museum, maybe. A university. We'll make some calls when we get back to the office.'

'Before we do that, let me 'ave a quick count up.'

'Of what?'

'Museums and universities on our manor. Right. I'm done an' you know 'ow many there are?'

Paterson knew where this was going. 'I didn't mean on our—'

'Zero. Turns out there's not one in Bermondsey anywhere. Nothin'. Not a carrot. It's the cultural arse'ole of the world, me ol' mate. Bermondsey is where brain cells go to die after they've been given their marchin' orders from Woolwich.'

'That's a bit harsh, John.'

'No it ain't. Not really. You've seen half the yobs that knock around the estates, same as I 'ave. Not too much in the way of schoolin', is there? It's been said that if the zombie apocalypse ever struck, it'd give Bermondsey a swerve.'

'Go on then. Why's that?'

'Zombies eat brains, don't they? They'd all fuckin' die of starvation round 'ere, mate. Bad enough bein' turned into a zombie in the first place, but fuck me, you know it's a shitty day if you can't even get summin' to eat.'

Paterson laughed. 'You're an idiot, you know that?'

Clocks gave him a grin. 'I like to think of meself as an undiscovered genius with a unique outlook on life. You'll see. One day they'll all hail Johnny Clocks the great an' good.'

'You reckon?'

'Nah.' He shook his head furiously. 'Fuck 'em. Let's go find ourselves an 'istorian. Put yer foot down, Batman my ol' son.'

CHAPTER SEVENTEEN

DCI Marcus Goodwin collected his bag from the overhead locker, gathered up his two kids and smiled at his wife. The seven-hour, forty-minute flight from Canada had frazzled them all and now they had the nightmare journey home ahead of them. Goodwin calculated it would likely take the best part of an hour to clear passport control and baggage reclaim and, assuming nothing went wrong at those two points, the first stop would be McDonalds for the kids. To tell the truth, he could murder a Big Mac and double fries himself.

He was pleased when they cleared the first two hurdles in under an hour and even more pleased when he could see that the queue for food wasn't as long as he expected. He left his wife and kids to find seats for them all and headed off to join the queue. As he walked past WHSmith, a headline in the *Daily Mail* caught his eye: *SAVAGE! Body found in park*. Intrigued, he picked up a copy and scanned the story: *brutal killing . . . back cut open . . . lungs torn out . . . Blood Eagle* . . . The report didn't give a name of the victim. Goodwin's heart skipped a beat when he saw that Paterson was heading up the investigation. *What the fuck is going on?*

He put the paper back on the stand and fumbled in his pocket for his mobile phone. He had no messages. Everybody knew he was on holiday for a week and he had given strict instructions not to be disturbed. Even if someone had called him, he hadn't planned to check his phone until he arrived back in England.

He dialled a number and waited. He joined the back of the queue, which had grown longer since his dalliance with the paper. 'Jane? It's me. I'm back. Yeah. Just landed. Listen . . . I've just seen something about a murder in the papers. Nasty by the sound of it. Yeah. And I've seen that Superintendent Paterson has caught the case. That right? Okay, it's just that I'm surprised, is all. I thought they'd both be suspended pending investigation. Why? Doesn't matter. I'll get it sorted. See you in a couple of days when I come back in. Bye.' He hung up the phone and pondered the situation.

Before he'd left for a holiday, he'd been present at a dying declaration. The victim was a Detective Chief Inspector Lambert, shot by a female assassin in his own office. Commissioner Anderson was convinced that Paterson and Clocks had ordered the hit but was unable to prove it until Lambert started to speak and, with his dying breaths said, *'A message. From Paterson . . . and Clocks. From Paterson . . . From Paterson . . . Clocks . . . Not personal. Not pers . . . No . . . Fuck off and die. Fuck off and die. Fuck off. . . and . . .'*

With presence of mind, he'd taken a bodycam from the armed policeman standing outside Lambert's room and recorded his words, and later had a copy made of the footage. He'd got what he thought was enough to at least warrant the arrest of the two of them and had sent a copy of the footage to Commissioner Anderson along with copies of statements from the witnesses present at Lambert's death: his wife, his daughter, an ICU nurse and the armed police guard.

He knew it wasn't unusual for investigations of this magnitude to get underway covertly but he thought that, at the least, the pair of them would be suspended. Something was wrong and he needed to make another call.

CHAPTER EIGHTEEN

Paterson and Clocks made their way along a lengthy corridor in the British Museum, their footsteps echoing as they went. DC Michael 'Monkey' Harris had made them an appointment to see a Dr Rakes, a renowned historian. Rakes was the only one he could find that had anywhere near the sort of specialisms Paterson wanted. Fortunately, Dr Rakes was free and happy to meet with them. Clocks reckoned it was because he was probably a sad old man covered in dust who had nobody to talk to and would be grateful that someone knew he was still alive and kicking. They were somewhat surprised when Rakes stepped out of the office to greet them. Dr Rakes was a good six feet tall, slender and a strikingly attractive woman. Paterson had her for being quite a bit younger than himself: twenty-six, twenty-eight, tops.

She beamed a smile at them. 'Gentlemen . . . I heard you were coming.' She held out her hand as Paterson walked up to her. 'I'm Linda Rakes, and you must be . . . ?'

'Paterson. Detective Superintendent Paterson. Good to meet you.'

'And you too. This must be Detective Inspector Clocks?'

'Yeah. 'Ow'd you know that?' said Clocks.

'Your colleague, Mr Harris, told me.'

'Oh, yeah. 'Course 'e did.' The two shook hands. 'Didn't bother tellin' us you were a bir— sorry, woman, though.'

'Does that matter, Mr Clocks?'

'Nah. Just would've been nice to get the 'eads-up. I thought you'd be an' old geezer smellin' of dust and books, but instead . . .' He eyed her up and down. 'Caught me on the 'op. You're so young as well.'

She smiled at him. 'Well, I'm the product of long days and nights hunched over books while my friends went partying. My father was determined I would make something of myself and not waste my life on hedonistic pleasures.'

'Good call,' said Clocks. 'Don't wanna waste yer life 'avin' fun, do yer? Nobody wants that.'

'Please, come into my office and make yourselves comfortable. Can I get you anything at all?'

'I could murder a drop of whisky if you've got any knockin' about?'

'I . . . er . . . yes. Yes, I have.'

'Tea is fine, thank you,' said Paterson. 'For both of us, please.'

Clocks's face dropped.

'Are you sure?' said Dr Rakes. 'I've got a ten-year-old bottle stashed away.' She nodded toward a large twin-door cupboard that looked as though it was installed on the day the museum was built. 'What do you say to a drop of that?' she said.

Clocks looked to Paterson.

'Well, I would have to say "happy birthday" to it,' said Paterson. 'So, thank you.'

Dr Rakes pulled out the bottle and three tumblers then poured them all large drinks, which she handed around.

Clocks took a big swig and screwed his face up, punched his chest and coughed. 'Oh, good gawd. That's a bit . . . 'andsome, that is. Nice one, love.'

Paterson sipped at his, rolled it around in his mouth before swallowing. 'Very nice indeed. Thank you.'

'You're welcome.' Dr Rakes settled back in her chair. 'Now, what is it I can do for you? Detective Harris said you needed to speak to someone with knowledge of the Dark Ages and forms of torture. He didn't tell me why, but I assume it wasn't just for the sake of it. So, how can I help?'

Paterson scratched his head and recounted the story of the Blood Eagle and the man in the bag. Dr Rakes sat and listened intently, making the occasional note as Paterson filled her in on the details. Clocks had taken up his default position of observing carefully as Dr Rakes spoke. He'd learned many years ago to watch closely as people spoke, looking for anything, any little twitch or tic that might point toward a lie. Paterson had no reason to suspect Dr Rakes of lying, but it had become an ingrained habit in Clocks now and it had served him well in the past.

'So, that's where we are,' said Paterson. 'And that's why we're here. We were hoping that you could give us some further insight into these forms of killing. We know that the Blood Eagle is purported to have been carried out by the Vikings, and for a moment we thought we may be looking for someone with a particular knowledge of that time period. But then we found the man in the bag, and it threw us out a bit. Someone said it was a method of punishment used by the Romans, but we were wondering if it has any links to the Dark Ages.'

Clocks snorted. 'Dark Ages. That's a funny thing to call a time period, ain't it? Must mean before electricity was invented. Everyone had to sit in the dark.'

'What?' Dr Rakes looked bewildered.

'No electric. Miserable existence I'd 'ave thought. Especially in the winter.'

She glanced at Paterson. He sighed. 'I'm sorry, Doctor. His mother shut his head in a door when he was small. Deliberately.'

Dr Rakes cocked her head to one side and pulled a face that suggested sympathy. 'Oh, I'm so sorry to hear that.'

'Don't worry about it. I deserved it. Me mum said I was being a right little sod. That's 'ow it was back then, none of this molly-coddling nonsense you get these days. You mucked about and got a bit lippy and *bosh*, yer 'ead got shut in a door.'

Dr Rakes looked across at Paterson. 'Is he . . . ?'

Paterson shrugged. 'He might be making it up, but quite honestly, I can hardly tell myself these days. But it would explain an awful lot. Let's just move on, shall we?'

'We'll call him Mr Big Sack!' said Clocks. 'We were gonna call him Noah, but I dunno . . .'

'O . . . kay.' Dr Rakes struggled to stifle a laugh. 'Let's take the first one, shall we? The Blood Eagle. Well, although it is mentioned in the folklore and writings of some Scandinavian historians and scribes, there is no actual proof that the Blood Eagle was actually committed by anyone. The most famous writings about it involve the great warrior Ivar the Boneless. He was the son of Ragnor Lothbrok, a great warrior, and Danish and Swedish king. It is said that Ivar the Boneless used it as a form of execution on King Aella of Northumbria as revenge for the murder of his father, Ragnor. But there is a belief among academics that if the Blood Eagle was used for execution, it was likely used for any crimes the Northmen felt were sufficiently serious to warrant it.

'Have no doubt, Mr Paterson, that if someone has done this, then they will have had very, very good reason to. Perhaps you're looking for someone who's avenging a murder. I don't know. TV has a lot to answer for too. Have you seen *Vikings* by any chance?'

Paterson rubbed his face a few times. 'Yep. That's where I got the idea from.'

'Blimey,' said Clocks. 'I must be the only bloke in the world not to 'ave seen this. I take it it's good, then?'

'Not bad,' said Dr Rakes. 'They've taken a great deal of liberty with the truth, but then again, that's what makes good TV, isn't it?'

'Liberties?' said Clocks.

'More than a few. For example, we're now discovering that perhaps the raiders from the North were not the bloodthirsty people history tells us they were. Aerial scans and digs can find no trace of the battles that have been written as fought between the various British kingdoms and the Northmen. The countryside should be littered with thousands upon thousands of skeletons and weapons, but it's not. It seems everything we believed about these people, and our own, is a lie. Still, it's early days yet. More work to be done before a definitive answer can be given.'

'We'll worry about that another time,' said Paterson. 'So, the bag man? Any ideas?'

'Remind me again,' she said. 'Any little details you have, please.'

Paterson quickly ran over the facts again and watched her as she jotted down some notes here and there. When he had finished, she sat back in her chair and cleared her throat.

'Well, yes. It sounds very much like a Roman method of execution. Have you ever heard of something called *poena cullei*?'

'Some sort of Italian food?' said Clocks.

'No, I'm afraid not. It's Latin. Means "penalty of the sack". Under Roman law it was a penalty imposed on someone found guilty of parricide. Being sown into a leather sack with live animals and thrown into water were all elements of this type of punishment.'

'What's a parrot . . . parry . . . what was it?' said Clocks.

'Parricide. The killing of one's father.'

Clocks nodded. 'So, our vic may have killed his father?'

'It's possible,' she said.

'I tell yer what, though, people back in the day were a bit brutal, weren't they? Get caught killin' yer ol' dad now an' it's off to a centrally 'eated cell, nice bed, a bit of telly, books, knife-makin' classes and a shit ton of body-buildin' so you can be even more intimidatin' when you get out after two years. And . . . *and*, as much coke as you can shove up yer 'ooter.'

Paterson ignored Clocks. 'What's the significance of the animals?'

'I don't know for certain, but I would guess it was to do exactly what it did to your victim. The animals would be in absolute terror and would no doubt inflict massive amounts of damage on the poor soul in with them as they fought for their freedom.'

'So, it seems like we've got two crimes that could be linked to the execution of fathers,' said Paterson.

'Possibly. It's bit of a stretch, though,' said Dr Rakes. 'The Blood Eagle could be used for killing someone for any crime, not specifically for the death of a father. The *poena cullei* . . . well yes, that *was* for parricide.'

'If I gave you restricted access to certain elements of this case, do you think you might be able to come up with some kind of connection between these types of crimes?'

'Of course,' she said. 'I'd be more than happy to. Can I just ask you something?'

''Course you can,' said Paterson.

'Have you ever heard of the Bermondsey Knights?'

'Nope. Who are they when they're at 'ome?' said Clocks. 'Are they a band?'

She shook her head. 'No. They're quite well known among internet chat groups.' She glanced at Clocks. 'As we all know, there are groups for everything and everyone these days. I'm a member of a private board on the internet that's used by serious academics with an interest in history. Every so often, a post would pop up, usually disputing some version of history and laying claim to a recent find of some kind. The general consensus is that they're just a nuisance — trolls, if you will — out to cause an argument among members, but they're a strange bunch.'

'Strange how?' said Paterson.

'Sometimes their posts become rants. They talk about taking revenge against their "oppressors", those that have held them down. Their posts are generally poorly written using what they think is a form of Old English. One of them is said to be spot-on. He knows his stuff. But the others . . . not so much.'

'Does he have a name, this spot-on chap?'

'No. He goes by "T". That's all. It's just that in one of their posts, one of them said they would be coming soon, ready to take revenge, and that the world would be in awe of their existence. It's been deleted since, I'm afraid.'

'They sound like a bunch of wankers to me,' said Clocks.

'So it's on Facebook or Twitter or Reddit or something?' said Paterson.

She smiled at him. 'No, sometimes we share academic ideas and papers that we would like to keep from prying eyes, and the commercial platforms are too easily hackable. As I'm sure you've heard it said, nothing is private online. But if you use it properly, then it can be.'

'Yeah, I guess. So, how do we get to look at his posts?'

'Er, you don't,' she said. 'The board is private.'

Clocks's eyes narrowed.

'I understand that, Doctor, but you've suggested someone who may be a suspect in these murders and I'm afraid I need to know a bit more — a lot more, actually. Now, I don't want to fall out with you, but I could get a warrant for seizure. That means I get to take your computer and as many servers as I can get my hands on and go through them with a fine-tooth comb. I'm sure you wouldn't want that, am I right?'

'Or,' said Clocks, 'Mr Paterson 'ere could distract you with 'is dazzling and very expensive smile. An' while 'e's got that on the go, I'll just nick yer laptop an' 'and it over to our tech boys. Believe me, they'll go through it like a dose of salts, so if you've got any dodgy pictures of yerself on there, doing whatever it is you 'istorians do, they'll find 'em and I'll 'ave a bloody good look at 'em.' He shrugged. 'Just sayin'.'

Dr Rakes looked horrified. 'What? Pictures? What are you talking about? There are no pictures.'

'Yeah, I know. You keep denyin' it. Convince yerself.'

She looked across to Paterson.

'He's winding you up,' he said. 'Take no notice of him. I'm not trying to be nasty, I'm really not. But I do need to take a look. I'm sorry.'

Dr Rakes sighed and looked resigned. '*You* can,' she said to Paterson. 'Not him.'

Clocks smiled. 'Got you worried, ain't I? You're not sure what you've posted now, are you? Last year's Christmas do, p'rhaps?'

Dr Rakes flushed. Clocks's eyes widened. She held her hand up to him.

'That's enough, John,' said Paterson. 'I mean it. No more.'

Clocks shrugged.

'Doctor, I'm very sorry,' said Paterson.

'It's . . . it's okay. Give me a moment to log in.' She opened her laptop and took a few seconds before she turned it around to face Paterson. She craned her neck over the screen. 'You're in.' Clocks stepped forward and looked at her.

'Of course you can look, Inspector. There really is nothing in there for you to see and nothing that would embarrass me.'

'Good to know,' he said. 'Me ol' mum always told me sister to keep 'er 'and on 'er ha'penny for as long as possible. Said the boys were only ever after one thing. I don't think she ever found out what 'er ha'penny was 'cos she 'ad her first kid at fifteen. Anyway, just as well there was no such thing as the internet when we were kids, 'cos gawd knows what she'd 'ave posted on there.'

'Thanks for letting me know,' said Dr Rakes. She turned her attention to Paterson. 'If you scroll down you'll be able to read all the posts in the latest thread.'

The room fell silent for the next few minutes as Paterson scrolled through. 'Have you checked this today?' he said without looking up.

'No. Why?'

Paterson spun the laptop back to her. 'The mysterious "T" posted this late last night.'

She read it. '*The penalty of the sack has been delivered and soon we bring forth the Bamboo punishment and the Sawn Man. Amen. T* . . . Oh, God!' She looked up at Paterson.

'What? What is it? What does it mean? D'you know?'

Dr Rakes nodded. 'Yes. Yes, I do . . . Well, not the Bamboo. I'll have to try to figure that out. But the Sawn

Man, yes.' She hurriedly left her chair and snatched out a thick book from one of the shelves in her bookcase. She flicked through its pages before tapping a perfectly manicured finger on a line-drawn picture. 'This . . . this is what you've got coming.'

CHAPTER NINETEEN

A cold autumn wind whipped at Paterson's jacket as he stood on the steps of the British Museum and contemplated what he had just seen in the book Dr Rakes had shown him.

'Don't s'pose you've got a plan, 'ave you?' Clocks unwrapped the Kit-Kat he'd bought in the gift shop on the way out.

Paterson sighed. 'Not yet. I'll think of something, though.'

'I bleedin' 'ope so. If that's what's going to 'appen to some poor sod, we need to nip it in the bud sooner rather than later.' Clocks shook his head at the thought of it.

Paterson pulled his collar up against the wind. 'We need someone who can use the internet properly. And I do mean properly.'

'We can get the Met's tech boys on it. I'm sure they're up to it.'

'You're probably right. But two problems I can see with that. One, we need someone *very* good. Someone who can follow a digital footprint as far as it goes. Two, we need to move fast. That means we can't hang around waiting to get through the system — requests, rubber-stamping, the usual shit. We need someone we can get to now. Today. Someone who knows their way around computers and who's not afraid to bend the rules.'

'Bend the rules? Us? Why would we need to do that?'

Paterson shrugged. 'It's what we do, isn't it? I'm just getting ahead of the game.'

Clocks nodded. 'Makes sense.'

Paterson pulled his phone out of his jacket pocket.

'You know someone then?' said Clocks.

'Nope. But I know a man who might.'

CHAPTER TWENTY

An hour later, they sat inside a café looking out across Greenwich Park. Clocks had wandered off to the counter to get a couple of teas and cakes and no doubt flirt with the teenage waitress behind the counter. Paterson had always liked this park, and while he waited for Clocks to return, he let his mind drift. He came here with his wife, Lisa, in the early days of their relationship, and they had spent countless Sundays just strolling hand in hand, busying themselves with the job of being young and in love. That he was wealthy and she was a highly sought-after model seemed to set them up for a lifetime of happiness.

For a while everything was rosy in their particular garden until Lisa's sister arrived on the scene with a bang. Quite literally. Within two days of meeting her, Paterson had bedded her, or perhaps it was the other way around. It didn't matter. Perhaps it was guilt or perhaps it was spite from a sister who was not the golden child in the family, but she decided to tell Lisa what had happened and that was that. Marriage over.

From then on, Paterson spent his days climbing the promotion ladder and his nights climbing on top of various women. In spite of his behaviour, Paterson always hoped that one day she would forgive him and take him back. She never did, and her brutal murder ensured she never would. Her death had sent him into a spiral of rage, which culminated in him shooting her killer in the head. Clocks had witnessed the killing and took the decision to cover up the crime. The two of them, now bound by a secret they would carry to their graves, were from that moment set on a very dark path. One that was slowly consuming them both.

'Ray!' Clocks's shout brought Paterson back from his thoughts.

'What?'

'What sort of cake you want? Got a sticky bun if you want one. I know you like 'em. Got a London cheesecake too. Don't see them very often. Want that?'

'I'll have the bun.'

Clocks turned back to the girl. 'Two London cheesecakes then, babe.' He paid and made his way back to the table.

Paterson looked at the tray and frowned.

'Oi, oi. I only got that bird's phone number, didn't I?' said Clocks.

'No, you didn't.'

'I did.'

'Show me.'

Clocks picked up the receipt and handed it to Paterson.

'There's nothing on it.'

'It's on the top.'

'That's the number of the café, you knob.'

Clocks grinned. 'I know, but still.'

'What the hell is that thing?' Paterson pointed to the cake, all pastry, jam and coconut strands. 'I asked you to get me a bun.'

Clocks shook his head. 'Yeah, I know. Thing is, they'd run out by the time I got to ask 'er. This is better, mate. Trust me. You ever 'ad one of these little babies?'

'Er, no. What is it?'

'That my friend is . . . a London cheesecake.'

'Where's the cheese?'

'Good question. No one knows.'

'So, why is it called a cheesecake?'

'No one knows that either. Just get it down you. I promise you, you'll be a changed man.'

Paterson took a bite and chewed it for a few seconds. 'It's all right. Nothing special. A bit dry.'

Clocks shook his head. 'You nobby people, 'onestly. You don't know good food when you see it, you lot.'

Paterson looked up sharply when he heard the door open. He smiled as his friend Wallace Young entered the café. Until his retirement, Young was the commissioner of police before Anderson. He was a rarity in the upper echelons of policing. He had worked his way through the ranks, always supported his officers and never shied away from speaking his mind no matter who he was talking to. Bullet-hard and with a mind like a steel trap, he was a formidable man. When he retired, he took the decision to go to America with Paterson and Clocks to track down the criminal Albert Tanner. He almost lost his life when he was stabbed while chasing Tanner. Paterson's money had saved him by paying for the very best medical care America could provide.

Technically, Young was still recovering, but he would never turn down a request from these two. His boys.

'Wally!' Clocks waved Young over to the table.

He strolled in and headed toward them. 'I trust you've ordered me a tea, Clocksy?'

'It's in the pot, guv. I'll go get it for you.'

'Good man. Oh, and I can't believe I still have to say this to you. Don't keep calling me "Wally".'

Clocks smiled.

'Or Wol. It's *sir*, to you.'

'Nah, it's not. You're Billy No-Rank now. Don't 'ave to call you sir at all. You know that, *Wally*.'

'Go and get my tea, you idiot!' He grinned as Clocks walked off to ask for the tea he'd already paid for.

'Hello, son. How are you?' Young scoured Paterson's face.

'I'm good, Wol. You?'

'On the mend. It's taking a while, but I'm much better than I was, thanks.' He dragged out the metal chair and sat himself down. 'The stubble does a good job of hiding the scar, doesn't it?'

Paterson raised a hand to his jawline and rubbed it. 'Does it? I'm not so sure.'

'Can't see it, I promise you.'

'Good. Thanks.'

'I thought you were still on the sick. No?'

Paterson took a sip of his tea. 'I was, but John called me in. A bad one.'

'Bad?'

'Yeah, the one in the papers.'

'Christ! You caught that? Very nasty by the sound of it.'

'It certainly was, and worst part of it all is, the victim was Anderson.'

Wallace stiffened. '*Commissioner* Anderson?'

'The one and only.'

'Shit!'

'That's exactly what we said.'

Clocks returned with Wallace's tea on a tray and set it down in front of him. He also plonked down a plate with a London cheesecake on it.

'And no, before you ask,' said Clocks, 'no china cup and saucer. It's still a café an' not the Ritz. Get it down yer neck.'

'Is that a . . . ?'

'It is.'

'My God. I haven't had one of these for years. Didn't know they still did these. Thank you, Clocksy.'

'More than welcome. There you go, Ray. Proper Lond'ner 'e is.'

Paterson smiled.

'How are you, John?' said Wallace.

'Yeah. Mustn't grumble. 'Ow you doin'? You're lookin' well, considerin' your age.'

Wallace turned back to Paterson. 'So, how did he die?'

Paterson spent the next ten minutes taking Wallace through the facts of the case and the meeting they had had with Dr Rakes. He explained about the group calling themselves the Bermondsey Knights and grinned through Wallace's jokey question about the Barron Knights before he got to the point of why he'd asked to meet.

'It seems these so-called Knights communicate through the internet, and I wondered — hoped really — that you might know of someone who may be able to help us with it.'

'What's wrong with our boys?' Wallace bit into his cheesecake, careful to catch the crumbs in his hand. 'Why can't they do it?'

'Time. I don't think we have much time at all. These crimes are coming in a day apart, starting with Anderson. It sounds like they could already have another one too. And, if they do, then maybe they're bragging about it online. You know what people are like, Wol. Maybe they've already killed another one. I don't know. But I do know I can't sit around cutting through red tape when I don't need to be.'

Wallace wiped his mouth on his paper napkin. 'Okay. I do know someone, actually. Carried out some off-the-books work for me back in the day. Knows his way around the internet like nobody else I know of. If he can't help, well . . .' He shrugged. 'I'll give him a call and set up a meet for you.'

Paterson was relieved. 'Cheers, mate. Knew I could rely on you.'

Paterson and Clocks stood outside to get some fresh air while Wallace made a call. He joined them outside a few minutes later. 'It's done. He's expecting you in an hour.'

'Brilliant. What's his name?'

'His real name is Reggie Coxson, but he's known as "Alice".' Wallace's eyes shot across to Johnny Clocks.

Clocks grinned. 'Alice? Alice? Who the fuck is Alice?' he said.

Wallace shook his head. 'That's how he likes to be known. It's what he calls himself both online and off. The flat he lives in — he calls it Wonderland.'

Clocks grinned. 'Alice in Wonderland? This sounds a bit odd, Wol.'

'Hmm.'

'All right, if that's what he wants,' Paterson said. 'Where's he live?'

Wallace handed him a slip of paper. 'I've written it down.'

'Thanks, Wol. I appreciate this,' Paterson said as he turned to leave.

'Listen, though,' said Wallace. 'Before you go over there, there's a couple of things you need to know about him.' Paterson cocked his head to one side. 'And you . . .' Young pointed at Clocks. 'You need to behave yourself over there. You need his help on this, so don't go pissing him off.'

'What yer talkin' about?' said Clocks.

'He's a bit . . . different. Unusual, shall we say. Brilliant, but unusual.'

'How'd you mean?' Paterson's curiosity was piqued.

'You'll see. It's not you I'm worried about, Ray. It's Mr Sensitive, here. He won't be happy, I can tell you that.'

'Why?' said Clocks. 'What's going on?'

'You'll find out soon enough. Oh, and . . . er . . . he's got some friends over. They'll be there when you get there, so don't worry about it, okay?'

'What *is* going on, Wol?' said Paterson. 'You're being a bit on the cagey side. It's not like you.'

'I don't want to tell you. It'll spoil the surprise.'

'Are we going to be able to talk to him? Get his help today?'

Wallace nodded. 'Should do. He said he's happy to help, if you don't mind a bit of noise.'

Paterson squinted. 'Noise?'

'Only a bit.'

'Okay,' said Paterson. 'You finished?'

'Yep. You can go. But listen . . . Stop at the sweet shop on your way over and get a few bags of sweeties for the kids.'

'Kids?' said Clocks. 'As 'e got bleedin' kiddies running around the gaff, then?'

'Yes.' Wallace had a wry grin on his face. 'About six of them, I think he said. You like kids, don't you?'

Clocks wrinkled his brow.

'Have fun boys. Clocksy . . . you be nice now, y'hear me?' Wallace walked back to his car, chuckling to himself and gently shaking his head.

'What d'you reckon the old boy's on about, Ray?'

'I really have no idea, but he seems bloody well amused with himself.'

'I fuckin' 'ope these bloody kids ain't runnin' about all over the place when we turn up. Little fuckers'll get a back'ander if they don't behave 'emselves.'

'I take it you're *not* a fan of kids, then?'

'Depends 'ow old they are. They're just shit and sick machines when they're babies, a bit more interesting when they get to about four. Can be fun until they're about twelve and then they become fuckin' teenagers. Different ball game then. That's when I wanna slap the shit out of the gobby, miserable little sods.'

'I bet your niece loves you. How old is she now?'

'She's all right, and never you mind 'ow old she is. I know what you're like around birds.' He sighed. 'She'll grow up an' become a right 'andful I s'pose. Still. Not my worry, is it? C'mon, let's go see what the ol' boy's stitched us up with.'

CHAPTER TWENTY-ONE

'Got something I want to show you before we go back and see this Alice person,' Paterson said. He put his foot down and the Ford picked up speed.

'Oh, 'ello, 'ere we go,' said Clocks. 'I ain't fallin' for that old one. Last time someone said they 'ad something to show me, it was my old uncle Dennis. "Dirty Dennis", my mum used to call him, and she would know 'cos 'e was 'er brother. Used to try and entice kids into the back of his van with the promise of a bag of Jelly Tots and a look at his little chicken. So I know what you're up to.'

Paterson chuckled. 'That's a load of bull again, isn't it? There's no Uncle Dennis.'

'Well, *you* don't know, do you?'

'I know you and all the shit you come out with, so there's no Uncle Dennis, is there?'

Clocks shrugged and turned to look out of the window. 'He's coming to the weddin'. You can meet him if you don't believe me.'

'What does he look like?'

'You can't miss him. He'll be the one with a bag of Jelly Tots, a little chicken and a load of kiddies under the age of five standing around him.'

'Har-de-har,' said Paterson. He flicked the indicator and turned onto the A21 from the Blackheath turnoff.

'Where we goin' then?'

'I've just bought another house.'

'Fuck me! Another one? What's wrong with the palace you live in now?' said Clocks.

'Nothing. Just wanted to buy this one.'

''Ow much is it?'

'That's a bit personal, isn't it?'

'Yeah, you're right. I don't care, though. 'Ow much is it?'

'I'll tell you later. You can throw a price at it and I'll tell you if it's close.'

Clocks shrugged. 'Where is it?'

'Not too far from me, actually. Beckenham way.'

'Nice.'

* * *

Fifteen minutes later, they pulled up outside a gated house in the more salubrious part of Beckenham. Clocks whistled softly as he stepped out of the car and looked around the street.

'There's a few quid 'ere, mate. You'll fit right in.'

'You think so?'

'Yeah, you all over, this is. Does it come with a maid?'

'I'll find out.'

Paterson pressed a combination of numbers on a small metal pad stuck on a wall, and the side gate opened. The two men walked up the gravel pathway to the house. Paterson let them in and stepped into the hallway.

'This is fuckin' huge, mate.' Clocks's voice echoed around the hallway as he took in the scene: solid wooden floorboards, a huge staircase dead centre and a large, modern chandelier at the foot of the stairs. He nodded his appreciation.

'Come on through.' Paterson led Clocks into the living room.

'Good gawd! This is bigger than my entire 'ouse laid out flat. It's amazin'. 'Ow many bedrooms?'

'Five. That's enough isn't it?'

Clocks nodded, nonchalantly. 'Oh, yeah. Just about. Might be a struggle if you 'ave people over for one of your poncey parties, but if you run out of room, I saw an 'otel on the way 'ere. You should probably buy that too. Just in case.'

'Not a bad idea, John. But considering I've never held a "poncey" party in my life, or any party come to that, I don't think I'll bother with the hotel.'

'Fair enough. It's your money.' Clocks looked around the room again. 'I couldn't afford the curtains for a place like this. Good luck t'yer, mate. Seriously.'

'Not finished yet. It's got an indoor and an outdoor swimming pool.'

Clocks looked at him, shaking his head. 'Oh, fuck off. You're ruinin' me, you know that?'

Paterson laughed. 'So, you like it, then?'

'Dream 'ome, mate. I'm sure you'll be very 'appy 'ere.'

Paterson, still with the keys in hand, tossed them at Clocks. 'I think you and Lyndsey'll be a lot happier here than me. I'm rattling around in my own place as it is.'

Clocks looked stunned. 'What?'

'It's your wedding present. I thought it best to show it to you now because I couldn't figure out how to wrap it.'

'*What?*' said Clocks, again.

'It's yours. And Lyndsey's of course. I bought it for you two. I remembered you saying to me once that you wanted me to buy you a five-bedroomed house with a swimming pool, so—'

'No. No, no, no, no. I was jokin', mate. You know that.'

'I know you were, but then I thought, why not? Seemed ideal. And it saved me traipsing round the shops looking for pots and pans or getting you Amazon vouchers. Be honest, did you really want a toaster?'

'Ray, I dunno what to say. I'm gobsmacked.'

'Then it was worth it just for that. C'mon, we gotta get over to see this Alice chap. When this is all over, bring Lyndsey here. See if she likes it. If she does, I'll get it signed over to you both.'

Clocks nodded. 'Yeah, yeah. I will, I will.'

They headed for the door.

'Oh, one more thing,' said Paterson. He reached inside his jacket, pulled out an envelope and handed it to Clocks. 'And you don't have to worry about decorating it either. This'll take care of that.'

Clocks looked at him.

'Open it then.'

Clocks did and his eyes went wide. 'No . . .'

'Yep. Now you've got a few bob too, John.' He smiled and patted Clocks on the shoulder before leading him out the door. Clocks, like someone glued to their mobile phone, kept staring at the cheque as he walked out. 'Next time we're in the pub, maybe you can get your hand down and buy me a drink for a change.'

'You can't . . . you can't do this, Ray. This is—'

'A better life for you and Lyndsey. Yes it is. And you both deserve it. Listen, though . . . when it's quietened down a bit at work, I'll take you to meet my people. They'll open up an account for you both and advise you as to the best way to keep hold of your money in the future. It's worked well for me. Don't just walk into Barclays with it, mate. They'll have a fit.'

'Bit like meself.'

Paterson chuckled. 'Yeah. I guess so.'

'Ray,' said Clocks as he opened the car door. Paterson looked over at him. 'I'm so, so grateful to you. I can't tell you what this means to me, to us. I really can't. Thank you so much.'

Paterson smiled. 'As you always say to me . . . "Get in the car you big 'ol tart!"' As he sat behind the wheel, Paterson thought that his friend's eyes were just a little bit moist.

CHAPTER TWENTY-TWO

'DCI Goodwin. Pleasure to meet you.' Assistant Commissioner Morne shook DCI Goodwin's hand and invited him to sit down. 'Can I get you a tea or coffee?'

'Tea would be nice, sir. Thank you.'

Morne nodded, picked up his desk phone and ordered tea. 'So, when we spoke on the phone you said you wanted to talk to me about Paterson and Clocks and that it had to do with the death of DCI Lambert. Is that right?'

'Yes, sir. Correct.' Goodwin fidgeted in his seat. He felt intimidated for some reason and he couldn't quite put his finger on why. On his way into Scotland Yard, he knew this would always be a difficult conversation to have. It didn't always pay to poke your nose into investigations conducted by people at Morne's level, but his conscience wouldn't allow him to not follow up on why Paterson and Clocks were back at work.

'Sir,' he said. 'I've just got back from holiday and I saw in the newspapers that Paterson and Clocks are investigating the case of a man who was found dead in a park. Horrific circumstances, from what I understand.'

'Indeed,' said AC Morne. 'Dreadful murder by anyone's standards.' He shook his head. 'Dreadful.'

There was a light tap and Morne's secretary, Kelly, opened the door carrying a tray with everything needed for tea making. Goodwin jumped up to hold the door open for her.

'Thank you.' She placed the tray down on Morne's desk. 'Would you like me to pour, sir?'

'No, thank you. That's splendid. Thank you.'

'Thank you, sir,' she said. Goodwin held the door for her until she left the room and closed it firmly behind her.

'Is there a problem with them investigating the murder?'

'I don't really know, sir,' said Goodwin. 'But I'm a bit confused.'

Morne frowned. 'What about?'

'I thought they would have been under investigation.'

'Why? What makes you think that?'

'Because of the video?'

Morne shook his head. 'What video? I've no idea what you're talking about.'

Goodwin searched the man's face. It could well have been that Morne was blanking him and keeping the investigation under wraps for the sake of security and Goodwin wasn't going to be let into the loop. None of his business now.

'The evening before I went on holiday, I sent a video to Commissioner Anderson.'

'What was on it?'

'It was the dying declaration of DCI Lambert, sir. His daughter asked that police be in attendance because he was repeating something over and over again. She was concerned and wanted someone from the police to record what he was saying. As you know, there was an armed guard outside the room and she made him come into the room and record her father on his bodycam. He did. I watched it and played it back and seized the video. I sent it to Mr Anderson via secure email.'

Morne looked stunned. 'I had no idea. No idea at all. Why did you send it to Anderson?'

'He was investigating them both, as I'm sure you're aware, and he was convinced that they were responsible for Lambert's shooting.'

Morne shook his head vigorously. 'No, no, no. That had nothing to do with them. They were in a pub full of witnesses at the time. Police witnesses. We also found out that the murderer was a woman — one of our own too. She had a rabid fixation on Paterson and shot Lambert for causing him problems. The evidence we found would suggest the poor woman had serious mental issues. Nothing whatsoever to do with Paterson and Clocks.'

Goodwin looked puzzled. 'I'm not saying they carried out the actual shooting, sir, but has anyone considered that they may have ordered this poor girl to kill him for them?

'What? No.'

'Why not? It's possible. The video shows Lambert pointing his fingers in the air, like a gun, and he was saying something like, "From Ray and John."'

Morne looked stunned. 'No . . . oh, no.'

Goodwin shrugged. 'I would have thought Mr Anderson would have shown it to you by now.'

'He didn't. And he can't.'

'Sir? Why can't he?'

Morne took a deep breath in and sat back in his chair. He rubbed his forehead before speaking. 'Look. This stays in this room and is strictly need-to-know, understand?'

Goodwin nodded. It seemed he was about to be let into the loop after all.

'The victim you read about in the paper . . .'

'No!'

'I'm afraid so. This stays in this room, though, you understand me?'

'Yes, sir. Of course. Jesus . . .'

'He was wearing only trousers when he was found. So, no video was on him. He always carried a bag to work, and we're looking for it now. I suspect that the video would have been in that.'

'I can get another one made and sent to you, sir. Shouldn't take long to do.'

'Yes, yes. Do that. Did you witness Lambert in hospital — this declaration, the finger gun, et cetera?'

'Yes, sir. I did.'

'Good. I'm going to set up an update meeting with my senior team and I want you there. Is that good with you?'

'Of course. I'll leave my number.'

Morne nodded.

'So, are you taking them off of this case?'

Morne rubbed his face with both hands. 'Not yet. There's another murder that they believe is connected to Anderson's murder. They're in deep.'

'The cases can be handed over, sir. It's not that difficult. Happens a lot.'

Morne's eyes flashed. 'I'm well aware of what happens, Mr Goodwin. The problem I have is that I genuinely don't believe they had anything to do with it.' He shook his head. 'I just don't.'

CHAPTER TWENTY-THREE

Paterson and Clocks stood outside the door of number 1909 on the Arnolds Estate. From inside, Paterson could hear the sounds of babies crying, but something sounded slightly off. He couldn't tell what.

'John . . .' he said.

'Yes, I know. I'll be'ave meself, I promise. Don't go on.'

'I've not said a word to you. But remember . . . Wol's doing this as a favour. We don't want to upset him, do we?'

Clocks rolled his eyes. 'No, Dad. We don't, Dad.'

Paterson rang the bell. Inside, the crying stopped instantly. He rang again and, after a few seconds, there came the sound of locks turning and chains rattling. A large round face poked itself between the door and the jamb. The man's face was red and sweaty and his eyes darted back and forth between the two policemen. On his head was a carefully balanced tiara. The sound of babies started up again.

'And you are?' said the sweaty man. His voice was deep and gruff.

'I'm Superintendent Ray Paterson and this is DI Johnny Clocks. I believe you're expecting us, yes?'

The man's eyes darted again. 'Yes. Yes, I'm afraid it's a bit noisy in here. It's the children's playtime. Do forgive me.'

The man pulled open the door and stood aside to let them in. Paterson got a full look at him. He stood about five nine, weighed about twenty-five stone and was squeezed into a pencil skirt that was at least one size too small for him. Paterson could see the outline of a suspender belt and that he was wearing stockings. He was also topless and didn't have a hair on his wobbly body. Paterson quickly turned to Clocks and gave him a sharp look. The two men stepped into the hallway.

'You must be Alice?' said Paterson, taking it all in his stride.

Clocks's eyes turned into saucers. 'What the fu—'

Paterson cut him off. 'Thanks for seeing us so quickly. Appreciate it.'

'Not a problem,' said Alice. 'Mr Young is a good man. He helped me out of many a tight spot.'

'I bet one of 'em wasn't that skirt, fellah,' said Clocks.

Alice gave him a non-committal look. 'Oh, I see. You're one of those, are you?'

'One of what?' said Clocks.

'You don't believe in people being who they are? Being different.'

'Of course I believe in 'em. You're standin' 'ere in front of me, ain'tcha? Unicorns I don't believe in.' Clocks shrugged. 'Anyway, mate, I don't really care what you do as long as you don't do it in the street an' frighten the 'orses. Knock yerself out, love.'

Alice nodded.

'Where do you want us to go?' said Paterson.

'Straight ahead. Into the living room. As I said, it's a bit noisy. Did Mr Young tell you what we do here?'

Paterson shook his head as he followed Alice. 'No, it'll be a nice surprise.' He pushed the door open and stepped inside. Paterson stopped dead.

'Oh, fuck me blind,' said Clocks as he looked inside.

'Come in, come in,' said Alice. 'My office is upstairs. Follow me. Tea or coffee?'

Paterson and Clocks stepped inside the room. Rolling and playing around on the floor in nappies and bonnets and nothing else were three fully grown men, one with a beard. Two were lying in overgrown cots. One was lying on his back playing with an overhead toy mobile while the other was chewing on a teething ring.

'Ray. What the fuck is 'appening?' whispered Clocks. 'What's goin' on? I don't like it.'

'You'll be all right, mate. Try not to look at them. You'll only upset yourself.'

'Too late. I can't not look. This ain't right. Say somethin' to 'em.'

'Behave yourself.'

'Poeaceman, poeaceman!' one of the babies said, pointing toward Clocks and giggling.

'The fuck . . . ?' Clocks said.

'I'm sorry,' said Alice. 'Wednesday is nursery day.'

'Fuckin' nursery?' said Clocks. 'They're grown men. The fuck are they doin'?'

Alice grimaced. 'Oh. You *are* one of them.'

'What? What'd you mean? I ain't one of *those* fuckin' idiots if that's what you mean.' He jerked his thumb backward.

'You clearly don't believe in free expression.'

'Oh, I believe in free expression, mate. What I'm 'avin' trouble with is grown men poncin' about in nappies and pretendin' they're fuckin' babies. That ain't right.'

'Who says?' Alice had a defensive tone now.

'Says me.'

'These men are doing no one any harm. They just choose to identify as babies.'

'Identify as babies? What'd you mean *identify* as babies? What for? What's the point of it?'

'The point is that they find a form of release from the suppression they feel in their daily lives. For some of them their job is extremely pressurised or they have a troublesome domestic life, and they find some measure of comfort and relief in going back to their early childhood to a time where they felt safe, free from any societal pressure.'

'Silly-born bastards. Don't make any sense to me mate, sorry. I mean, they can identify as a four-slice electric toaster if they want to, good luck to 'em, but what's the chances of ever gettin' a toasted 'am sandwich out of 'em? I'll tell yer . . . none. An' I'll tell yer why. It's because they're not a fuckin' toaster, they never will be a toaster an' they're not fuckin' babies either so what's the bleedin' point pretendin' they are?'

Alice shook his head.

'An' what's that fuckin' smell? Jesus!'

'That'll be David.' Alice, nodded to one of the men on the floor. 'He has a little tummy trouble.'

'Oh, turn it in!' Clocks looked at David. 'You dirty bastard. Whassa matter with yer? Get a fuckin' grip an' sort yerself out.'

David looked embarrassed and his bottom lip wobbled.

'Oh, no. You're not gonna cry. You are *not* gonna cry. Don't you dare cry, you fuckin' idiot.'

David's eyes welled up and he began to sniffle.

Clocks turned to Paterson. 'Is it just me? Or do you see it too? Tell me you see this . . . malarkey.'

'Take it easy, mate,' said Paterson. 'You've upset him.'

'I've upset *'im*? Good gawd.'

'Treat it as a learning opportunity for you.'

'A learnin' opportunity for what?'

'For how to be more understanding. To be more tolerant of other people. They're not doing any harm. They're just expressing themselves in a way that makes them feel comfortable. It's their right.'

'Whaddabout my rights? They're makin' me feel fuckin' *right* uncomfortable.'

Paterson shrugged. 'It's their nursery. We came into it.'

'Oh, don't. Not you an' all. Nursery? If this is a nursery then I reckon a call to Ofsted's in order. Where's me phone?' Clocks fumbled around in the back pocket of his trousers.

'Ow! Fuck!' he shouted as a small wooden brick hit him on the back of the head. He spun around, fury etched on his face.

'Which one of you soppy cunts did that?'

The babymen all acted innocently.

'Don't fuck about with me. Who did it?'

'Mr Clocks,' said Alice. 'Please calm down. Shouting at them will only upset them and they'll all start crying.'

Clocks balled his fists and dropped his body slightly lower.

'John, no!' Paterson said. 'Don't!'

Clocks ignored him. 'Was it you, mate? Did you chuck that at me? Did yer?' He headed toward the man with the beard. 'C'mon. Hands up.' The babymen all giggled and clapped.

'Right then. Fuck the lot of yer. I'm about to identify as a right 'orrible bastard an' I'm gonna punch each an' every one of yer back into yer suits.'

Alice intervened. 'Now come on, children. That was naughty. Uncle Johnny is upset now. Look at him.'

'What? I'm not their bleedin' uncle. Don't drag me into this bloody . . . whatever this is. Nightmare.'

'Say sorry to Uncle Johnny or no one's going to get any of Mummy's milk.'

Clocks frowned deeply. 'Mummy's milk?'

With that, a heavily pregnant woman stepped out of the kitchen. Her two large breasts were fully exposed either side of the flaps of her dressing gown. The babymen suddenly became excited and toddled across to her. 'Come on, my darlings,' she said. 'Who's hungry?'

'Oh, no, no, no,' said Clocks. 'Turn it in. This is all kinds of wrong, Ray? I've 'ad enough of this. I'll be in the car diggin' me eyeballs out with a pen an' dippin' 'em in a bucket of bleach.' He turned and stormed off along the hall and out of the street door, banging it behind him.

'Sorry, about that,' said Paterson, with a loud sigh. 'He's trying hard, but the 1970s keep calling him back.'

'No worries,' said Alice. 'We're used to it, I'm afraid.'

As the man with the beard clamped his mouth over one of the woman's nipples she looked over at Alice. 'I've made the teas for you. In the kitchen. They're a bit milky, though. Sorry.'

'A glass of water is absolutely fine for me,' said Paterson.

CHAPTER TWENTY-FOUR

Paterson slid into the driver's seat next to Johnny Clocks. 'Okay. It's done. He's on the case for us. Can't give us a definitive time but he understands that time is of the essence.'

Clocks was staring out of the window.

'You okay?' Paterson asked.

Clocks nodded. 'Yeah, 'course. Sorry about that up there. Just freaked me out a bit. Lost it.'

'I noticed. Why does it bother you so much?'

'I dunno. I just 'ave an 'ard time gettin' me nut around the world these days. I just don't understand the need for it.'

'It's complicated, John. Very complicated. As Alice said, people sometime need to get away from the pressure they're under. I drink and do the odd cheeky line of the white stuff and that's how I deal with it. You . . . well now you're off the drink a bit more, you get all outraged and indignant with the odd punch thrown in. But, come to think of it, you always did that. So, each to their own, mate.'

'I've gotta stop being so judgemental,' Clocks said, matter-of-factly.

Paterson turned to him. 'What?'

'You 'eard.'

'Jesus! I never thought I'd hear you say that. Ever. Sounds like you're evolving into a human. Want me to run you up to the hospital? Get your head tested?'

'You're a hoot. I know you think I'm a knob—'

'No, I don't.'

'I am a knob. But I'm trying to be better, Ray.'

Paterson squinted at him. 'You're on a wind-up again.'

Clocks grinned. ''Ad you going there, didn't I? Fuck all that understandin' malarkey. Punching people's good for me. Not for them, but for me. Besides, what would all me fans think if I went soft?'

'Fans? Don't kid yourself, Johnny boy. You haven't got any fans. Only me and Lyndsey, and I can't figure out why she's not kicked you into touch by now. I mean, she knows you and yet still she's going to marry you.'

Clocks shrugged. 'What can I say? I'm just a big ol' cuddly teddy bear.'

Paterson laughed and drove off.

'What did that Alice geezer say, then?'

'As I said, he's on it. I filled him in on everything we know. He'll call us as soon as he's got something. *If* he's got something. Pity you left really. He took me into his office and, mate, you've never seen anything like it. All of his computer gear is in a big Faraday cage, which he says stops people picking up on his communications. That and better-than-military-grade encryption. He has about ten big screens and a shitload of laptops lying around everywhere and servers dotted about all over the place. He runs everything off just a couple of laptops. Amazing really. The bloke clearly knows his onions.'

'So, where are we now?' Clocks fidgeted to get comfortable in his seat.

'Fucking nowhere. Two dead, no suspects apart from this silly Knights group, no idea who they are and it looks like a third dead'un on the way. We're kind of stuck until Alice gets back to us.'

Clocks shook his head 'Nope. Not good enough. We need to be rattlin' a few cages on the street, mate, an' a lot 'arder than we 'ave been.'

'Don't see how that will help.'

'It always 'elps. Trust me.'

'What's happening with Anderson's wife and daughter? Have we heard anything yet?'

'Not a carrot. I'm worried about those two.'

'Yeah, me too,' said Paterson. 'So, who's looking after the boy?'

'Dunno. Colin Yorkshire's been keeping an eye on the place, but I've not 'eard anything, so I'm guessing he's still on his own. There's a nationwide alert gone out for the two of them, but we've held back the fact that it's the commissioners family and that he's dead. We've just said they're people of prominence.'

'Okay. That's good. Shall we send in social services for the son, d'you reckon?'

'What for? We tell 'em a twenty-something man is strugglin' to wipe the spit off his chin. Can't see 'em droppin' everythin' to go rushin' round there, if I'm honest.'

'John, you can be a real callous bastard sometimes, you know that?'

'Yeah. I don't mean it like that, do I?'

'Then don't fucking say it. It's not his fault, is it? Have some compassion.'

'Nah. Makes yer weak.'

'Makes you human.'

'I'll give it a swerve if it's all the same to you, Muvver T'resa.'

'I think we need to go back and check on him. This is all kinds of wrong. Something's not adding up.'

'Okay but, so you know, the more I think about it, the more I think Anderson's ol' woman an' daughter topped 'im an' then fucked off together.'

'I thought that was off the table? I honestly don't think it's them.'

'Perhaps he diddled them against their will, they'd 'ad enough of it and decided to Blood Eagle 'im.'

'*As you do.* No, John. It's not them.'

'So, where the fuck are they then? People don't just disappear in the night, do they? Do they?'

'Not as a rule, no. We're going back to the house.'

'I'll call Tetley an' let 'im know we're on our way. He will be pleased.' DC Colin Yorkshire had had the misfortune to be gifted with the same surname as the historic county he was born in, a place with a long association with the British tea industry. Clocks therefore decided that, going forward, Colin Yorkshire would forever be known as Tetley, the largest tea manufacturer in the UK, themselves based in Yorkshire.

* * *

Thirty minutes later, as Paterson and Clocks drove up, DC Yorkshire got out of his car to greet them.

'Any joy?' said Clocks.

'No, sir. I haven't seen any movement in or out. No one's been by or near the place.'

'So, 'e's still inside?'

'He should be.'

'He better be,' said Clocks. 'If 'e ain't, then I'm gonna wanna know why 'e slipped out on your watch, Tetley, me ol' cocker. Now . . . let's try again . . . Is 'e inside?'

Yorkshire glared at his senior officer. It was no secret around the station that the two men had little time for each other. DC Yorkshire considered Clocks to be an ill-mannered, uneducated moron. For his part, Clocks considered Yorkshire to be a first-class fuckwit. 'Yes,' Yorkshire said. 'He's inside.'

'Then let's go an' 'ave ourselves a little chinwag with 'im, shall we?'

As they walked toward the house, Paterson noted that everything was exactly as it had been during their earlier visit. No new tyre tracks in or out of the garage, nothing parked on the driveway. He rang the bell. No answer. Clocks looked at Yorkshire. Paterson rang the bell again.

'It took him a while to answer last time,' he said. 'Let's give it a couple of minutes.'

'Fuck this,' said Clocks. 'I'm off to look for an open window.' He bent down to pick up a large stone. 'Ooh, look! One of them new-fangled window keys.' He walked off toward the side of the house.

'John! What are you doing?'

'Climbin' through this open window.' Without turning to look back, Clocks disappeared around the corner of the house. Yorkshire rolled his eyes. Paterson caught it.

'Problem, DC Yorkshire?'

Yorkshire dropped his eyes slightly. 'No, sir.' He sighed. 'No problem.'

There was a loud crash of glass from around the corner, and Clocks reappeared. 'Fancy leavin' yer window open! You comin'?'

'You'll be the death of me.' Paterson watched Clocks tap out the rest of the broken glass from the frame.

'Nobody lives forever, mate. Enjoy life while you can.' He started to wiggle open the window frame.

'Did you check for an alarm?' said Yorkshire.

Clocks stopped. 'What? Er, no. Did you?'

'No. Why would I? This was your idea, sir.'

'An' it was a blinder until you 'ad to chuck a spanner in the works. Dunno what to do now. Guv?'

'A bit late now, isn't it? You might as well lift it an' see what happens.'

Clocks nodded. 'Let's 'ave it then.' He raised the window a couple of inches. Nothing happened. Clocks looked hopeful and raised it a foot. Still no alarm. 'Cracked it!'

'Seems odd,' said Paterson. 'The commissioner of police's mansion and it's not alarmed?'

Clocks pushed it up as far as he could reach. 'Gimme a leg up, Tetley.'

DC Yorkshire cupped his hands into a makeshift stirrup and took hold of Clocks's foot. In the distance a siren wailed quietly.

'Shh!' said Paterson. 'You hear that?'

Both men stopped what they were doing.

'Oh, bollocks,' said Clocks. 'Fuckin' silent alarm weren't it?' He took his foot out of Yorkshire's hands. 'Plan?'

'We could run,' said Yorkshire.

'Good boy,' said Clocks. 'Welcome to the real police.'

CHAPTER TWENTY-FIVE

Ronald Lavery checked his watch as he drove through streets, slick with rain. Lavery had made his mark in the world. He had started a successful clothing business that now had over 170 employees in the UK and branches opening up across Europe on a monthly basis. He owned a big house in Kent just off the A21 where he lived with his wife of forty years and two red setters. His only child, Toby, was at university studying for a degree in history, and from what he had been told, was doing well and with expectations of a BA with first-class honours. Work kept Lavery busy and out of the home most of the time, and it was those absences he attributed to a successful marriage that had lasted so long. That, and a string of lovers dotted around everywhere. He figured that, as he worked so hard and had built such a thriving empire that kept him and his family in luxury, he was entitled to extra perks. Being a handsome, muscular man who had taken good care of his body over the years, the perks were not in short supply.

He checked his watch again and cursed under his breath: 10.58 p.m. He was going to be late for his meeting. Not much — five minutes at most — but he hated being late, hated it with a passion. Time was money. Although this wasn't a business meeting, the maxim was deeply ingrained in him. Old habits were hard to break.

He debated calling Toby to tell him he'd be late but thought better of it. He hadn't seen his son for the best part of two years now so didn't feel the need to. Work was always in the way. Always had been. Always would be. Lavery felt no guilt or shame over his 'perks' or his lack of interest in his wife and son. He paid for everything, made their lives better and slept soundly at night.

The fact that Toby had called him didn't really interest him, one way or the other. He knew he was never going to follow him into the business and so wouldn't be able to take over when he eventually retired, but he knew that if his son was calling and asking to meet, then he wanted something. Money probably. He thought for a second that perhaps he'd got some girl pregnant but laughed that off. He doubted whether Toby had even had sex with anyone other than himself.

He pulled into the industrial estate at 11.07 p.m. and pulled up outside a large brick warehouse. As he flashed his lights at the figure standing in the distance it suddenly crossed his mind that it was a strange place to meet so late at night.

CHAPTER TWENTY-SIX

DAY 3

'Mr Goodwin, thank you for coming back,' said Morne. 'This is Peter Stannard, the assistant commissioner, crime; Elizabeth Boyle, the deputy assistant commissioner; and I've also asked Lorna Ellis as the Met's senior legal advisor to sit in on this meeting.' The small group said their hellos and got down to business.

'Lorna, let me brief you in a bit more detail, if I may. DCI Goodwin has brought to my attention that he sent a video to Commissioner Anderson the night before he died. That video is the dying declaration of DCI Lambert, who you know was shot in his office by an assailant we now know was Detective Constable Carrie Gedmine. Our investigation discovered that Miss Gedmine was extremely obsessive and had a very unhealthy crush on Detective Superintendent Paterson that had become an all-consuming fixation. Papers found in her locker show quite clearly that she planned Lambert's murder. Only she botched it up and Lambert didn't die at the scene. He died later in hospital.

'His daughter called for the police to be in attendance because of what her father was saying before he died. He was recorded on a bodycam and DCI Goodwin here took possession of the footage sometime after. That footage was sent to Mr Anderson and, as you know, he was the first victim of . . . of . . . whoever the hell it is.

'That footage would seem to suggest that, while not directly involved in the shooting itself, they may have had a hand in ordering it.'

The room stayed silent.

'And Paterson and Clocks are the investigating officers into Commissioner Anderson's death.'

DCI Goodwin shook his head and looked down at the floor. Morne watched Lorna Ellis scribble something on her pad and scratched at his chin.

'I realise that this doesn't sit right with you, Mr Goodwin, but there was no reason to suspect them of any involvement in Mr Anderson's death and, until you came to me, nothing to suggest they had anything to do with DCI Lambert's murder. Nothing. I know Anderson had a grudge against them — we all know that. But I do not see him having a grudge as a valid reason for not putting the two best detectives I have on the case. I trusted their professionalism. I still do.'

'Then with respect, sir, I think your judgement is seriously flawed,' said Goodwin.

Morne fixed Goodwin with a cold stare. 'Mr Goodwin, please watch your tone. I've invited you into this meeting because of your involvement with the Lambert shooting. We both know that your being here is a courtesy, not a requirement.'

'Sir, I understand and I apologise for my manner. But, I have to ask. How on earth can you think that these two . . . *cowboys* would be the best people to investigate the death of a man they hated? I just don't get it.'

'Why do you say they hated him?' said Morne. Goodwin sat up straight. 'What evidence have you got to even suggest that?'

'Commissioner Anderson made no secret of his dislike for them. Didn't he have them placed under observation because he suspected them of being involved in Lambert's shooting? I don't suppose there would have been any love lost between any of them. It's just common sense.'

'And with respect to *you*, DCI Goodwin, I would argue that you are not in a position to say that. You have no idea what they thought of Anderson, and it will do no good to suggest otherwise. Not once have they complained about Anderson's behaviour toward them. They've taken it on the chin like men, and from my conversations with them, I'm of the opinion they found him no more than an irritation.'

'An irritation? The man is . . . was the bloody commissioner! He had a perfect right to put them under investigation if he suspected them of wrongdoing.'

'I'm not denying that. All I will say is that they'd become his pet project. His hatred of them consumed him so badly that in the end he lost the confidence of his entire senior management team, who actually called for him to be put on gardening leave.'

'Gentlemen,' said Lorna Ellis, 'this isn't helping. Can we please calm down and look at this video? I take it we have a copy? Didn't you say that it was sent to Anderson?' She looked across to Goodwin.

'Yes, ma'am. But I managed to get a copy sent over to my tablet.' He spun it around and hit *play* before turning it so that everyone had a clear view. A minute later he hit the stop button. 'Seems cut and dried to me,' he said.

'It's far from that,' said Ellis.

ACC Stannard turned to her. 'How so?'

'Look. Dying declarations are notoriously difficult to be taken as solid useable evidence. I can promise you we're going to have a huge problem getting anyone to take that as anything other than a man's dying hallucinations. From what I recall, I understand *he* wasn't a fan of Paterson and Clocks either. I remember reading somewhere that he thought they were involved in the murders of a number of young girls, isn't that right?'

Morne nodded. 'That's correct. But we now know that Gedmine carried out those murders too. Both Lambert and Anderson were way off the mark with these two. Way off. It seems to me that both of them had it in for Paterson and Clocks. Why, I don't know, but let's be honest, they're not the conventional coppers that this politically correct government and police service want to see, are they? And that, I believe, shoved a stick up Anderson's arse.'

Ellis grimaced.

'I can't speak for Lambert,' said Morne, 'but I understand they pissed him off by disagreeing with him over the murders he was looking at.'

'What are you saying?' said Ellis.

Morne sighed. 'I honestly think these two have been given a bad deal by the establishment and have been the victims of extreme confirmation bias. All the job has done is treat them as guilty and look hard for evidence to confirm that belief. Trouble is, there is none — never has been — and this looks like another desperate attempt to hang them for something.' He turned to Goodwin. 'No disrespect to you, Mr Goodwin. You did exactly the right thing in bringing this to my attention. So . . .' He turned to face Stannard. 'We can go on looking at them as suspects for God knows what else we want to try and stick on them or we can get out of their way and let them do their bloody job! Personally, I'm all for the latter. Now, let me state on record, I do not believe for a second that Paterson and Clocks had a hand in either Lambert's or Anderson's death. And if I'm ever proved wrong, I will resign my post immediately.'

'Just to be clear,' Stannard said, 'the PM does have her concerns over them. She's had numerous reports come across her desk about their behaviour.'

AC Morne sighed. 'Frankly, I don't give a toss. She's only been fed biased information herself, so any judgement she's making is based on someone else's opinion. If she wants a *balanced* opinion, she can talk to me.' He turned his attention to Ellis. 'Lorna, you've seen it now. Your opinion, please.'

Her elbows on the table, Lorna Ellis rubbed her eyes. 'I wouldn't be happy to take this any further based on what I've seen here. Any competent defence lawyer would punch holes straight through it and I know that Paterson can afford the best legal team in the business. That would extend to DI Clocks too, I suspect.'

'Explain the problem for me in clear terms please, Lorna,' said Stannard.

'There's nothing there that directly implicates either of them in Lambert's shooting. What we have is a man who was literally on his last knockings. There are hundreds of scientific papers that suggest that the dying hallucinate all sorts of things moments before they die . . . visions of Heaven . . . white lights . . . tunnels . . . dead family . . . old friends . . . cars they owned . . . favourite football players . . . all sorts of things. It's the brain's way of shutting down gently and easing the person into death. We also have to consider that Lambert was no doubt drugged up to the eyeballs. The paperwork associated with his hospital stay will no doubt show us to what degree, but gentlemen, this case will be strangled at birth, I can assure you of that. As I said, dying declarations are a nightmare to use as evidence.'

AC Morne seemed satisfied. 'Peter? Anything to add?'

Stannard shook his head. 'Not yet. Please, continue.'

'Elizabeth?'

'No.'

'Mr Goodwin, then. Anything from you?'

'Not really, sir. I'm not happy, obviously, but I take Ms Ellis's point.'

'Well, that's that. Paterson and Clocks will not be investigated for DCI Lambert's murder and, while we're all here, I strongly suggest, Elizabeth, that if it hasn't already been done, you contact our tech guys and get them to make an appointment with both of them to strip out all the surveillance equipment in their houses.'

Elizabeth stared at him.

'Oh, come on. There's no point in dragging it out and every day you leave it there the stronger their lawsuit will be, especially after they've already informed us they know.'

Stannard huffed and tapped his pencil rapidly on the table.

'What's all this?' said Lorna Ellis.

'Lorna, you need to know that both men have all kinds of documentation relating to the surveillance in and on the grounds of their properties. Thick files that they are prepared to use to launch a legal action against the Met. So, you might want to have a word with Elizabeth sooner rather than later and make sure that all the warrants for this surveillance operation were obtained properly — all the i's dotted and all the t's crossed — because we are about to get our arse kicked by these two, big time. And it fucking well serves us right.'

'Let's not be hasty, Mr Morne,' said Stannard.

Morne looked at him. Something was coming.

'Look,' said Stannard. 'I've listened to everything you've said and you've made your point, but the fact is I'm prepared to believe that Paterson and Clocks *did* have a hand in Anderson's death. Maybe not directly. I'm not saying they were the ones that killed him, but I strongly suggest that the investigation into them remains open and that they be brought in and questioned about it at length. No more half jobs. That way we can never be accused of covering up the actions and behaviours of two senior police officers.'

'Jesus Christ! Lorna?' said Morne. 'What's your take?'

She sighed and sat herself back into her chair. 'To be honest, it might be prudent. I'm sure the dying declaration won't stand the test as substantial evidence, but Mr Stannard makes a good point about us covering our backs if anything comes out at a later date.'

'This is bloody ridiculous.' Morne threw his hands up in the air and shook his head. 'You're seriously suggesting that I have them arrested?'

'Yes, sir. I am.'

'For God's sake. No. I won't do it.'

'Sir,' said Elizabeth, 'just for your information, when I briefed the prime minister, she was unhappy about their involvement. Now, we both know she cannot interfere with police business and she can't tell us what to do, but I got the distinct impression that if anything goes wrong with this operation, the government will show you no support.'

'This will fall on your shoulders if it all goes sideways, sir,' said Stannard. 'You know what these two are like. They *will* fuck up at some point and this will come back on you. Order their arrest, sir. For your sake. Protect yourself. Let's get them properly investigated. I'll get the warrants actioned.'

'So, that's it, is it? None of you are willing to back me, then?' Morne snorted and shook his head. 'I believe we're done here. Show yourselves out.'

CHAPTER TWENTY-SEVEN

Paterson, Clocks and DS Suzi Rocket climbed the last set of stairs to the roof and made their way over to a small group of uniformed police officers. Behind them was a large make-shift plastic tent, the sort of thing put over strawberries or tomatoes to help them grow, only taller. Monkey Harris was holding open one of the tent flaps and looking inside.

'Monkey boy!' Clocks shouted. Harris pulled his head out.

'All right, guv . . . guvs,' he said, giving Paterson and Rocket a nod of the head.

'Whatcha got, then? Anythin' good?'

The trio breezed past the uniformed officers without saying anything to join Monkey Harris.

'Yeah,' said Harris. 'Say hello to Christine Lord. She was a sitting judge here.'

'A judge?'

'Yep.'

'How do we know that? Any ID on her?'

Harris shook his head. 'A maintenance man came up here to fix something or other. He saw the tent and poked his head inside. Bad mistake on his part.'

Paterson frowned.

'Take a look.' Harris stood aside.

Paterson and Clocks poked their heads through the flap.

'Fuck me,' said Clocks. 'I bet that 'urt.'

'I reckon,' said Paterson.

'Is that even possible?'

'Yeah,' said Paterson. 'It's possible.' He grimaced at the thought of the agony the victim would have endured before death. 'But it takes time — maybe a week, maybe less — and the pain would have been excruciating. It would have taken a good amount of time to die. She's been here a while.'

All four stepped inside the tent and took a proper look at the victim. A female in her mid-fifties and completely naked, lay flat on her back with arms and legs stretched out and secured on a thick bed of what looked like soil. Her mouth and eyes were covered with duct tape. Around her body were several bamboo stalks. Bursting out through her face, throat, arms, torso and legs were ten sticks of bamboo.

Clocks crouched down to take a closer look. 'So, you're sayin' that this poor cow was plonked down 'ere on the earth, on top of what, bamboo seeds or whatever they are, and these things grew *through* 'er?'

'Looks like it.'

'Nah. I'm not 'avin' that. It can't grow through a body. Can it?'

'The Japanese were rumoured to have used it as a form of torture in World War Two,' said Harris, nodding his head sagely.

'S'right,' said Paterson. 'Heard of *Mythbusters*?'

Clocks shook his head.

'They were on the telly a few years back. Couple of Americans who go about busting . . . well, myths. Someone asked if it were possible to kill someone like this and they tested it with a body made out of ballistic gel. It's the nearest thing they could get that approximated a human cadaver. Turns out it went right through the thing in a few days. You can still find it on YouTube. Type in "Mythbusters bamboo" and see for yourself.'

'Jesus! Who knew? Wait a minute. I'll tell you who knew.'

Paterson looked at him. 'Who?'

'Dick Van Dyke. 'E sang a song about bamboo in one of 'is films, didn't 'e? Oh, shit. What was it called?'

Paterson shrugged.

'You must know it. Bloody 'ell. What was it?'

'Don't worry about it, John. It's not important.'

'It is to me. That'll drive me mad, now. I can 'ear it in me 'ead. A fuckin' earworm, that is.'

Paterson watched as Clocks nodded his head from side to side and twitched his elbows.

'What's he doing?' said Rocket.

'I've seen him do this before. I think he's singing to himself. John! What are you doing, mate?'

'Singin' to meself. Can't quite get it.'

Paterson nodded. 'Thought so.'

'It's gonna drive me mental all day.'

'Christ almighty. What's wrong with him? Bloody singing to himself.' Rocket turned away. 'I'll be downstairs.' Under her breath she said, 'Man's a fucking moron.'

Clocks stood up. 'Fuck's got up 'er kilt, the miserable cow? No sense of humour, some people.'

'Some people would say it's a tad unprofessional, Clocksy.'

'Only people with no sense of humour. People need to lighten up a bit. Everyone's so fuckin' serious these days. Jeez.'

Paterson ignored him. 'Monkey, can you give Jock Hudson a bell for me and get him out here. He's gonna want to see this.'

'Yeah, course.' Harris took out his phone.

'And while you're at it,' said Clocks, 'give London Zoo a call and tell 'em we've found their panda, Chi-Chi, an' she's overdosed on bamboo.' Harris gave him a wry grin and stepped outside the tent.

'Same killer?' said Paterson.

'Gotta be,' said Clocks. 'Different method but the theme's the same. Bloody weird. So you reckon she's been here about a week?'

'Honestly? I don't know. I know bamboo's one of the fastest-growing plants on the planet and that all plants grow toward the light. Weather's been shitty the last few days, so maybe the dull light slowed it down. I'm guessing. That said, I read somewhere once that one particular species of bamboo grew thirty-six inches or so in twenty-four hours.'

'Oh, fuck off! Three foot? I don't think so.'

'Didn't say it was true. Said I read it somewhere. I'm not a botanist. What do I know?'

'Does this stuff grow in the cold?' said Clocks.

'Well, by the look of it, I'd say yes. Yes, it does.'

'But you reckon she was alive when she was plonked down?'

'Yeah. If you're going to torture somebody it's a bit pointless doing it if they're dead isn't it? Makes no sense. No. She was alive, same as Anderson. Whoever's doing this is making a point of torturing his victims first.'

'Nasty fucker.'

'Indeed.'

'I'm confused.'

'That makes a change.'

Clocks ignored him. 'Is this some sort of Dark Ages murder too?'

'No idea.'

'If it's not, then that blows up that particular line of thought. Instead of dealin' with Ragnar bloody Whatsisarse or Ivor the Engine, it's just yer run-o'-the-mill, sadistic nutjob. Boring.'

Monkey Harris stepped back inside. 'Hudson's on his way, guv. About an hour.'

'Cheers, Monkey,' said Paterson. 'Okay. We're not hanging around for Jock this time. I'll give Mr Morne a bell and let him know what's happened and that we *think* it's connected. See what he says.'

'Go on then. I'll try and find out if anyone's seen this ol' bird's clothes. She must be freezin' 'er bloody tits off out 'ere.' Clocks chuckled to himself as he walked away.

CHAPTER TWENTY-EIGHT

Paterson's phone rang and he answered the call, routing it through the Bluetooth system. 'Paterson,' he said.

'It's me. Alice. Got something for you.'

'Go on.'

'I've traced the point where the emails originate from.'

The boys stayed quiet.

'It's coming from a boat, the *Liberty*, which is permanently moored in St Katharine Dock, just north of Tower Bridge. I assume you know where that is?'

'Yep. Know it well,' said Paterson. 'How d'you know it's permanently moored?'

Alice chuckled. ''Cos I'm really good at this, Mr Paterson. I hacked the dock master's computer, and the last time that boat moved anywhere was about nine months ago. Fair to say it's not going to go anywhere tonight either.'

'Why'd you say that, then?'

'Ah, is that Mr Clocks?'

'The one an' only,' said Clocks.

'How are you today? Have you recovered from your trip to another reality?'

'Recovered? I don't bloody think so, matey. I've bought meself one of those little eyebaths and I'm sloshin' bleach in me eyes every ten minutes or so.'

Alice burst out laughing. 'You are a funny fucker, Mr Clocks. You do make me laugh. I don't suppose you're free on Saturday by any chance?'

'Er, why?'

'I'm hosting a Ken and Barbie party. I think you'll enjoy it. Please say you'll come.'

'Alice, me ol' darlin', there's more chance of me kissing the Queen than there is of that 'appening, so stop all yer flirtin' and let's get on with it. Why isn't that boat likely to move, then?'

'Ah, yes. Well, I also checked with the Marine Registration Database and it's registered to one Scott Anderson.' Paterson and Clocks snatched a glance at each other. 'There's a second person shown on the registration document too. A Mr Temple Anderson.'

'Who the fuck's that?'

Paterson shrugged. 'Alice, do you know who it is?'

'Not yet. I assume it's his son, perhaps. Maybe a brother?'

'Can you dig into it for me, please?' said Paterson.

'Of course. I just wanted to give you the boat information first.'

'I appreciate it, Alice. Listen, top work there, fellah. Keep me posted on anything else you find, yes?'

'For the wages you're paying, Mr Paterson, I'd likely have your babies. Ciao, my lovelies.' Alice hung up.

Clocks's face was screwed up when he spoke. 'That's disgustin'.'

'I don't suppose it was meant literally.'

'Maybe. But he's an odd one. Wouldn't surprise me if 'e 'ad a womb tucked up 'is arse somewhere.'

'Yeah, okay. Forgetting that. This boat . . . we've got to get a warrant and get over there asap. Make a call for me, John, and I'll ring around the squad, make sure they're all available. Once we've rounded up the troops, we'll head over and have a chat with the harbour master, see what he can tell us.'

Clocks nodded. 'That's a stupid name, ain't it? *Temple*. Who calls their kid Temple, for fuck's sake?'

'Dunno. What bothers me is why we didn't know about him. His son's name was Fane, wasn't it?'

'Yeah. Another dopey name. Fane and Temple. Poor little bastards. I bet they got the granny kicked out of 'em at school. They wouldn't 'ave lasted ten minutes at my school.'

'I don't want to sound snobby, but I doubt they would have gone to the same reform school for wayward boys as you. What was it called? Borstal, wasn't it?'

'You cheeky bastard. I 'ad the best edumacation our failed school system could provide, I'll 'ave you know. I left with all Es and Ds on me report card.'

'And you're proud of that, are you?'

'Too right, matey. I was the school brainbox. Everyone else got straight Fs.'

'Dear God,' said Paterson. 'Get the warrant, John. I need to make a call.' He disconnected the phone from the speaker so as not to disturb Clocks and dialled a number.

'Dr Rakes? It's me . . . Superintendent Paterson.'

'Mr Paterson. Wasn't expecting to hear from you yet. What can I do for you?'

'I'm sorry to call so late, but I have an important question to ask.'

'If you're going to ask me on a date—'

'What? Er, no. I wasn't. That is . . . I will, sorry. Wasn't expecting that.'

She laughed. 'Don't worry about it. Just my sense of humour. How can I help?'

'Does the word *Fane* mean anything to you?'

'Fane?'

'Yeah. F.A.N.E. Somebody gave me the name and I hadn't heard of it before. I just wondered if it was an old name or something? Thought you might know of it or have it on one of your databases. Save me the time having to dig around.'

'Hold on,' she said.

Paterson could hear a keyboard being tapped.

'Found it. According to Google—'

'You use Google?'

'Yes. Don't you?'

Paterson felt a bit embarrassed that he hadn't thought of that. 'Er, yes, but to be honest, it never crossed my mind.'

'Well, it doesn't matter. Let me read what I've found. It's not very much I'm afraid. *Fane is an archaic word. It has its root in the Latin word* fānum. *It means temple or shrine.*'

Paterson hit the brakes. Johnny Clocks shot forward and cursed.

'Fuck me! Whassamatter? What's goin' on? What? No. Sorry, sir. Didn't mean to swear. I'm in a car and the driver just slammed the brakes on for no reason. Nearly 'it me nut on the dashboard. I'll call you back. Sorry.'

Paterson didn't move as cars behind honked at him to get out of the way.

'Did you say *Temple*?'

'Yes,' said Dr Rakes. '*Temple or shrine*. Why?'

Clocks frowned. 'What's going on?' he said to Paterson. A car drove past slowly, window down.

'Get out of the road you fuckin' arse'ole!' the driver screamed. Paterson ignored him. Clocks gave him the finger. The driver stamped on his brakes and wrenched up the handbrake. He made to get out of his car, and as he did so, Clocks pulled out his badge and held it across Paterson's face so the driver could see it.

'Whenever you like, mate!' Clocks shouted to him. The driver gave him the finger and screeched off.

'What's going on?' said Dr Rakes, a hint of concern in her voice.

'Nothing,' said Paterson. 'Listen, thank you for that, and I'll give you a call. We'll sort out dinner soon.' He hung up.

'What's goin' on, guv? I nearly shit meself when you slammed the anchors on.'

'Yeah, sorry about that. Did you hear any of my conversation?'

'Not much. I was too busy swearin' at a magistrate. I don't think he was very 'appy.'

'I asked her if she'd heard of the name Fane.'

'Yeah, I 'eard 'er say something about a temple. What was that about?'

'It turns out that Fane is an old, archaic name that means Temple.'

The penny dropped for Clocks. 'Oh, shit in an 'at an' punch it!'

'Exactly. The boy Fane, that was bollocks, mate. That whole mental disability thing. All bollocks. A show. I'll bet his name is really Temple and I'll bet he's behind all of this.'

'The slippery little fucker. He's due a clump when I get 'old of 'im.'

Paterson pulled away and joined the traffic. 'We go tonight, John. We storm this boat and nick whoever's there. If it's not Fane or Temple or whatever he calls himself, we'll keep whoever we do nick incommunicado. They speak to nobody. Nobody. I don't want him getting wind that we're onto him. Then we go straight over to Anderson's house and nick the little fucker on the spot. Up for that?'

'Fuck, yeah. An' that, me ol' mucker, sounds like a plan.'

CHAPTER TWENTY-NINE

Paterson and Clocks stood side by side at the front of the office. Behind them was a sparsely populated whiteboard, evidence that they were lacking in suspects and clues. A picture of Anderson looked out at the room, hanging precariously from a small piece of masking tape. There were at-the-scene images of all three victims dotted all around the board.

'Evenin' all,' said Clocks. 'Thank you all for coming back in at such short notice. I know it's probably upset yer families an' all that, but while you were at 'ome watchin' the box with yer feet up, me an' the guv were creepin' about tryin' to get a lead. Turns out we got one.'

'Yeah, thanks for coming back,' said Paterson. 'I got a call earlier this evening from a tech guy who's doing some under-the-table work for us and he's put the email messages as coming from a boat moored in St Katharine Dock — just the other side of the Thames, for those of you new to the team. Interestingly, the boat was registered to our dearly departed Commissioner Anderson. Even more interesting . . . also shown on the paperwork is one Mr Temple Anderson. I put in a call to Dr Rakes and she discovered that the name *Fane* is an old word for temple.

'So, working off that, we figured that Anderson's son had us over when we visited his house, and we now strongly suspect that this son of his is involved in all three murders. We haven't quite worked out how yet, but we're hoping there will be someone, perhaps Temple himself, on this boat who we can nick.'

'We've got a couple of CID from Leman Street to keep an eye on the boat for us while we assembled everyone together,' said Clocks. 'Now, given that whoever's responsible for these murders is a tasty fucker who knows 'is way around a blade, we're all toolin' up. So, those of you who are authorised, get yerselves down to the armoury and book out a firearm an' then meet us in the yard.'

The small team of officers began to disperse amid the usual hubbub of excitement. They grabbed property bags, notebooks, pens, radios, coats and hats.

'Before you all go,' said Paterson. 'If we blow our cover at St Katharine's, we head straight over to Anderson's house. DI Clocks has got warrants for the boat and the house waiting for us from a friendly magistrate, and we'll stop and pick them up on the way. Are there any questions?'

'Yes,' said Suzi Rocket. 'Do we have boat police on standby?'

Paterson shook his head. 'Hadn't thought of that to be honest. From what I understand, the boat is moored and, knowing St Katharine's, it won't be possible for a quick getaway. Besides, we'll be swarming all over it.'

'I was just thinking of evidence, sir. If anything comes out of a window and into the water, that's pretty much destroyed. Maybe a couple of boats on a silent approach could liaise with us and move in at the same time.'

'Yep, good point,' said Paterson. 'Get onto that for me, please.'

She nodded and went back to her desk to make the call.

'Anyone got anythin' else?' said Clocks. 'No? Let's do it then. See you downstairs.' Everybody in the office started to move. Meeting over.

'Why didn't you think of that, John?'

'What?'

'The boats.'

'I can't think of everythin', Ray. Why didn't you think of it?'

'I can't think of everything, John.' He smiled.

'An' that's why we've got 'er, innit? Ms Rocket. Gives 'er summing to do when she's not making the tea.'

'Ooh, you're in so much trouble, Clocksy.'

He shrugged. 'Put it on the list. C'mon, let's go an' get a gun. It's been ages since we had some fun.'

'You going to be sensible?'

'Moi? 'Course I am. Trust me.'

* * *

'Evening, Polly,' said Paterson. Jimmy Brown, the inspector in charge of the armoury, smiled as Paterson approached his cage. He was given the nickname 'Polly' a few years ago by Johnny Clocks for the simple reason he sat in a cage all day and, like most nicknames, it had stuck. It cemented itself when Clocks took a picture of him and stuck it on the canteen wall with the words 'Polly wanna cracker' emblazoned in red marker along the bottom.

'Evening, sir,' he said. 'You off out to play too? Just sorted out a few of your crew a couple of minutes ago.'

'Yeah. Clocksy here hasn't held a gun for a few days now and was getting withdrawal symptoms.'

Polly looked over his glasses at Clocks, who was standing behind Paterson. 'Evening, John. Didn't see you there. They still letting you have a gun, eh? Bloody dangerous if you ask me.'

'All right, Pol? Fuck me, you've put on some weight, ain'tcha? Fat as a barrel now. Must be sittin' in that cage all day eatin' crackers.' Polly frowned. 'An' what's with the glasses? You look like you've turned into a fuckin' owl now, don't 'e, Ray?'

'You do a bit, Pol. Has to be said,' said Paterson.

Polly sighed. 'What can I get the two of you?'

'We'll 'ave a couple of nuts if you've got em. Failing that, some of yer millet. I don't want you goin' 'ungry, though. Winter's comin'.'

'Two Glock nineteens coming up,' Polly said, ignoring him. He walked over to the safe. 'Ammunition?'

Clocks screwed his face up. 'No, don't bother about that. We're 'appy just throwin' the guns at 'em.'

'I meant, how much?'

'Oh. Sorry. I dunno. Whatever you can spare from your winter stash.'

Polly walked over with two handguns in holsters and set them down on the small shelf. He pushed a piece of paper on a clipboard at Paterson. 'Be careful, Timex. These aren't toys. You could hurt someone.'

'Polly, you realise you're about the only one left in the job that still calls me Timex?' said Clocks.

'Nope. Don't care either. You were introduced to me as Timex and Timex it will be.'

Clocks clipped the gun to his belt. 'Fair enough. Listen, I was thinkin', now you're an owl, do you want me to see if I can shoot some mice for yer dinner? Make a nice change for yer. Give you a break from nuts an' seeds. 'Ow's that sound?'

Polly shook his head. 'Sounds lovely. Thank you.' He handed over four clips of bullets. 'Two each,' he said.

'Jesus. You're no fun, are you?' Clocks dropped his jacket down over the holster.

'Come back next week. We're trialling a Bazooka, if you're interested.'

Clocks raised one eyebrow. 'Stop it. I'm getting' a twinge in me pants.'

Polly laughed. 'Seriously, be careful out there.'

'Cheers, Pol,' said Paterson. 'Ready?' he said to Clocks.

Clocks fumbled about in his pockets until he pulled out a small, opened and half-eaten packet of biscuits. He held them out to Polly and, mimicking a parrot, said 'Polly wanna cracker?'

CHAPTER THIRTY

Paterson drove out of Tower Bridge police station and made his way north across Tower Bridge. Following the one-way system, quiet at this time of night, he pulled into St Katharine Dock. The journey from the station to the dock was less than ten minutes. In the car with him was Johnny Clocks, DS Rocket and DC Gunn. Clocks hadn't spent much time with either of the newcomers and wanted to see for himself how they performed under pressure. The car behind was staffed by DC Ronnie 'Dusty' Doneghan, DC Michael 'Monkey' Harris and DC Colin 'Tetley' Yorkshire. Dusty and Monkey were carrying firearms. Yorkshire had declined to take a firearms course on ethical grounds. This was yet another thing that failed to endear him to his colleagues: his apparent lack of moral fibre.

As they approached the harbour master's office, a pair of plain-clothes police officers stepped out. One of them held up his warrant card. Paterson dropped his window. 'Evening,' he said. 'Superintendent Paterson. You from Leman Street, mate?'

'Yes, sir,' said the officer. 'Austin Gaye.'

Clocks grinned. 'Probably are an' all,' he muttered to himself. 'Leman entry, my dear Watson.'

'Nice to meet you, mate. Anything we need to know before we move in?' Paterson looked at all the different boats dotted around the dock.

'No, sir. All quiet on the Western Front.'

'Good. Do we know which one it is?'

'Yeah. It's over there.' He pointed into the distance.

Clocks bent forward to get a look at the officer on Paterson's side. 'That's 'elpful, son. Any chance you can narrow it down a bit?'

'Sorry, sir. See where that jetty is?' He pointed with his head. 'That's the one. The one you're after is the sixth one in on the left. It's a big lump.'

'I'm sure it is,' said Paterson. 'Got the code so we can get through the gate?'

'Yeah.' He handed over a slip of paper with the number written on it.

'Cheers, mate,' said Paterson. 'Appreciate you keeping an eye out for us. You can go now.'

DC Gaye tapped the roof of the car. 'Good luck, gents,' he said, and disappeared off into the night.

'Clearly didn't see you sittin' in the back did he, gel?' said Clocks to DS Rocket.

'People rarely see us.'

'What'd you mean?'

'Women.' She shrugged. 'I'm used to it.'

'What? Oh, don't start with all that. I saw you, didn't I?'

'You saw my tits, is what you saw.'

'Yeah, but to be fair, we all did. It's not like you can't see 'em, is it?'

Paterson winced. 'John . . .'

'What? She started it.'

'Pack it in.'

Clocks sighed heavily. 'I don't know why everybody's so uptight these days. It's not personal.'

'Not personal?' said DS Rocket. 'Every time I speak to you, you're looking at my chest.'

'Well, I can't help that. They've got a gravitational pull on me eyes. P'rhaps you should stand with yer back to me in future. Might be easier for both of us.'

DS Rocket shook her head. 'Are you fucking kidding me? The last thing I'm going to do is let *you* stand behind me. You're supposed to be a grown man, not a fourteen-year-old boy.'

'Err . . .' said Clocks.

'Don't go there,' said Paterson. 'Personally, I think he's about twelve at most.'

'That's not particularly helpful, guv, is it?' said Rocket. 'You're supposed to be putting a stop to this kind of behaviour. I shouldn't have to be the object of men's ogling.'

'True enough,' said Paterson. 'But the reality is, you will be. Fact.'

'I don't believe this. You're as bad as him, for Chrissakes.' She pushed herself back in her seat. 'This is why women have such a hard time in the workplace.'

'Oh, shut up, you soppy tart!' said Clocks. 'We're only muckin' about. I'm sorry I looked at your bangers. I'm a very bad boy and I won't do it again. I promise.'

'We'll see,' she said, an almost defeated tone in her voice.

'I won't need to. They're up here now,' he said, tapping his temple. 'Tucked away in the wank bank.'

'That's it!' she said. 'That's enough. I want a transfer out of this . . . this . . . homage to *The Sweeney*. You're all pigs.'

'DS Rocket,' said Paterson, 'I'm sorry. I really am. Look, we were just testing you, really. We need to know if you fit in. See if you could take a joke. Admittedly, it was in bad taste, but . . . there you go. If you want, you can have a transfer by all means, but can I suggest you stay? I would like you to stay. This will stop as of now. You have my word.'

Rocket took a deep breath and nodded curtly. 'I'll think about it.'

'Good enough for me,' said Paterson. 'C'mon, we've got work to do.' All four let themselves out of the car. Behind them, the others did the same. Chugging slowly into view were three police boats. 'Yorkshire, go talk to them. Tell them what we're up to and where we're going.'

'Sir.' He ran off along the quayside, waving a hand.

'So, what's the plan, guv?' said Monkey Harris.

'Simple,' said Clocks. 'We let ourselves in the gate, creep along as quiet as possible an' once our boats are in position, we storm Anderson's boat, boot the door in if it's got one, shout and scream a lot to frighten the shit out of anyone who's inside, nick 'em, then back to the factory for tea an' toast. Who's with me?'

Harris shook his head. 'Mr Paterson?'

'Similar plan, but not quite. Clocks and I will wait until our boats are in place, then I'll do a quick and quiet walk past, having a little peek inside the cabin if I can. Then we'll get ourselves onto the boat and try to ascertain if anyone is actually inside. If they are, we'll call you all in for backup before we enter. Now, that boat looks like a big lump, so I want only the two of us to go in. I want the rest of you to take up position on either side of the jetty where both sides of the boat can be seen. If you see anyone else creeping about, let them know you're there. If you hear shots from inside, wait until one of us calls you in. But if you hear shots and someone else comes out but us, shoot the shit out of them. Goddit?'

Harris nodded. 'See, guv?' he said to Clocks. 'That's a plan.'

'Basically what I said, wasn't it?'

Harris laughed. 'We going now?' he said.

'We go now,' said Paterson. 'Stay behind until I wave you in. Once we're on board, take up your positions quietly. I want complete radio silence, so make sure no one fucks it up by letting their radio squawk at the wrong time.' Everyone turned their radios off as Paterson and Clocks made their way toward their target.

'So, 'ow we workin' this, Ray? You goin' in first or me?'

'I'll go. You're getting married. Don't wanna lose you, do I? Lyndsey will fucking kill me.'

'Yeah, she would. Got a temper, that one.'

Paterson watched as the police boats got within fifty yards and cut their engines to drift into position. When he was happy they were ready, he and Clocks made their way to the side of the boat. He took a walk past with a crafty side look through the windows. The window blinds were down, but he could make out a dull blue light coming from inside. He assumed it was the glow from a computer screen, but he needed to actually see for himself.

'Look at the size of this thing.' Clocks let out a low whistle. ''E must 'ave been proper loaded, ol' Mr Anderson, or else 'e was bent as a nine-bob note.'

'What the hell is a nine-bob note?' Paterson whispered as quietly as he could.

Clocks shook his head. 'It's an expression. I'll explain it later, if I can be bothered.'

'Clocksy,' Paterson whispered. 'I'm going on board to get a proper look, see if anyone's at home. Keep an eye on me and I'll signal yay or nay.'

'What?' said Clocks. 'Yay or nay? The fuck is yay or nay when it's at 'ome? D'you mean yes or no?'

'Yeah,' said Paterson.

'Then bloody say that. Fuckin' yay or nay.' Clocks shook his head. 'Whassamatter with yer?'

Paterson ignored him and headed off again. He waved to Monkey Harris and watched as he moved into position. The rest of the squad deployed either side of the jetty, where they could good get a good view of the sides and back of the boat.

Paterson drew his weapon and very quietly stepped onto the boat, his eyes fixed firmly on the door ahead of him. Inside, the glow from the monitor filled the small round window in the centre of the door and spilled out from underneath it.

He tiptoed his way down the steps and headed for the door, noting that there was no cover to be had. If anyone fired a shot he was a goner. He forced the thought out of his mind and crouched close to the door. On the jetty, weapon drawn, Clocks was watching him carefully. Paterson put his ear to the door and strained to listen for any sounds inside. He stepped back and waved Clocks toward him. The sound of a keyboard being tapped furiously from inside was enough for him. It was a go.

Clocks moved quickly to join him.

Paterson held a finger to his lips.

Clocks slowed himself down and tiptoed down the steps of the boat. 'What you got?' he whispered.

'Someone's tapping a keyboard.'

Clocks nodded. 'We goin in?'

'Yep,' said Paterson. The rest of the squad had closed in a bit tighter, still able to see and close enough to storm the boat if Paterson and Clocks were in trouble.

Clocks rapped on the door. 'Pizza!' he shouted.

Paterson glared at him. 'The fuck are you doing?' he whispered angrily.

'Coming. Hold on a sec,' said a voice from inside.

Clocks pointed back along the jetty. Ambling along was a young man carrying a pizza box. 'I saw him open the gate. You see any other boats with lights on? No. Bet he's comin' 'ere. Nerds love a pizza, don't they?' Monkey Harris stopped the man from getting closer.

The door opened and Clocks pointed his gun straight at the face of a young man, who jumped back in fright.

'Boo!' said Clocks. He kicked the door in, pushed his way forward and rushed toward the young man as he fell backward. Paterson burst in behind him, gun high, two-handed. 'Police!' he shouted. 'Stand still!'

'All right,' said Clocks. 'There's no need to 'oller, guv. Anyone else in 'ere, kid?' he said.

The young man, flat on his back and his eyes wide with terror, stuttered, 'N-n-no. No. No one.' Paterson moved forward, checking under the table and in cupboards before he disappeared below deck.

Clocks kept the gun pointed straight at the young man. 'You sure? You're not lyin' to Mr Clocks, are you?'

'No, no. Who's Mr Clocks?'

Clocks looked offended. 'Me. I'm Mr Clocks. You not 'eard of me?'

The young man shook his head.

'Get up,' said Clocks. 'C'mon. Chop-chop. Let's 'ave yer. What's yer name, son?' He holstered his gun.

'Jamie Lord, sir.' Clocks raised an eyebrow.

Paterson, finding no one else on board, walked outside and shouted to the rest of the squad to stand down before re-joining Clocks.

'What are you doing on this boat then, Jamie?' said Paterson.

'It belongs to a friend of mine. He said I could use it. Am I in trouble, sir?'

'Could be,' said Clocks. 'Thing is, you've gotta be honest with us. If you're not, well . . .' He looked at his wristwatch and pretended to press a button. 'Right, I've just started Mr Clocks's naughty clock. You know what that is?'

'No.' Jamie looked puzzled.

'Well, this clock tells me if you're lyin' or tellin' the truth. Don't ask me 'ow it works. I don't know meself.' He shrugged 'I think it's magic, I really do. It's never let me down before.'

Jamie Lord looked at Clocks in such a way that implied he doubted him very much.

'Don't believe me? I'll show yer. Before I do though, I 'ave to tell you that every time you lie to me, I'll smack you in the mouth. That's the rules. Okay?'

Jamie said nothing.

'Rules accepted then. Let's go again. What you doin' 'ere?'

'My friend let me use it.'

'What's 'is name?'

'Laurence.' Jamie licked his lips.

'Laurence? You sure?'

He nodded.

'You don't look sure. You sure you're sure?

'Yes, sir.'

'Laurence what?'

'Sellars. Laurence Sellars.

'Is it 'is boat then, this Laurence?'

'Yeah.'

'Is it registered to him?'

'I think so. Yeah. I dunno.'

Clocks held his watch up to his ear. 'What's that, Mr Naughty Clock? Oh, okay.' He put his hand down and gave Jamie a hard stare. His hand shot out and backhanded him hard enough for him to feel the sting but not hard enough to really hurt. Jamie's head rocked back from the blow.

'You're lyin', son. What did I say about lyin'?'

Jamie held a hand to his face, red and smarting from the backhander. 'You said not to do it.'

'Or?'

'Or, you'd smack me in the mouth.'

'Correct. But, I noticed you 'ave a very nice set of teeth. Don't want to damage them if I don't 'ave to. That's why you got a slap instead. Now, let's 'ave another go, shall we? What're you doin' on this boat?'

'My friend let me use it, honestly.'

'Okay. What's yer mate's name? An' don't say Laurence.'

Jamie became agitated. Paterson and Clocks said nothing. Silence could be an effective tool if you had the patience to wait it out. Clocks couldn't. 'Name? C'mon.'

'Sir, I can't . . . I can't . . .'

Very slowly, Johnny Clocks lifted his wristwatch to his ear and gave a few slow, deliberate nods.

'Okay, okay,' said Jamie. 'Look. It's his and his dad's boat.'

'Name?' said Clocks.

'Fane. Fane Anderson.'

'Real name?' said Clocks.

'What?'

Clocks's hand shot out again and made a loud cracking noise as it connected with Jamie's cheek again. He yelped in pain and stumbled back into Paterson, stepping on one foot as he did so.

'Oi, you little shit! Mind the shoes. Cost a bloody fortune, they did.' He shoved him back toward Clocks.

'Real name?' said Clocks, his tone serious.

'That is it. Fane. Fane Anderson.' Jamie rubbed his face again, tenderly.

Clocks shot a glance over his shoulder at Paterson. Paterson shrugged.

'Right. What'd you know about this mob that calls themselves the Bermondsey Knights? Fuckin' bunch of wankers, they are.'

Jamie frowned.

'Yeah. We know all about them,' said Paterson.

Jamie turned to look at him.

'We also know that you're one of them, so you might as well tell us what we want to know and do it a bit quick. It's pretty simple, really.'

'I don't know what you're talking about.'

'Thing is, you do. You most definitely do. Ask me how I know.'

Jamie eyed Paterson suspiciously. 'How do you know?'

'Because the guy who found you for us is a lot better than you. Plus he's found out a shitload of other stuff, and all done from the comfort of his nursery.'

Clocks grinned. 'You're what we in the trade call *fucked*, me ol' son.' He spun him around. 'Jamie Lord. You are nicked for murder. And you're cautioned.'

'What? What does that even mean?'

'It means you're nicked. Deprived of yer liberty. And you've been cautioned. That means you can keep yer trap shut if you want.' Clocks glared at him. 'But I wouldn't advise it.' He grabbed him by the collar while Paterson pulled out a set of plasticuffs.

'Put yer 'ands behind yer back,' said Clocks.

Paterson fastened the cuffs and pushed him down into a chair. On a little table stood a laptop, the source of the blue glow. Paterson walked around the table and looked at the screen. 'This is odd, Jamie. You don't know who the Knights are and yet here you are sending an email in their name.' Paterson looked over to where he'd sat him. 'That is a bit odd, isn't it?'

Jamie's head drooped to his chest. 'I'm not sayin' anymore. I want a brief.'

'Oh, what's that?' said Clocks. 'You want legal representation now, do yer?'

Jamie didn't answer.

'Well, good luck with that, son. We're investigating some right 'orrible murders, an' at the moment you're bang in the frame for 'em. An' 'cos we both think you're plotting to do another you don't get to call a lawyer. As of right now you're what we call *incommunicado*. Understood?'

Jamie scowled at Clocks. 'You can't do that. I'm entitled to a lawyer. I know my rights.'

'No you don't. You only think you do. And that's yer problem, son. You think you know more than you actually do, but don't feel bad about it. Lots of people are as dumb as you. You're not alone.'

Jamie Lord looked at Paterson and then back at Clocks. Gone was the look of fear. In its place were eyes burning with hatred. 'Get me my fucking lawyer, you dumb pig!'

Paterson stared at him from behind the desk.

Clocks's eyes widened. 'What'd you say to me?'

'Clocksy . . .' Paterson held his hand up.

'Oi, snot gobbler! What'd you fuckin' say?'

'Stupid as well as violent, eh? A fucking walking cliché, no less. I said to get me my lawyer. This will cost you dearly.'

Now Clocks was intrigued. 'Cost me, will it? How so?'

Jamie snorted. 'You two idiots have no idea what you're dealing with. How powerful we are. You do not want to make us come for you.'

Clocks bent forward and rested his hands on his knees, all the time keeping eye contact with his prisoner. 'You can come for me if you like, sonny. I don't mind. In fact, I'd like to meet all of your silly little playmates. Tell me which little Wendy house they're all playin' in an' I'll pop round to see 'em after I bang you up in the nick.'

'You will beg for mercy before you die, heathen.'

Clocks sniffed. 'Guv,' he said, without looking at Paterson, 'he's gettin' on my fuckin' wick.'

'Yeah, and mine,' said Paterson. 'Fire at will, Clocksy.'

Clocks shot forward and with one hand grabbed Jamie by the throat and shoved him onto the floor. Crouching over him, Clocks went nose to nose with him. 'Listen up, fucknuts. In a second, I'm gonna take your cuffs off an' then you're gonna be what we call *resistin' arrest*. When you do that it empowers me by law to kick you all around this fuckin' boat an' then drop' you in the drink outside when I'm done with you. Goddit?'

Jamie's eyes blazed. 'Get off of me, you heathen coward.'

Clocks pulled him up off the floor by his hair and stood him up. He pulled out a penknife from his jacket, cut the plasticuffs and pushed him away from him. Jamie Lord spun around, dropped low and charged forward. Clocks brought his knee up and connected with Jamie's chin. He dropped onto his knees, stunned. Clocks grabbed a clump of hair again and jerked his head up. He drove a right-hander straight onto his jaw, dropping him back onto the floor. He rolled over onto his back, unconscious.

'And a good knight to you, you little prick.' Clocks looked over at Paterson. 'Geddit? Good knight — good-night. He thinks he's some sort of knight, so . . .'

'Oh yeah,' said Paterson. 'Cracking joke. I dunno how you think of them, I really don't. If you've finished playing, come here and look at this message he was sending.'

'What's it say?' He joined Paterson in front of the laptop and read the message.

Brothers. Our work is nearly done. We have avenged the wrongs bestowed upon us. Now we face the greatest challenge of all. The Sheriff's men are hunting for us. We must be stealthy and tread warily on our righteous path to the light. We are summoned to Temple on the full moon to fight for our liberty. We must meet the Heathen army on our chosen battleground. To ensure we weaken their numbers we must take one . . .

'It's not finished,' said Paterson.

'Well, that sounds like an admission of guilt to me. What's all this bollocks about sheriffs? We ain't gotta go after a bunch of cowboys now, 'ave we?'

'No. Back in the day, a sheriff was a lawman in this country too.'

'So, you reckon 'e means us?'

Paterson nodded. 'I do indeed. Looks like they got wind that we were looking for them.'

Clocks squinted at the screen. 'An' what's this about 'eathen warriors? Who's that then?'

'That's us, mate. All of us. The police.'

'Oh. So, we're a couple of 'eathens then?'

'Yeah. I imagine a few people think so. It must be obvious.' Paterson grinned at him.

'Okay, good. I just don't wanna be called summing I'm not.'

Paterson read from the screen again quietly to himself. '*Work is nearly done.*' He repeated the sentence. '*Work is nearly done. Nearly done.* Okay. Not yet finished, maybe?'

We have avenged the wrongs bestowed upon us.

'*We have avenged. We have avenged*. Implies that they've finished what they set out to do.'

Now we face the greatest challenge of all. The Sheriff's men are hunting for us. Him and John.

We must be stealthy and tread warily on our righteous path to the light — whatever that meant.

'*We are summoned to Temple on the full moon to fight for our liberty*, blah, blah . . .'

We must bring the heathen warriors to our chosen battleground.

'*Fight for our liberty . . . heathen warriors . . . chosen battleground.* Okay, they're gonna let us know where and when this all goes down.'

To ensure we weaken their numbers we must take one . . .

'*Weaken their numbers . . . take one . . .*' Paterson tapped the screen with his finger. 'What'd you think that means, Clocksy?'

Clocks shrugged. 'Dunno, mate. Maybe they're planning on grabbing one of us. Use whoever it is as an 'ostage to ensure they get their sticky little mitts on the other one.'

'Yeah, maybe. In which case, we stick even closer together from now on.'

'Agreed,' said Clocks.

'Let's get him back to the nick. I'll get Yorkshire to wait with him until the van arrives. The rest of us are going over to Anderson's house. Now.'

CHAPTER THIRTY-ONE

Once again, Paterson and Clocks stood outside Anderson's house looking through the wrought iron gates. Behind them, Rocket, Doneghan and Harris waited. The house itself was in complete darkness. No one had twigged they had triggered the alarm and Paterson didn't see the point in setting them straight.

'You reckon he's in there, Clocksy?'

'Dunno. Only one way to find out. D'you wanna bunk-up?'

'Excuse me?' said Paterson.

'You bloody wish. No. Not that sort of bunk-up.'

'I thought you meant—'

'I know what you thought. Freudian slip an' all that. Just leave it. Do you want me to give you a leg over . . . a boost? A boost over the gate, I mean. Got me at it now.'

Paterson smiled. 'I know what you meant.'

'Hmmm. Did you? I'm not so sure. C'mon. Up you go.'

'You coming with me?'

''Course I am. Monkey can chuck me over in a minute.'

Two minutes later both men were crossing the lawn, crouching low and careful to avoid stepping on the gravel path. They took up positions either side of the door and drew their weapons.

'You got a torch?' said Paterson.

Clocks shook his head. 'You?'

'Nope.'

'Lovely. Into a nutjob's 'ouse without a light between us. What could possibly go wrong?'

'Once we go in I reckon that silent alarm will bring the locals running again. You rang to tell them we were coming this time, didn't you?'

'Hmm,' Clocks looked down at the ground.

'Oh, for fuck's sake, Clocksy. Do I have to think of everything on this team?'

'It'd probably be 'elpful if you could, Ray. To tell the truth, me memory ain't what it used to be.'

Paterson gently pressed the front door, testing it for tension. 'Locked.'

'Want me to boot it?'

'Sounds reasonable,' said Paterson.

Clocks stepped away from the wall and stood in front of the door. He pressed his foot against it, gauging the pressure he'd need. 'Ready?'

Paterson nodded. An image flashed into his mind.

Clocks kicked the door once. It gave slightly. He lined up for a second kick.

'John!' Paterson yelled.

Clocks's foot connected with the door and it gave.

Paterson dived forward knocking Clocks flying a second before there was a loud bang and wood splintered out of the small hole that appeared in the door. Paterson yelped as he fell on top of Clocks.

'Ray!' Clocks shouted as the two men scrambled about. 'Fuck! Ray! You okay?' He pushed Paterson off of him. 'Jesus!'

'Yeah, I'm all right. Caught a few pellets in my arm, I think.' Paterson sat up. Clocks pulled the shoulder of his jacket down. There were several small holes in the fabric and the sleeve of Paterson's jacket was red with blood. 'Ah, fuck! That stings.'

Paterson heard the cries from the other members of the team outside and looked toward them. 'I'm all right!'

he shouted. 'I'm okay!' He saw headlights come on, heard the engine rev and watched the gates clatter to the ground as Monkey Harris rammed his way onto the property. Rocket and Doneghan ran in behind.

Monkey braked hard and slid the car across the gravel. He was out of the car in a flash. 'Guv! You all right?'

Paterson nodded. 'Just a scratch, mate. I've had worse.'

'Monkey, get on the blower,' Clocks barked. 'Get an ambulance an' SCO19 over 'ere. Now!' Monkey dived straight back in the car and picked up the radio.

'Sir . . .' DS Rocket looked around her, anxious.

'I'm fine. Stay away from the door. You and Dusty get back and keep your eyes open for any movement. Don't go round the back on your own. Understood? Monkey's onto Nineteen now.'

'Sir.' She and Doneghan took off back to the main gate.

Clocks helped Paterson to his feet and looked at him in the eyes. 'You saved my life.'

'So it would seem.'

'And you took the bullet that was meant for me.'

'Not all of it. A few bits of it. And some splinters I think.'

'Still . . .' said Clocks.

'Still,' said Paterson.

'So 'ow'd you know?'

Paterson shook his head. 'That it was rigged? No idea. I just got a flash of a hole being blown in the door. Premonition, maybe.'

'Yeah, maybe. Maybe. Thank you, Ray.'

'S'all right, mate. You'd have done the same for me.'

'Yeah, right. Would I, bollocks. I'm not as thick as you think I am, matey.' He smiled at Paterson. 'You've got yerself wounded again.'

'Nah. This is nothing compared to last time.' A memory flashed into his vision of Marcus May, the Childmaker, slicing open the skin along his jaw line. 'A couple of Band-Aids and I'll be fine.'

'Hmmm. You sure?'

'Yes! I'm fine. Don't worry about it — I'm not. What I am worried about is how the fuck he knew we were onto him. The kid in custody couldn't have tipped him off, so who?'

'Maybe 'e figured it out. Maybe 'e knew it was only a matter of time and rigged the 'ouse.' In the distance, half a dozen sirens wailed their way toward them.

'Which still leaves Mum and Sis unaccounted for. Where the fuck are they?'

The sirens drew closer.

'Not a clue. We'll 'ave a good nose around once Nineteen 'ave declared it safe. Might be something in there that will 'elp us.'

The first police car came tearing through the open gate, followed by two more. In the distance, more sirens wailed their way along the country lanes.

'One of them should be an ambulance,' said Clocks.

'I don't need an ambulance, Clocksy. I'm all right.'

The next car through the gate was SCO19. Their two cars screeched to a halt and the officers inside bailed out the second the cars stopped.

'Officer in charge?' one of the men called out.

'Over 'ere, mate!' Clocks called.

'Sergeant Egan,' said the officer as he hurried to join them. 'What we got?'

'DI Clocks. This is Superintendent Paterson. We tried to execute a warrant on this place. I kicked the door in. Fuckin' place was rigged. Shotgun. Caught the guv'nor in the arm.'

Sergeant Egan frowned. 'I take it you're okay, sir?'

'I'm okay. Copped a couple of pellets, is all.'

'We need you an' yer boys to sweep the building,' said Clocks. 'Make sure nothing else is lurking around the corners.'

'Sure. Do you have a map of the place?'

Clocks looked at Egan, straight-faced. 'A map? We're not surveyors, fellah. '*Ave we got a map?*

'John, don't start,' said Paterson. 'Please.'

Sergeant Egan gave Clocks a hard stare.

Clocks nodded. 'Sorry, skip. Just shook us up a bit. Didn't mean to snap at you. No, we don't have a map. Sorry.'

'No worries,' said Egan. 'Forget about it. I'll go brief my team and we'll get started.'

They watched Sergeant Egan jog back to his car.

'Was that all right?' said Clocks.

'Well done, mate. You did well. Very polite. In the end.'

Clocks smiled. 'I told you before. I'm a total fuckin' delight since I met you. You do know you complete me, don't you?'

'Piss off you little gobshite,' said Paterson. His face suddenly creased with pain. 'Fuck!'

A female paramedic came running over to them. 'Evening, boys!' She sounded altogether too chipper. 'Which one of you got shot then?'

Clocks shook his head. 'That'll be 'im, love. The one with the 'oles in 'is coat an' an armful of claret.'

She started for a second. 'I'm . . . sorry. I couldn't see in this light.'

'Ah, you're all right, love. Just windin' you up. It's been yet another fuckin' day in paradise. Sorry to snap at you.'

'That's OK. Being snapped at is de rigueur for this job, I'm afraid.' She dropped her bag on the floor and opened it up.

Clocks looked at Paterson, who was gently easing off his jacket. 'What's she say? Is she foreign?'

Paterson sighed. 'No, de rigueur means it's demanded by fashion or custom.'

Clocks shrugged, his face blank. 'Are you foreign too?'

'You asked. Now, be a sweetie and fuck off while I get fixed up.'

'Fuckin' off now, sir.' Clocks whirled around and mimicked marching away.

'He's a one, isn't he?' said the paramedic as she pulled Paterson's shirt away from his shoulder.

'Yeah. He's a one all right. Wouldn't have him any other way, though. He's a good man.'

'Sounds like you're in love.' She wore a cheeky grin on her face.

Paterson grinned back.

CHAPTER THIRTY-TWO

'All clear, sir,' said Sergeant Egan. 'We've gone from top to bottom. Nothing.'

'Cheers, skip,' said Paterson. 'Appreciate it. Can you hang fire for a while, just in case we stumble across something? It's happened before.'

'Absolutely. Give us a shout if you need us. Oh, by the way, the gun was on an electronic breaker. All wireless. No strings, trips or anything. Clever stuff. It's safe now.'

'Thank you.'

''E's a bit friendly,' said Clocks as he watched Sergeant Egan return to his team. 'Don't normally get the cowboys talkin' to us like that.'

'That's because you wind them up all the time.'

'Can't 'elp meself.'

'I know that. You nearly pissed him off as well.'

The two of them entered Anderson's house and stood in the hall.

'Fuck me! 'E weren't pissing about was 'e?'

In front of them on a metal stand, a Remington shotgun pointed straight at the door.

'What we lookin' for anyway?' said Clocks.

'Don't honestly know. Hopefully we'll find something that'll give us a clue as to where the boy and the rest of the family might be. I'll start in here.' Paterson stepped into the living room.

Clocks wandered into the kitchen and stood in the doorway. 'Ray!'

Paterson stepped back out into the hall. 'What?'

'There's one of those chalk board reminder thingies 'ere. It says '*I've got 'em both. Their arse is grass. You'll never take me alive, coppers!*' That's a clue isn't it?'

Paterson extended his middle finger and went back into the living room. Forty-five minutes later, Paterson, Clocks and the rest of the squad met up outside on the lawn.

'Anything?' he said.

Everyone shook their heads except for Dusty. 'I picked up an address book that was on the wife's side of the bed. Might be something useful in here.'

'You had a look inside?' said Paterson.

'Just a quick one. Nothing jumped out.' He handed it to Paterson.

'She's well organised.' Paterson flicked through the book. 'Everyone in here is filed correctly and under their surnames. There's two entries under "Anderson". One has the word "Mum" in brackets, but that one has a neat line drawn through it. I guess she's dead. And the other has "Sister" in brackets.'

'So the wife and daughter could 'ave gone to the sister's place?'

'Maybe. It's a place to start,' said Paterson. 'If they haven't gone to her then maybe she can tell us when she last heard from them, how they seemed and where they may have gone.'

'Give us it back, guv, and I'll get on checking it back at the nick,' Dusty said.

Paterson tossed the address book to him.

'We done here?' Dusty said.

'We're done. Call me when you have something.'

CHAPTER THIRTY-THREE

Ron Lavery was sweating profusely. He'd made a mistake. A very bad mistake. In business, he'd learned to trust his instincts, and that same instinct that had made him very rich and powerful had been screaming at him not to get out of his car. But it was his son standing in his car headlights. His son. He ignored his instincts, got out of the car and went to him. When he was close enough, Toby Lavery quickly pulled out a taser and drove it against his father's stomach. As big as he was, Ron Lavery didn't stand a chance. He vomited on the spot then fell like a bag of wet cement onto the cold, hard ground. And now he found himself upside down, hung from two thick chains that separated his legs. His hands were bound behind his back. Fear spiked his brain as he found himself at the mercy of his captor. His son? He squinted in the half-light of the cavernous building, trying desperately to make out his surroundings. The cold hit his body and he realised he was naked.

'Toby!' he called. 'Toby!'

His voice echoed around the warehouse. He struggled to free his wrists and ended up spinning lazily around on the chain. He saw a figure — three figures — standing about six feet away from him. He couldn't make out who they were.

'Toby? Is that you? What's going on?'

Nobody answered.

'Toby! For fuck's sake! It's me. Dad. What are you doing to me?'

A figure stepped forward out of the shadows. 'Hello, Dad.'

'Toby! Why you doing this?'

His son stood in front of him, his face impassive.

'The fuck have I done to you, son? You want money? Is that what this is about? I'll give you money.'

Toby chuckled. 'No, Dad. It's not about money. That's your answer to everything. It's about you.'

'What do you mean? I don't understand.'

'Of course you don't. You never did, did you?'

'Look, Toby Boy. Whatever I've done to upset you, I'm sorry. Just let me down and we can talk. I know it's a bit overdue.'

'Don't call me *Toby Boy*. You know I fucking hate being called that. Or you would if you'd ever taken any notice of me.'

'Is that it? Is that what this is about? You think I don't care about you?'

'I know you don't. Or Mum. All you care about is money. Lots and lots of money. That's all you've ever cared about.'

Lavery's panic was rising fast. Clearly his son was pissed at him, and he figured he'd have to use all of his powers of persuasion to get himself out of this one. He realised he might get a beating, that was probably what the friends were for. He'd take that. But when he was free, people were going to get hurt. His son especially.

'Look, c'mon son. You know I love you. I was just trying to make a nice life for the both of you, that's all. I had to be away.'

'Maybe,' said Toby. 'But you never had to beat the shit out of me when you came home in a foul temper, did you? When one of your deals went wrong. No. But you did, and God only knows you were in a foul temper most of my life. So save the I-love-yous for your mistresses. It doesn't mean shit to me or to Mum.'

'Ahhhh. Is that it, then? Did your mum put you up to this? Is she still bloody well whin—'

Toby punched him hard in the solar plexus, forcing the air out of him as he swung back and forth on the chains.

'You . . . you . . . little . . . fucker . . . I'll fucking—' Lavery gulped in big breaths as he issued his threats — 'kick the shit out of you. And . . . your pussy . . . friends.'

'Ronald John Lavery . . .' A deep male voice came from behind him.

'Who's that?' The man stepped into his eyeline. He was dressed in chain mail beneath a long, white surcoat emblazoned with a large red St George's cross on the left breast. On his head was a simply designed crown.

Lavery laughed. 'Oh, fuck me! Who you supposed to be? King Arthur?'

'You have been judged by the good Knights of Bermondsey and have been found guilty. Do you wish to speak before sentence is pronounced?'

Lavery's heart pounded with a blend of fear and rage. He licked his lips as he gathered his thoughts and went for the bravado option. 'Yeah, I do. Because I've had enough of your little fun and games, son. If you don't let me down right now, you little prick, I swear I'll fucking kill you. You hear me? Toby! Tell him. Tell him what I'll do to him. Toby! Answer me!'

'The son of Ronald Lavery has gone to ready himself for the sentence that is to be meted out.'

'Sentence. Sentence? Who the fuck are you to sentence me to anything? What are you talking about?'

'I am King Temple the Wise.'

Lavery chuckled. 'You're a fucking lunatic, son. That's what you are.'

'Ronald Lavery, you have been found guilty of the offences of wanton abandonment of your son, gross physical violence inflicted upon your son, neglect and abandonment of your wife and the sin of adultery. These are the charges laid against you. You have no right of appeal.'

'Oh, yeah? Can I say something?'

'Speak.'

'Look, to be fair, I did leave the boy and my missus alone a lot, but that was to build up a business. A business he'll get when I'm gone. Violence? Yeah, a bit, but it wasn't that bad, y'know what I mean? He got the odd clump when he got out of line, nothing heavy. And adultery? Well, that's not the worst thing a man can do, is it? You'll see what I mean when you grow up to be a proper man. Play the game, son.'

'This is not a game and it is the judgement of King Temple the Wise that you be summarily executed for your crimes.'

Lavery felt the blood run cold in his veins and his mouth instantly dried up. 'What? Executed? You can't be seri—'

'The sentence is to be carried out immediately. Toby the Brave! Come forth.'

Toby stepped back out of the shadows. This time he was dressed in the same chain mail and surcoat as King Temple.

'Toby! What the fuck are you doing? That's enough! You win, okay? You win. You've scared me, okay? It's gone far enough. Lemme down.'

In his hands, Toby held a long double-handled saw, the kind used for cutting down trees in older times.

'What the . . . you're kidding. Toby!'

His son Toby stood in front of him and tossed one end of the saw between his legs. King Temple took the other end.

'No! No! No! Tobyyyyyyy . . .' He screamed a second before the third man stepped forward and stuck tape over his mouth. He squirmed and raged against his loss of voice. No more pleading. No chance of manipulating the outcome. The reality hit him on the first bite of the saw against his perineum. He was going to die. Painfully.

* * *

Fifteen minutes after it was done, King Temple made a call to Paterson.

CHAPTER THIRTY-FOUR

Paterson and Clocks stopped off at the Embankment and grabbed two teas each. The day had been productive, but frustration was setting in. They took themselves off to a section of wall and stood looking over the River Thames, so beautiful at night. They stood in silence as they sipped at their teas, both lost in their thoughts.

Paterson watched entranced as the lights from the building opposite danced rhythmically to the tide and the boats bobbed gently in the water. He'd always liked working nights when he was a probationary PC. He'd liked the excitement of the first two hours when the pubs turned out and the fights started, and then at about one in the morning the domestic calls would come in. Someone's husband would come home all pissed up and decide his wife needed a bit of a talking-to and all hell would break loose. Police would be called and a snot-nosed young kid like him, with very little experience of the world, would come between a man and wife who generally had kids older than him, and he would break up the fight and give them advice. *Him.* Giving advice to couples who had more years under their belt than he'd been alive. Being a police officer was a strange job sometimes.

His phone rang. 'Paterson,' he said.

'Is this Superintendent Paterson?' said a deep voice on the other end.

'It is.'

'Do you know Shawn and Sons? The meat packers.'

'I know of it. Why?'

'Who's that?' Clocks whispered. Paterson held up a finger.

'Can you get here in thirty minutes?'

'I doubt it. Why? Who is this?'

'This is the man you are looking for. You have thirty minutes to stop us before we deliver unto you the Sawn Man. You and your partner only.' The phone went dead.

Paterson threw down his styrofoam cup and ran for the car.

Clocks spat out his tea and spilt some more before chucking his cup too.

'Ray! What the fuck?'

'Move, John!'

Paterson slid across the bonnet of his car and landed neatly on the driver's side of the road. He was in the car and had the engine started before Clocks had wrenched his door open. He was halfway in as Paterson gunned the engine, nearly tipping Clocks back out into the street.

'Fuckin' 'ell, Ray! What's goin' on?'

Paterson glanced quickly into his wing mirror and pulled out, causing a black cab to swerve and brake before he ploughed into a lamppost. 'Call was from someone claiming to be one of the Knights. We've got to be at Shawn's the meat packer in thirty minutes or someone else cops it. Put some music on. Play our tune, Johnny boy.'

Clocks turned on the siren and lights then pushed his feet into the footwell as Paterson gunned the engine, weaving in and out of the late-night traffic, barely slowing down for a red traffic light and just missing a group of drunken city boys, one of whom lobbed his can of beer and a few choice expletives at the car.

'What else 'e say?' said Clocks.

'That he was going to deliver the Sawn Man if we didn't get there in time.'

'Jesus, Ray. We're not gonna make it in 'alf an hour. Not even with you drivin' like a knob.'

'I know, but we've gotta try.'

'You know why 'e only wants the two of us there, don't you?'

Paterson, on the wrong side of the road, swerved to avoid an oncoming bus and pulled back into his lane. 'Of course I do. It's probably a trap.'

CHAPTER THIRTY-FIVE

They stood a good hundred yards from Shawn and Sons. From where they'd stepped out of their car, Paterson eyed up the outside of the building, looking to see if there were any signs of life — an ambush awaiting them, perhaps. There was nothing obvious. He walked forward and touched the bonnets of several cars either side of the streets. Clocks crossed the road and did the same.

'Cold,' Paterson said.

'Same 'ere. These 'ave been parked up 'ere a while.'

'Can you smell something?'

Clocks sniffed. 'Yep. Know what it is?'

'Not off the top of my head, but it smells familiar.'

'It should do. Dead meat. Blood. Guts. Usual stuff.'

Paterson jerked his chin up slightly. 'Oh, yeah. So it is.'

'What was you expectin' outside of a meat packers? Roses? Perfumes?'

'All right, don't go on. So, if they're in there it would seem they didn't get here by car.'

'Nah. An' I can't find any 'orses tied up either, so we know they're shit at this Knight malarkey.'

Paterson grinned. 'C'mon, then. Let's see how we get in there.'

As they walked around the back of the building, they made their way through a wasteland of rubbish, dumped there by fly-tippers. The rubbish pile went on for as far as Paterson could see until it melded with a building site in the distance. He noticed an unmarked police car and a marked police van parked up in a nearby side street. 'John. Looks like uniform's already here.'

'That's a bit worryin'. Didn't 'e say that 'e only wanted us comin' 'ere?'

'That's what he said.'

'So who the fuck's in there, then?'

'No idea. But we go in quietly and carefully. Keep your eyes and ears open.'

The two men crept toward the back door.

'It's open, John. Padlock's been prised off.' Paterson pointed to the lock lying in a shallow puddle. He gently pushed the wooden door open and poked his head inside. A crowbar lay on the floor. He stepped through.

Clocks followed him in. 'They got any lights in 'ere?'

'Keep your voice down, Clocksy. There's a light on up ahead. See it?'

Clocks stepped to one side. 'Yep.' His voice was quieter now.

Ahead, dangling on hooks and chains either side of them were the carcasses of dead pigs, their stomachs slit wide open, their ribs exposed. Lifeless, glassy eyes stared up at the ceiling.

'Bleedin' 'ell! This place stinks. An' it's bloody cold. Like the bleedin' Arctic in 'ere, it is.'

'Trust me. It's a lot colder in the Arctic. I've been.'

'Of *course* you 'ave. I shoulda known, shouldn't I?'

Paterson stopped.

'What? What is it?' Clocks whispered urgently.

Paterson said nothing.

'What?' Clocks whispered louder.

'I thought I heard something. It's nothing. It's okay.'

'Bloody well 'ad me goin' there. Listen up . . . before we go wanderin' through the dangly pig graveyard together, I'm gonna 'ang back a bit.'

Paterson turned to him. 'Why?'

'Well, I don't know if anyone's 'iding in the dark mate, an' if they are, they'll get you first. Then I can pile in on 'em if needs be. Just thinkin' of you, as usual.'

'You're too kind.' Paterson wandered off toward the pigs. The closer he got to the first pig, the more he slowed his pace. He cocked his right fist and stepped carefully past the first carcass.

'John,' he whispered.

'What?'

'It smells a sight worse in here now.'

'The smell ain't gonna kill yer, is it? Don't be a tart. Get in there.'

They stepped further into the dark, toward the faint glow of light ahead.

'Looks like some sort of room ahead of us,' said Paterson.

'Ray . . .'

'What?'

'I thought we weren't supposed to go toward the light. Ain't that what 'appens when you die?'

'So they say.'

'Well, don't you know? I mean, seein' as 'ow you snuffed it for a while in America, I thought you'da seen somethin' or other. Didn't you see anythin'?'

'Nope. Didn't hear anything either. Mind you, that was a blessing with you around. Nice to have a rest from all your yapping.'

'Charmin', that is. Saved yer bleedin' life an' all, I did.'

Paterson ignored him.

'Ray . . .'

'Oh, for Chrissakes. What now?'

'I was just gonna say, you're right. It's mingin' in 'ere, ain't it? I knew a bloke with breath like this once. Dead Pig Dave we called 'im.'

‘No you didn’t. Now, shut up for a minute, will you? I need to listen. I can hear something.’

Clocks turned his head to one side and looked at one of the pigs. He gave it a little push and it swung gently. He pushed it a bit harder. The chain clanked slightly.

Paterson stopped. ‘Shh!’

Clocks gave it a bigger nudge and smiled as it made slight contact with Paterson. Paterson whirled and struck out, his fist making a hollow slapping sound as it thudded into the dead pig’s flesh.

‘Fuck!’ Paterson, his heart beating its way out of his chest, realised what he’d hit.

‘Sorry, Ray. I caught it with me shoulder.’

‘You idiot! Well, if there is someone in there, they know we’re here too.’ He strode forward faster, toward the light. ‘Sod it.’

CHAPTER THIRTY-SIX

Paterson burst into the room to find two things: a pale Inspector Norris, bent double in the corner, and something hanging from the ceiling that his brain wasn't yet ready to take in.

'Stuart . . . what are you doing here?'

Norris held his hand up and heaved.

Clocks strolled into the room and looked around. 'Ooh, fuck! That must 'ave really, *really* 'urt.' He winced and shook his head as he stood in front of the dead man.

Paterson turned and stared at the man who hung before him: naked, upside down and completely severed in half, the left and right half still swinging ever so gently on its chains. Beneath was a thick pool of sticky blood, its surface tension disrupted only by the drip-drip-drip of what little blood remained in the two halves. On the floor was a pile of roughly cut, glistening intestines. He baulked as he made out bits of bone sticking out of the pile of offal. He nearly threw up when he saw half of a brain lying two feet or so away from where it had fallen out of the victim's skull and bounced around the floor. From both sides of the body the odd gob of gore and sawn bones were either hanging out or falling loose. 'What the hell?' His thoughts were disrupted by the sounds of Inspector Norris throwing up. He turned his attention back to the Sawn Man.

'Well, that bird was right — whassername . . . Cakes . . . Bakes . . .' said Clocks.

'Rakes,' said Paterson. 'Dr Linda Rakes.'

'That's the one. Just like in the picture she showed us. She wasn't wrong, was she?'

'I've seen some stuff in my time but . . . this? What the hell is this?'

'Well, I'm goin' with it bein' the Sawn Man, Ray. Clue's in the two 'alves swingin' about.'

'How do you murder someone this way?'

'My guess would be that someone sawed 'im in 'alf. What d'you reckon?'

'How does someone even do this? How fucking sick are they?'

'I'm gonna go with *as sick as fuck*. You?'

'I'd say you're on the money, Clocksy, but how?'

'Well, again, I'm goin' with the obvious. A saw, maybe?'

'Yeah, obviously a saw. I know that, but what sort of saw?'

'A big'un, if I 'ad to guess.'

'You know what I mean. Surely this wasn't done with a handsaw? An electric saw maybe. Industrial strength, yes. I can see that.'

'Oi!' Clocks shouted to the retching inspector. The officer heaved again.

'Fuck's sake.' Clocks walked over to him. 'All right, No-Nuts? Listen, when you're done delivering the ol' pavement pizza there, I need to know if you've 'ad a look around the place, maybe found something. Take yer time.'

Inspector Norris, exhausted, sat down on the floor, pulled out a handkerchief and wiped the dribble from his mouth.

'Every time I see you lately you're chucking yer ring up. You can't 'ave much left in yer, surely?'

Norris looked up at Clocks with bloodshot, tear-filled eyes.

'Bloody 'ell, son. You don't look too clever. You're white as a sheet. Rough coupla days for you, eh? Again. You might wanna think about gettin' out of this game. You ain't got the stomach for it, 'ave yer? Not really. Good news is, there's one layin' about over there you can 'ave, but it needs repair work.'

Norris took a few deep breaths before speaking. 'You're a sick bastard, Clocks. Do you know that?'

Clocks shrugged. 'Just tryin' to be 'elpful. No need to get personal.'

Norris wiped some stringy spit from his chin. 'Sorry. Never seen . . . never seen anything like that.'

Clocks shrugged. 'Me neither. What's the problem?'

Norris closed his eyes, screwed them tight, then looked up again. 'I'm a human, Clocks. A human. Give it a try sometime. I just found it a bit disturbing, that's all.'

'Ah, you'll be all right. Nothing a drink addiction, a suicide attempt and a coupla years of therapy won't put right. Trust me.' Clocks held his hand out. Norris took it and Clocks hauled him to his feet.

'Thank you so much for being such an understanding soul,' said Norris.

'Think nothing of it, mate. Always 'appy to 'elp. In fact, I'm thinkin' of volunteerin' for the Samaritans. What'd you reckon?'

'I'm not convinced it's the best idea you've ever had,' said Norris.

'Here's a bit of advice for yer. Always remember, you're a copper, not a member of the Royal fuckin' Ballet. Man up a bit. There you go. Words of wisdom for you, free of charge.'

'What do you want?' Norris spat out a thick gob of spit and wiped his mouth again.

'Er, I'd 'ave thought that was obvious. Someone's been murdered. Over there.' He pointed back toward the dangling body halves. 'You the first on scene?'

'No. The van driver was stopped by someone in the street, a woman who said that she'd seen three people coming out of the building. Said they looked a bit suspicious. Nervous.'

'Where's the van driver now?'

Norris shook his head. 'When I got here, he was wandering around in a daze. I've arranged for him to go to hospital. Shock.'

'Where's the rest of your troops, then?' said Paterson.

'This is it,' said Norris. 'We only paraded five officers tonight. Two on the area car and they arrested a burglar earlier on, so they're tucked up with paperwork. We had the message car out double-crewed and they've gone off to hospital with the van driver. Only me left.'

'You came in here on your own?' said Paterson, looking surprised.

'Yes. Just me.'

'Why the fuck didn't you call for some sort of help? You know other districts would have come running. That's just stupid.'

'Didn't seem that stupid at the time. I thought someone might need help inside.'

'Way beyond 'elp that one,' said Clocks. 'But respect to you for goin' in alone. That took balls, and 'ere's us thinkin' you ain't got any. Goes to show, eh?'

'Did the van driver see anyone?' said Paterson.

'No. Place was empty. He said he saw what he thought were two lumps of meat hanging up. Thought no more about it given where we are. Something about it seemed wrong, though. Doesn't know what. Went to look and saw . . . this poor bastard.' He looked past Clocks toward Paterson. 'What's he doing?'

Clocks turned. Paterson was on one knee, up close and looking carefully at one half of the gently swinging corpse. 'Dunno.'

'Don't let him screw up the scene.'

'He won't. We've done this before.'

Norris shook his head. 'Of course you have. How silly of me to forget.'

'You found anything? Murder weapon, p'rhaps?'

'Yeah. Possibly. Outside. Go left out of the back door, turn left again and walk down the side of the building. On the ground is a big, old-fashioned double-handed saw. I scouted around before I came in. Surprised you didn't see it.'

'Too busy thinkin', mate.'

'I'm sure if you ask nicely the ambulance crew can drop you a couple of paracetamol when they get here.'

Clocks frowned, then his face lit up. 'Oh, yeah. I get it. I must 'ave an 'eadache 'cos of all the thinkin' I was doin'. That was funny, No-Nuts. Really funny. C'mon, let's go an' see Mr Paterson.'

'No, it's all right. Don't need to see him yet. I'll catch up with him outside.'

'Oh, stop being a woozy an' get yer arse over there. Fuckin' thing's not gonna 'urt you, is it?'

Norris drew in a deep breath and, shaking his head, blew it out. 'I said no. I'll be outside.'

'Suit yerself. Before you run away, do we 'ave *any* description of these three suspects? Anything to go on?'

'No. Nothing. They were long gone before the driver got here. How did you two get here so quickly? I've only just called in the scene investigators.'

'The guv'nor got a call from somebody. Said we 'ad to get 'ere a bit lively or he'd kill someone. *This* someone I presume.'

'I'm off outside,' said Norris. 'Enjoy yourselves.'

Clocks nodded and walked back to where Paterson was still down on one knee looking closely at the man's face. He stood up when Clocks got closer.

'These fucking "Knights" lied to us. He was dead before I got the call.'

'Yeah. Don't surprise me. We're not much further on, though. No description of 'em. Nothing.'

'Male or female?'

'*No description. Nothing.*'

'Sorry,' said Paterson. 'Miles away.' He stood himself up and patted the dirt off of the knee of his trousers.

'No-Nuts reckons we've got the murder weapon too. Big ol' double-'anded saw round the side of the buildin'. Looks like whoever did this did it manually. That takes some doin'. Must 'ave taken a fair ol' while.'

'Yeah.'

Clocks looked at the dead man. ''Ow long you reckon it took 'im to die?'

Paterson grimaced. 'What? I dunno. Why?'

'Just curious. I reckon by the time they cut through 'is nadders, he'll 'ave died. I fuckin' know I would.'

'Stomach, I reckon.'

'Really? Nah. I'll put a tenner on his nadders.'

'Might as well give me your tenner now. There's no way he'd have died by then. Look, they would have only just started sawing. Granted, he wouldn't have been too happy about the way things were going for him and I don't doubt he was in a shitload of pain, but I doubt he would have died when they cut into his balls.'

'Yeah maybe. But you're not takin' into account the fright factor. I reckon 'is ol' ticker was going like a trip hammer when he felt the saw teeth resting on his arse. First cut and he'd 'ave been squirtin' out claret like a fountain.'

'Stomach.'

'Well, we'll soon know. The CSIs 'ave rolled up.'

Behind Clocks, two men in white paper suits made their way toward them. From previous crime scenes, Paterson recognised them as Tony Kent and Charlie Kennedy. He had Kent down as a pompous knob. Kennedy was all right. He got on all right with him.

'Gentlemen. That was quick,' said Paterson.

'Hello, Mr Paterson,' said Kennedy. 'We've just come from a stabbing in Tower Bridge Road. Male victim. Twice in the gut, three in the neck and one in the face. The cheek. He may be next on your list.'

'Get anything?'

'Knife was dropped at the scene. Got a few decent prints off of it. Got some other stuff too. All solid for a conviction so far.'

'Good stuff,' said Paterson.

'Mr Paterson and Mr Clocks,' said Kent. 'Lovely to see you both again. How badly have you fucked up my crime scene today?'

'Done a right number on it, Mr Kunt,' said Clocks.

'Kent, Mr Clocks. Kent. As well you know.'

'I'm sorry, Mr Kunt. Me ears ain't what they used to be. Anyway, we thought you two might show up, so me an' the guv 'ad a chat before you got 'ere and we decided to really fuck it up for you. It's *proper* fucked up, so you're gonna 'ave to work double 'ard for the same pay. Good to you, ain't we?'

Grinning, Charlie Kennedy put on his face mask on and pulled the white hood up over his head. 'This looks choice,' he said to Paterson and nodded toward the body.

'Yeah. It's what we call a two-part job,' said Paterson. Kennedy chuckled.

'It isn't funny, Kennedy,' Kent snapped. 'Death is never funny.'

'I beg to differ,' said Clocks. 'I remember we got called to a bloke once who was found 'anging in a tree. He was in the nod apart from 'is strides, an' they were round 'is ankles. Turns out he'd been looking through the windows of a nurses 'ome an' 'avin' 'imself a Sherman Tank.'

CSI Kent wrinkled his nose.

'I'm tellin' yer. The theory goes he was chokin' his chicken with one 'and an' tweaking his nipples with the other. Dunno 'ow they figured out that bit about the nipples, but there you go. Anyway, for some sort of weird thrill, he'd chucked the rope over an 'igher branch 'an tied it off. Apparently if you lean forward a bit, you start to choke and get a bigger sexual thrill. Dunno 'ow that works either, but all this chokin' caper seems to be popular with the kids these days. Anyway, we reckon 'e was gettin' to the good bit when his legs buckled, his foot slipped an' wallop! He 'ung 'imself. That *was* funny. Made me roll up when I got there.'

CSI Kent looked at Clocks with an expression of utter disdain. 'There's something wrong with you, Clocks. You know that, yeah?'

'Oh, where's yer sense of humour? He'd only 'ave gone on to be a rapist or summin', so no real loss to the world, was it?'

'You don't know his story.'

'I don't give a fuck about 'is story. Any bloke standin' around in trees 'avin' a wank is a wrong'un as far as I'm concerned. Got what 'e deserved. Tree wanker, mate.'

Kent ignored him and put his mask on.

'I've got loads more funny ones like that. Next time I see yer, remind me to tell you about the bloke in the cupboard wearin' an 'arness round 'is body and a dildo up 'is bum. That's comedy gold, that one.'

'C'mon, John. Let's leave them to it. I want to have a look at this saw,' said Paterson.

'We're going now, Mr Kunt. Bye.'

'Fuck off, Clocks,' said Kent.

Clocks gave Charlie Kennedy a thumbs up and walked off with Paterson. 'He's a miserable bleeder, that Kent.'

'He's all right. Just takes things a bit too seriously. Not necessarily a bad thing.'

'Wait a minute,' said Clocks. He stopped walking.

'What?' said Paterson.

'I've got it. I've only figured it out.'

'Figured it out? What? The case?'

Clocks looked at him. 'No, not that. CSI. I figured out what it really stands for.'

Paterson took a deep breath. 'Go on, then.'

'Can't Solve It!' Clocks laughed to himself all the way to the officer who was now standing guard at the entrance to the building.

'You staying here, officer?' said Paterson.

'Yes, sir. There are more of us on the way and we're putting in cordons around the building as we speak.'

'Good. You know the drill, I take it?'

'Yes, sir. Unfortunately, I've done this a few times.'

'Okay, well, make a note that me and DI Clocks were here and we'll sign the paperwork later. D'you know where the alleged murder weapon is?'

'Over there, sir.' He pointed toward the corner of the building.

Clocks was already walking in that direction. He stopped at the corner. 'Has this been photographed in situ, son?' he shouted back to the PC.

'Don't think so, sir. Not yet. Photographer is on his way. Shouldn't be long.'

'Fair enough. Listen, if it starts to rain, get it covered up with something.' Clocks got out his mobile phone and took a few pictures of the saw.

'Nasty-looking thing,' said Paterson as he joined Clocks. 'He must have shit himself when he saw that coming toward him.'

'He probably did, but given 'e was upside down I doubt anything came out. Well, not in the conventional sense, anyway.'

Paterson looked around. 'So, quick recap. We got ourselves a call from the Grand Poobah himself, telling us we had thirty minutes to save a life. That was a lie. We've got a witness who saw three people running from the building. We have no identification, no sexes, no vehicles, nothing. We have no details for the woman who saw them running away. We have a bloody big saw and a man split in two with no ID on him. We need to find out about CCTV, John.'

'Yeah. I would think there's some around the entrance an' exit, but from what I can see, there's nothing in the actual building. Doubt they'd want any film of what goes on in this place to leak out. Certainly wouldn't want the Humane Society gettin' a hold of it.'

'Good point. Still, we'll ask. Would be nice to catch a break for a change.'

CHAPTER THIRTY-SEVEN

The sudden ringing from his mobile phone jerked Paterson out of his thoughts. He looked at the face of his phone. 'Shit!'

'What?' Clocks was sitting opposite him in Paterson's office.

'It's Morne.'

'Don't answer it. Let it go to voicemail. Fuck 'im.'

Paterson pressed the answer button. Clocks sighed.

'Mr Morne. How can I help you?'

'Paterson. Listen to me.' Paterson noticed the edge in his voice.

'I've been at a meeting that included my senior team and the Met's legal advisor. They're none too happy with you two investigating Anderson's murder and there's some outstanding issue they want cleared up about DCI Lambert's murder.'

'Fucking hell. Not again. Go on. And what's the next bit? There's always a next bit.' Paterson pressed the loudspeaker button. Clocks perked up.

'And I'm under pressure to have you both brought in for questioning.'

Paterson took a sharp intake of breath. 'Define *questioning*.'

'They want you both arrested and questioned as possible suspects in Anderson's and Lambert's deaths.'

Paterson said nothing, gathering his thoughts. Clocks's eyes widened.

'Right. Who's this telling you what to do? Your senior team, yes?'

'Yes.'

'Okay. Just a thought, sir . . . You're the boss, tell them to go fuck themselves,' said Paterson.

'It's more complicated than that, I'm afraid.'

'What's complicating it?'

'I'm informed the prime minister has intimated that it would be better if you were removed from the job and is apparently not averse to your arrests.'

'That's nice isn't it? But, if I remember rightly, policing operations are a matter for the police, not government officials, whatever their positions. Am I right?'

'Technically, yes. But this is an arse-covering operation. They believe that you two will make a mistake somewhere and bring the reputation of the police into disrepute, which will then bounce onto the Home Office or Number 10.'

'Us? Bring the service into disrepute? Can't see that happening, sir. Never done that before, have we?'

Morne chortled. 'Hmmm.'

'Look,' said Paterson. 'You've got to do what you've got to do, but where does that leave us now? Are we supposed to just give ourselves up?'

'Technically, of course you are. But you won't do that, will you?'

'Not a snowball's, sir.'

'I thought not, so I'm afraid I will have to issue warrants for your arrest. Listen though . . . I wholeheartedly disagree with this course of action. It is, however, out of my hands for the time being. If I stand against my entire senior management team I'll no doubt be put on leave, the same as Anderson was. But for now . . .'

'For now, we're royally fucked,' Clocks spat out.

'Yes. Yes. I'm so sorry.'

'I know,' said Paterson. 'It's not your fault. How long before you get the warrants?'

'Not long. I can delay for a couple of hours, but that's about it. I can't do any better than that, I'm afraid.'

'Okay. Just so we're clear: Anderson's murder had nothing to do with us. Nothing. So we won't be giving ourselves up until we find whoever's doing this.'

'But how will you do that without the Met's resources?'

'It'll be bloody difficult, but we're well versed in keeping our heads down and out of the way while we get on with things. We'll find a way. We always do. Have to ask . . . do me and you have a problem now?'

There was a moment's silence from Morne. 'Technically, yes. Practically, no. Go and do what you have to do. Just call me if and when you get something of significance. Otherwise, go dark and stay dark. I'll do what I can to keep you in play for as long as possible.'

'Thank you,' said Paterson. 'Sir?'

'What is it?'

'Why are you condoning this? You could lose your job.'

'It's possible. That's a chance I'm willing to take. I genuinely believe you two and I believe in you. You came with the highest recommendation from ex-commissioner Young, and if he vouches for you, that's good enough for me. And, for the record, not everyone up here in the Ivory Tower has it in for you.'

Paterson chuckled. 'I know. Thank you. And, sir, just to give you a head's up, we've just come from another murder. We're here now with the duty inspector. This one's bad too. Really bad. It's a man sawn completely in half. Lengthways. Don't see that every day.'

'Jesus . . .'

'No, it's not him, sir. I've checked. Trust me.' Paterson bit his lip as soon as he'd said it. He was getting to be more like Clocks every day. And it bothered him. He recounted the facts that he had to Morne and waited for him to say something.

'I don't understand. Why would he call you to go there and lie about the man being already dead?'

'I'm not sure, but I'm wondering if he was trying to set us up, y'know. Think about it. We're in the building with a dead body and then the police show up and, on the face of it, we're caught bang to rights. Only, it went off a bit earlier than they would have liked thanks to the witness flagging down the van driver. The uniforms got there before we did.'

Morne was quiet for a second. 'Okay, I see that, but why would they want to set you up? Seems odd.'

'I agree but, let's be fair, everyone and their brother is trying to set us up for something. Makes a change to be set up by a couple of murderers instead of coppers. Just saying.'

'Indeed,' said Morne.

'Look, I'll be in touch when we have something.' Paterson hung up.

Elbows on the desk, Clocks rubbed the heels of his hands into his eyes. 'Didn't fuckin' see that one comin', Ray.'

'No. Nor did I.'

'Plan?'

Paterson stood up and walked out into the office. Clocks followed.

'Everyone! Gather round. I have something important to say.'

Everyone left what they were doing and paid attention to him. He recounted his conversation with Morne and carefully watched the expression on each person's face as he laid out the facts.

'So, that's it. DI Clocks and I will soon be wanted men. I'll tell you straight, we have no intention of giving ourselves up and we're going dark to keep working on this. Anyone have a problem with that?'

The room stayed silent.

Paterson nodded slowly. 'Good. Because if you do, now's the time to make your move.' He looked at each of them in turn, scanning their faces for any sign of a wobble.

'What can we do to help, guv?' said Monkey Harris.

Paterson grinned. 'Just your jobs. No doubt someone else will come in to take our places. Play the game with them. It's not their fault they're getting saddled with this. But . . . keep us in the loop, yes?'

''Course,' said Monkey.

'We'll pick up a coupla burner phones,' said Clocks. 'Soon as we've got 'em, I'll give you a bell an' then you'll 'ave me number. Call us on that if you get anythin'.'

'Last chance . . .' Paterson slipped on his jacket. 'Anyone want to nick us?' Nobody moved.

'Good luck, guvs,' said Dusty. 'Be careful out there and keep your heads low.'

'Yeah. Good luck guys and thank you,' said Paterson. 'Stay safe.'

Paterson and Clocks said their goodbyes and walked out of the office, taking the fire escape stairs just in case.

'So that's that,' said Paterson as they walked out of the station yard.

'Yep. That's that.'

'John . . .'

'What?'

'We're going to have to get ourselves another car. We can't be using our own. Not now. Any ideas?'

Clocks looked at him. 'Yeah. I know someone who can get us some wheels.'

'Won't be nicked, will it? No point running around in a stolen car. May as well use our own if that's the case.'

'Nah. It'll be clean. Might even be 'is own. 'E's an old friend of mine. Bit of a wide boy but good as gold. I trust 'im.'

'Good enough for me. Can you give him a call and ask him to meet us?'

'Yup. 'Course I can.' Clocks grinned from ear to ear. 'I fuckin' love this. We're on the run, mate. Me 'n' you. A right coupla bandits.'

'Yeah. That's me and you, John. Thelma and Louise.'

'Exactly. Fuck 'em all, Ray.'

CHAPTER THIRTY-EIGHT

Clocks listened to the ringing tone in his ear. This wasn't a conversation he ever thought he'd have to have and wasn't one he was looking forward to. He knew Lyndsey wouldn't take it well.

After the sixth ring, she answered. 'Hello?'

'All right, sweet'eart? 'Ow you doin?'

'I'm good, love. Everything all right? What time you coming home?'

'Yeah, I'm all right, babe. What's 'appening?'

'Not much. Sorting out a last few minute bits for the wedding.'

Clocks cringed. 'That's good.'

'Yeah. My mum called. Something else about a present. She doesn't know what to get us. Did we want anything in particular? Blah-blah. Usual stuff. Anyway, I'll tell you when you get home.'

Clocks said nothing.

'Johnny. You there?'

'Yes, love. Sorry. Got distracted.'

'So what time are you coming home?'

'Er, yeah . . . About that . . .'

'What? What does that mean, *about that*? Has something happened?'

Clocks nodded to himself. 'You'll laugh an' laugh when I tell you.'

Her tone took on a frosty air. 'Tell me what, John? What have you two done now?'

'We ain't done anything, love. It's just that . . .'

'What?'

'Er . . .'

'What?'

'Well, look. Here's a funny thing. It only turns out that there's a warrant out for us. Tch. What can you do, eh?'

Lyndsey said nothing.

'So, it's not really a matter of *when* I'm comin' 'ome, more a matter of *if* I'm coming home.'

'Excuse me?' she said eventually. 'Did you say a fucking warrant?'

'No. I said warrant. Not a fucking warrant.'

'Don't make silly-bastard jokes with me, John. What's happened?'

'Not sure, really. Got a tip-off that someone higher up wants us dragged in for questioning over Lambert, remember him? And Anderson?'

'Oh, Jesus.'

'Yeah. That's what we said. Ray's getting onto a good brief for us now.'

'Where are you now? Do you need a lift? I'll come and get you.'

'Nah, you're all right, babe. We've got wheels.'

'Are you going into the nearest nick? What one is it?'

'Sorry?'

'What nick are you going into? You're giving yourselves up, right? Get it all sorted out quickly.'

'Oh, no, no, no, no. We're not 'anding ourselves in, babe. That's not 'ow this is goin' to work. We're goin' to find out who killed Anderson and the others first and then we're fuckin' off to Brazil for the rest of our lives. Wanna come?'

'You make one more fucking joke, John, and I swear I'll shoot you myself when I next see you.'

'That's a bit 'arsh, innit? Thought you might wanna beach wedding. S'posed to be lovely.'

'Oh, God! The wedding! What are we going to do? How can we get married if you're on the run? That's the first place they'll look for you. You've ruined everything.'

'No, babe. Now don't get upset. We've almost cracked the case, so once it's done, the warrant will be withdrawn and we can go back to normal. And, just for the record, I've not ruined anything. The bloody job has. They issued the warrant.'

'Yes, and you and Ray are going on your toes. Whose fault is that?'

'Well, if you're gonna split hairs . . .'

'What happens now, then?'

'What happens is, we go dark for a while. I'll call you on the downstairs phone and keep you up to date with what's 'appenin', so make sure you keep it on you.'

The 'downstairs phone' was code they used that referred to a cheap, pay-as-you-go phone. Untraceable. Paterson insisted they all have one as soon as he realised that their homes were bugged.

'What? Why?'

'Don't be surprised if you get a knock on the door from someone looking for us. They may well have a search warrant and, because of our involvement with each other, might just suspend you to make sure you can't use any of the Met's resources to tip us off. Might even nick yer mobile.'

'Yes, of course, okay. I'll make sure it's with me all the time.'

'Good girl. I'll give you a call when I can.'

'I love you, John.'

'Yeah, I know you do. Love you too, sweet'eart. Look, hun, please don't worry yerself about it. It's just another day at the office for us. We'll be fine. Trust me.'

'You two take care. If you want or need anything, call me. Understand?'

''Course. But there's no need. We're not gonna drag you into this.'

'Oh, my darling, I'm already dragged in. Give my love to Ray.'

'Nope. He's got enough love as it is. He don't need any more.'

Lyndsey chortled and then sniffed. 'Stay safe.'

'Always. Ooh, before I go, a bit of good news.'

'What?'

'Ray's got us a coupla really nice presents for our weddin'.'

'What are you talking about?'

'Tell you when I see you. Love yer. Night, night.' He hung up.

'She all right?' said Paterson.

'Over the moon, mate. She's got the house to herself for the next God-knows-when. She'll probably binge-watch something on Netflix. I told 'er to get on an' do a bit of housework and washin' up. I'm not 'avin' her lolloping around the house doing nothin'.'

Paterson smiled at him. 'You are a new man, for sure, Johnny Clocks.'

Clocks smirked.

'I'm going to give Dr Rakes a call,' said Paterson. 'I've got an idea to flush these little bastards out.'

'It's a bit late, innit?' He looked at his watch. Half past midnight.

'She gave me her number. It's her fault.'

A flash of lightning lit the sky and a rumble of thunder followed along somewhere in the distance.

'C'mon. We have to go,' said Paterson. 'There's a storm coming.'

CHAPTER THIRTY-NINE

They stood in the shadow of a small tea hut tucked back from the main road when the car they had been waiting for parked up. The driver switched the engine off and stepped out of the vehicle. Kevin Letts was the old friend Clocks had mentioned to Paterson and, just as he'd said, Letts hadn't let him down.

Letts was a semi-pro bodybuilder. A big man, six-four, big chest, arms like tree trunks and thighs that could crush a cow. They rarely saw each other these days, being on different sides of the fence, but old ties still bound them to each other.

'Oi! Oi!' said Clocks as he stepped out into the light of a streetlamp.

'Johnny Clocks. Fuck me blind, son. 'Ow are yer?' Letts said in a gravelly voice brought about by a brush with throat cancer in his early twenties.

'Yeah. Good, mate, good. You?'

'You know me. Duckin' an' divin' still.'

Clocks grinned at him. 'No surprise there, then. 'Ow's everybody doin'?'

'Yeah, all right, I s'pose. Paulie Mason's got 'is own business floggin' computer software. Tony Hardiman made a few quid from stocks 'n' shares. Always was the bright one. And Shotgun, remember 'im?'

Clocks nodded.

'He pulled a fifteen stretch for armed robbery. Forgot that it's not the seventies anymore and security vans are shit targets these days. Ended up shootin' two people. What about you? You in trouble again, Clocksy, me ol' mucker?'

'Why d'you ask?' said Clocks.

'It's about the only time I 'ear from yer these days, when you need a bit of 'elp. Whatcha done now?'

Clocks smiled. 'Best you don't know, mate. And, you're right, I don't see enough of the old mob. We need to get together soon.'

Paterson stepped forward.

Letts nodded to him. 'Aye, aye! You're that Paterson fellah. One in the papers, yeah? Done a few people in, yeah?'

Paterson nodded. 'Yeah. Unfortunately, I have. Nice to meet you.'

'You too,' said Letts.

They shook hands.

'Anything I can 'elp you boys with?' Letts said.

'Nah, you're all right, Kev. We can manage now. Just needed wheels. Whose is it?

'It's mine. You said it 'ad to be straight.' He chucked the keys to Clocks.

'I'll drop the car back asap. Full tank of petrol.'

'Fuck me! You're gettin' generous in yer old age. Not like you to get yer 'and in yer pocket. You 'ad a pay rise or summin'?' Letts grinned at his old friend.

Clocks looked across at Paterson and smiled. 'You could say that, mate.'

'Can we drop you anywhere?' said Paterson.

'Nah, you're all right. Train station is a fifteen-minute walk from 'ere. It'll do me good.'

'Listen, Kev,' said Clocks. 'If this goes bad on us, I nicked yer car from outside yer 'ouse, okay? We don't know each other and you don't know anything about it.'

'Yeah, all right, mate. Thanks, though. Listen, take it easy, John.' He glanced at Paterson. 'You too, boss.' Then he turned and left without looking back.

'He's a big old lump,' said Paterson.

'Mean with it an' all,' said Clocks. 'Not the sort of bloke you wanna piss off. Salt of the earth, though, mate. One call, bosh! He turns up with a car. No questions.'

'Must be nice to have friends.' Paterson gave a wry smile.

CHAPTER FORTY

Dr Rakes opened her door to Paterson and Clocks. 'Gentlemen . . . good to see you both again.'

'Thanks for agreeing to see us at such short notice. Sorry it's so late,' said Paterson.

'No worries. It sounded urgent on the phone. What is it I can do for you?'

'I need you to send a message to these Knights for me.'

Dr Rakes gave him a blank stare. 'What?'

'I need you to send them a message. You can do that, right?'

'Er, yes. Technically. But that's not how this has been working. I told you, they normally post onto the forum spouting their bullshit and we give them a bit of aggravation. Then after a few arguments, they disappear again.'

'Yeah, I know that. But I was wondering, perhaps they monitor the forum regularly. If they do, there's a good chance they'll see the message.'

'I guess so. What do you want to say?'

'I need you to send them this.' He handed her a slip of paper with a scribbled message on it.

Temple Anderson. Detectives Paterson and Clocks have asked me to inform you of this. Earlier tonight they raided your father's boat. They have arrested Jamie Lord, and he remains in custody. They know who you and your fellow conspirators are. They want you to know that you are now living on borrowed time. Your names and pictures have been circulated to the press and to social media outlets. They suggest that you give yourselves up immediately and, to that end, they are willing to meet you at a place of your choosing to facilitate your being taken into custody and concluding this game you are playing. If you are the brave knights you consider yourselves to be, you will understand that you have been beaten and will surrender without a fight.

'Seriously?' Rakes said. 'You've arrested one of them?'

'Oh yes, babe,' said Clocks. 'Right little pussy 'e was. No fight in 'im at all. Gave 'em all up like a shot. Not a lot of honour there.'

'Yes, of course. But, as I said, I can't guarantee anyone will read it tonight.'

'I know,' said Paterson, 'but fingers crossed and all that.'

Dr Rakes pulled her laptop close to her and switched it on. 'I'll do that now. What happens if he can't reach you? Shall I put the number of your office down too?'

Paterson shook his head. 'No. We won't be there for the foreseeable future.'

'What's happened? Are you in some sort of trouble?'

Clocks chortled. 'Trouble? Trouble's what 'appens to normal folks. We're always about two levels deeper than that on a good day. Right now, we're about ten levels deeper in the shit. We're wanted for the Anderson murder.'

She stopped typing and looked up. 'What? You're wanted?'

'Yep. It's true,' said Paterson. 'So you see the urgency. We need to nick these little bastards and hand them over. That way all the shit flying around us goes away.'

'Oh, wow!' she said. 'I never expected that.'

'*You* didn't, love?' said Clocks. 'Bit of a shocker for us too.'

'So, you're both on the run and yet still working the case. How exciting!' She resumed her typing.

'Depends on what excites you, I guess,' said Paterson.

She gave him a quick glance and a little grin. 'I guess it does.'

'Right, come on you two,' said Clocks. 'Pack it in. We ain't got time for the flirties. Save that nonsense for after we sort all this out.'

'We have to go,' said Paterson.

'Go where?' she said.

'You're a bit on the nosey side, ain'tcha?' said Clocks. 'Big boys' work. That's all. He'll call you later. C'mon, Ray. Places to go, people to see.'

With that, they hurried out of her office.

CHAPTER FORTY-ONE

Lyndsey sat in the kitchen nursing a cup of coffee when she heard the dull crack of a terracotta pot break from somewhere in the garden, quickly followed by an angry, muffled voice. She rose calmly, walked to the kitchen drawer and pulled out a large chopping knife. She turned off the light and walked out into the hallway. From where she stood, she had a clear view of both the front and back doors to the house. She was used to being in tense situations; she had rushed headlong into danger more times than she could remember and had waited many times in the dark before she and the officers under her command in SCO19 made a move that could mean life or death. For someone.

She closed her eyes for a moment and strained her ears for the next sound that would confirm someone was coming for her. All she heard was the whoosh of blood in her ears as her adrenaline level spiked.

She hoped that it would be the police and not someone else Johnny Clocks had pissed off. She dropped low and waited.

Voices came from outside the front door, followed by the squelch of a Met Radio. She stood, walked back into the kitchen, put the light back on, dropped the knife on the countertop and put on the kettle.

Seconds later, the doorbell rang. She made whoever was there wait until the third ring before she ambled out into the hallway toward the street door.

'Who is it?' she called.

'Police! I'm DCI Lymes,' said a male voice. 'Can you open the door please?'

'This time of the morning? I don't think so. Show me your warrant card first.'

'Yeah. I apologise for the lateness. I can't actually show you my card until you open the door.'

'And I'm not opening the door until I see some ID. If you're police, you should know that, shouldn't you? Put it through the letterbox.'

'I'll hold it up to the letter box. You can bend down and have a look.'

'Can't.'

'What? Why?'

'Bad back.' John had been right all along: winding people up could be fun.

'Inspector Kitchener . . . I'm Detective Chief Inspector Lymes. Just open the door please.'

'When you post your ID through the letterbox. Never heard of you. You could be anyone, for all I know. You've got five seconds to drop your warrant card through the door or I'm calling the police myself.' She heard a loud sigh, smiled to herself and heard the letterbox flap as the card dropped on the mat. She picked it up and looked at the picture of the officer called DCI Harry Lymes. He looked like a barrel of laughs, she thought, and opened the door to him.

A gust of cold wind hit her and for a second she saw Clocks in her mind's eye. She imagined him somewhere dark, and he was cold, wet and shivering. Standing in the doorway looking peeved was DCI Lymes and two other detectives. Behind them, a uniformed officer was speaking into his radio. She knew he was probably advising the officer in her garden to be aware that she'd answered the door and he could stand down.

'Sorry, sir. A girl can't be too careful.'

'No,' he said. 'I suppose not. Warrant card, please.' He held out a hand that had more hair on the back of it than the average chimpanzee. Monkey Harris's soulmate, she mused to herself.

She handed the card back. 'What can I do for you? Is everything all right? Is it John? Is he hurt? Oh, God! Please, no!' She staggered back and fell against the wall.

'What? No!' said DCI Lymes. He lurched forward and caught her arm. 'No, it's not that sort of a call. John's fine. He's fine.'

Lyndsey stood herself up and looked at him, then at his hairy hand on her arm. He pulled it back sharply.

'So, what is it then?' she said. 'Frightened the shit out of me, you did, coming here at two in the morning. I thought you were here to tell me he was dead.' She managed to look suitably relieved and annoyed at the same time. She had him on the back foot and wasn't letting him go yet.

'I'm sorry,' he said. 'Should have phoned ahead but . . .'

'But what?

'But I couldn't. It would've defeated the object.'

'What object? What do you want?'

'I'm here about John. I'm looking for him.'

'Why?'

DCI Lymes was getting a bit bolder now, getting back on track. 'I have a warrant for his arrest. Both him and Superintendent Paterson.'

'What? A warrant? What for? Why?'

'I'm afraid I can't discuss that with you at this time.'

Lyndsey scowled at him.

'Is he here?' Lymes looked over her shoulder.

'No, he's not.'

'Where is he then?'

'How the fuck should I know? He went to work this morning. Haven't seen him since.'

'Has he been in touch?'

She shook her head.

'Do you mind if we come in and look around?'

Lyndsey knew this is where things were about to take a darker turn. 'Yeah, I do mind. You got a warrant to search? 'Cos if you ain't got one, you're not coming in.'

The two CID officers behind DCI Lymes suddenly perked up a bit.

'I was hoping you'd co-operate, officer.'

'Officer now, is it?' She gave an exaggerated nod of her head. 'I see. Well, you're wrong, *sir*. You come to my door at stupid o'clock and tell me you're hunting down my ol' man and his boss and then think you can come in and start ferreting around everywhere, pulling open cupboards, tipping the bed up, climbing about in the loft and looking in my drawers. Not happening. You're not looking in my drawers.' She smirked. 'I bet you'd like to though, wouldn't you?'

DCI Lymes shook his head, his face a mask of confusion. 'What? What're you talking about?'

'My drawers. I bet you'd like to go through them, wouldn't you?'

'I would,' an Irish accent piped up from behind Lymes. 'If the offer's there darlin'.'

'Oh, yeah? Well, it's not there for you, you ugly bastard!' she shouted, acting up, deflecting away from the real issue. The Irish DC laughed.

Lymes bit his lip. 'Look, I have reason to believe you're harbouring two wanted police officers and it would be in your best interest if you just let us in and gave them both up.'

Lyndsey stood square onto him. 'Is that right? You think I'm hiding them, yeah?'

DCI Lymes stared her directly in the eyes. 'I do now, yeah. Let me in or you'll be in trouble as well, and I'm pretty sure you don't want that.'

'You've no idea what I want. Now it sounds like you're threatening me, and I don't like being threatened by anyone, job or not. So, *are* you threatening me?'

DCI Lymes sighed. 'Look, just let us do our job, Inspector. If they're not here, we go and we go with an apology.'

'I said no. You need to tell me what grounds you have to think they're here and what grounds you've got for thinking I'm harbouring them.'

DCI Lymes set his jaw and moved forward.

Lyndsey jumped back and cocked her fist. 'You do and I promise you'll regret it, guv'nor or not.'

Lymes stopped. 'Are you . . . threatening *me*? For God's sake, woman. I'm your superior officer.'

She snorted. 'You're not my *superior*, mate. You're just my senior. And if you try and force your way into my house without a warrant then I will break your fucking jaw, senior officer or not. This is *my* house and I've told you — you can't come in without a warrant. Understood?' Lyndsey planted her feet, sideways on, fists up.

Lymes looked back at the CID officers. Both of them had smirks on their faces. The Irish detective moved to push past Lymes.

'Yeah? Come on then,' she said to him. 'Give it a try, mate. See how far you fucking get an' all!'

Lymes put his hand on the officer's shoulder. 'Stand down, man. Stand down.'

Lyndsey's heart was going ten to the dozen as it fought to break out of her T-shirt. This could go either way. The Irishman stopped and glared at her.

Lymes swallowed hard. 'Okay, okay. Fair enough. We're going. But if I find out they're hiding here—'

'You won't,' she snapped.

'If I find out they're hiding here or that you've been lying to me about their whereabouts, you'll be suspended pending prosecution.'

Still in a defensive pose, Lyndsey shrugged. 'Big deal.'

DCI Lymes turned on his heels and stormed off down the garden path. Lyndsey relaxed her stance and went to close the door. The Irishman stood in the doorway looking her up and down.

'What you looking at?' she said.

'Nice tits,' he said.

She looked down at her chest then up at him. 'Thanks. They are, aren't they?' Then she butted him in the face. The crack of his nose breaking stopped DCI Lymes just as he got to the gate.

'Thanks for noticing,' she said as the man staggered back, blood pouring from his nose. 'Us girls really do love a compliment.'

Lyndsey looked at DCI Lymes as he ambled back along the path to the injured officer, who was holding his face, blood streaming through his fingers. 'You can nick me if you want, guv, but I'll put in so many complaints against the two of you, you won't know what's hit you.' DCI Lymes shook his head.

The Irishman was up now, furious. He shook off his partner, who had helped him to his feet and steadied him. 'I'm gonna fuckin' nick yer meself,' he said, forcing his way past his colleague.

'Danny!' shouted Lymes. 'Enough!'

Danny stopped, eyes blazing at Lyndsey.

'Leave it!' Lymes stood in front of him. 'Leave it. Look at me. Look at me!'

Danny spat a gob of blood onto the pavement before looking at Lymes.

'She didn't do that for no reason, did she?' said Lymes. 'Did she?'

Danny shook his head.

'No. Thought not. You need to watch that mouth of yours, son. You've been told enough times. Now let it go.'

Lymes turned to Lyndsey. 'Go inside, Inspector. It's over. For now.'

She shut the door.

CHAPTER FORTY-TWO

DAY 4

Monkey Harris was in a tricky position. The investigation had thrown up the possible whereabouts of Mrs Anderson and her daughter, Trisha. Monkey knew what he was going to do with it, he just wasn't sure of the best way to do it and keep himself out of the frame if the proverbial shit hit the fan. He looked at the printout left on his desk by the stand-in superintendent, Susan Tin, herself a member of the Met's Homicide and Crime Command. She was a highly respected officer throughout the Met and was lauded for having a 96% clear-up rate with respect to murders. Her conviction rate stood at 97%. The 3% failure bugged her immensely.

What bugged him was the fact it was sitting on his desk and not, as would be the usual way, handed to him by Paterson, Clocks or the office manager, Leon Molton. Paranoia was a nasty thing. It ate away at the mind and sent you off in all manner of directions, and nearly always where you didn't need to go. His paranoia at that moment was telling him that Superintendent Tin had left it there to see how he dealt with it. Would he deal with it immediately or would he inform Paterson and Clocks first? Would Superintendent

Tin have someone already plotted up at the address to see if Paterson and Clocks went there? Was she using him to get to them? What would be the outcome for him if he did inform them? Or was it nothing more than a request to pop into the office to see her and discuss next steps?

All of these things crossed his mind in a matter of seconds before he pulled out the cheap, throwaway burner phone he kept in his drawer. Paranoia aside, he knew where his loyalty lay.

CHAPTER FORTY-THREE

'So, 'ow we doin' this? If Mrs Anderson's in there, she's not gonna be too friendly toward us, I wouldn't 'ave thought.'

'Why not?'

Clocks shrugged. 'If Anderson told his ol' lady that he's been 'avin' grief with us, now that he's turned his toes up she might think we're involved. Hence, won't be too pleased to see us. Might even call the police on us, an' to be honest, I can't do all that running shit again.'

'We'll be fine.'

Paterson rang the doorbell and they waited. Eventually, a woman in her sixties answered and peered through the gap. 'Yes. Can I help you?' she said.

'Good evening. Mrs Meard, is it?' Paterson flashed her a smile.

'Yes,' the woman said, her voice wary.

'Hi. We were hoping to speak to either Mrs Anderson or her daughter. I understand they're staying with you. Is that correct?'

'Who are you?' she said.

'Oh. I'm so sorry. I'm Detective Superintendent Paterson and this is Detective Inspector Clocks.' He held up his warrant card for her to look at. 'We need to have a word with her about her husband, if we may.'

'I'm sorry, she doesn't want to be disturbed.'

Paterson flashed the smile again. 'I understand, but we wouldn't be here if it wasn't very important. I'm sure you understand.'

The woman frowned, gave a curt nod and stood aside, allowing them entrance to her home. 'Wait here,' she said, and walked off without a word.

Clocks was all eyes, having a good look around the place. 'Nice gaff, this. Must 'ave a few quid, I'd 'ave thought.'

'So it would seem.' Paterson started looking around too. Clocks was right. There was money in this place. Paterson recognised one painting on the wall as being worth at least fifty grand.

A minute later, Mrs Meard appeared at the end of a long hallway. 'Come this way, please, gentlemen.' She beckoned them through. 'My sister will see you, but she has asked that I be present also.'

'Not a problem,' said Paterson. 'In fact, that's a very good idea.'

She showed them into the living room. Mrs Anderson was herself in her sixties, a very smart, twin-set and pearls type, who greeted them without getting up. Paterson noted the quality of her clothing, expensive but not ostentatious. 'Gentlemen. Please take a seat.'

'Thank you for agreeing to see us.' Paterson sat himself down on the sofa. 'I'm so sorry to disturb at you this time of the evening.' He glanced at the grandfather clock stood behind the sofa she sat on: a quarter to nine.

'Why are you here?' said Mrs Anderson. Her voice had the raspy edge of a smoker he once knew.

'It's about your husband,' said Paterson.

Mrs Anderson sneered. 'I've left him, if that's why you're here.'

Paterson, surprised, shook his head. 'No. No, it's not that.' He paused for a second. 'Would you mind if I asked what happened?'

Mrs Anderson picked up her teacup from a silver tray and took a sip before answering. 'I won't go into detail, but it had been floundering for years. He was not — how shall I put it — a particularly kind man, I'm afraid. He was obsessed with his work, and once he took promotion, he became even more of an insufferable fool. His obsession with you two was the straw that broke the camel's back. Every morning it was Paterson and Clocks this and Paterson and Clocks that, and it was the same every evening when he came home. You two became his sole focus of attention, and now you're here. At last I get to meet you both.'

'I'm genuinely sorry to hear he was like that,' said Paterson. 'Do you happen to know why he had such an obsession with us, by any chance? Did he ever mention anything that sparked it off?'

She shook her head. 'Nothing specific. He just believed that you two sailed far too close to the wind and that your continued presence brought the police service into disrepute. He hated the fact that you were so often in the papers or on the internet. He believed your methods, whatever they were, had no place in the modern police force.'

'More than a few people believe that, love,' said Clocks. 'Gets the job done, though.' He went back to looking around the room.

'Yes, so I understand. So, to the point please, Mr Paterson. Why are you here? Did he send you to look for me?'

'No. To be honest, we had to track you down as we were worried for you and your daughter's safety.'

A frown creased Mrs Anderson's forehead. 'Our safety?'

'Yes. Look . . . is your daughter here, by any chance?'

'She is,' Mrs Meard interjected. 'She's actually with my husband out in the stables. Both are mad keen on horses. A very good horsewoman, that one.'

‘Okay . . .’ said Paterson. ‘Mrs Anderson, I’m so sorry to have to tell you this . . . There is no easy way to tell you, but I’m afraid Mr Anderson is dead.’

Mrs Anderson’s face drained of colour and she dropped her teacup. It bounced around on the carpet before emptying the remaining drops of tea onto the Wilton.

Paterson looked to Mrs Meard. She also looked pale and lowered herself into the nearest chair.

‘Dead?’ said Mrs Anderson. ‘No. There must be some mistake. Are you sure?’

Paterson gave a slow nod of his head. ‘I’m afraid so. His body was found on Monday, and I’m afraid I have more bad news.’

Mrs Anderson flashed her gaze at him.

‘Mr Anderson was murdered.’

Her face crumpled, and like a river getting ready to burst its banks, the tears suddenly streamed down her cheeks. She put her hand on her chest and fell back deeper into her chair.

Paterson and Clocks stayed silent, allowing a few moments for her to process what she’d just heard, but time was pressing on.

‘That’s why we were all concerned for your safety. We didn’t know if the person who killed your husband had perhaps taken you and your daughter. That’s obviously no longer the issue.’

‘I know it’s a shock, love,’ said Clocks ‘but you an’ yer daughter ’ave each other. And yer sister. You’ll get over it. I mean, you’d already given ’im the old heave-ho, so . . . y’know?’

Paterson shook his head. Luckily, it appeared that neither woman had heard him, or if they had, hadn’t been able to process his words.

‘I’m so sorry for your loss, Mrs Anderson, I really am,’ said Paterson, his face a mask of sympathetic responses. ‘But, rest assured, we have everyone on this. We’ll find whoever did this and bring them in. You have my word.’

Mrs Anderson pulled out a dainty hanky that she kept tucked between the cushion and the arm of the chair and dabbed at her eyes. Paterson had seen this before. She wasn't going to lose it here in front of them. Too British. Too much of the old stiff upper lip about her for that. She'd wait until they'd gone and then the grief would come.

'Mrs Anderson,' Paterson said softly. He held out a card. 'That's my number. And on the back is the number of the current acting commissioner, Mr Morne. He's the one you need to speak to in the first instance and he'll tell you exactly what happened and what will now happen. I'm afraid we have to leave now. We have a lot to do. I'm sure you understand.'

She wrapped her index finger in the little hanky, pressed it into the corner of her eye and nodded.

Paterson stood to leave. 'Before I go . . . you have a son too. Am I right?'

'Yes.' Mrs Anderson's voice was suddenly full of fear. 'Is he all right?'

'Yes, yes,' said Paterson. 'He's fine, as far as we know. I understand one of our officers was in contact with him earlier this evening to find out your whereabouts.' Lies came easier to Paterson these days.

'Does he know about his father?' she sobbed.

'Oh, yeah,' said Clocks. 'We're pretty sure of that. You got any idea where he might be stayin'?'

Mrs Anderson stopped dabbing at her eyes. 'Why would you ask me that? You just said he'd spoken to one of your officers a little while ago.'

'Yeah, but that was on the phone. We wanted to tell 'im in person. It's just 'ow we like to do things,' said Clocks.

'He could be anywhere, I'm afraid. Temple tends to stay with his friends mostly. He's stayed in touch with them since university.'

'Do you happen to have their names and addresses, by any chance?' said Paterson. 'Might help us find him faster.'

'No.' She went back to dabbing her eyes. 'Not here with me. I have them in a notebook back at the house somewhere. I can't think . . . No good to you now, though.'

'No, not really,' said Paterson. 'Not to worry. We'll find him.

'Can I just ask you summin', please?' said Clocks.

'Of course,' she said.

'Has your boy got a few problems with 'is nut by any chance?'

Mrs Anderson stopped dabbing again. 'I'm sorry? I'm afraid I don't understand. His *nut*?'

'Yeah. 'Is nut. Is 'e flyin' a bit lower to the ground than 'e should be?'

She looked at Paterson. Translation was required.

'What Mr Clocks is trying to ask in his own clumsy way is whether your son has any form of mental illness that you know of? Some sort of split personality, perhaps?'

Mrs Anderson frowned and cast her eyes down before raising them again. She stiffened and looked to her sister. 'I'm sorry, Mr Paterson, but how is this relevant? You said you were looking for him to tell him what had happened to his father and then you ask a question that makes me think you're looking at him as a suspect.'

'Mrs Anderson, please. It's important we know.'

She gave a weak nod and then straightened her shoulders, head up. 'Yes. Yes, he does. He was diagnosed with a mild form of multiple personality disorder. Mild.'

'Can I ask how that manifested itself, please? I don't mean to pry, it's just that . . .'

'He has always had a fixation with the Middle Ages — the Dark Ages, whatever it was he called them. Children get fixated on lots of things when they're young, don't they? But they usually grow out of it in time, so we thought no more about it. However, he didn't grow out of it. There were times that he believed himself to be a "Knight of the Realm", as he called it. Silly, really. But he was doing no harm to anyone. Just . . . playing. It wasn't his fault.'

Paterson raised his eyebrows. It never was. 'How was his relationship with his father, if you don't mind me asking?'

Mrs Anderson stiffened again. 'Actually I do mind, Mr Paterson. But I will tell you for the sake of completeness. Scott — my husband — and he had a complex relationship. Of course, you know that my husband's role kept him away from home most of the time. He certainly spent more time at the office than he did with us. I tried to explain to him that his father loved him, but as he grew older that wore a bit thin. Later, he and my husband used to fight a lot — not physically, you understand — but some of the things my husband said devastated him. Scott could be something of a bully, I'm ashamed to say.'

'So, would you say that there wasn't much love lost between them, or is that too strong?'

She shook her head. 'No, no it's not. They didn't get on at all, especially in the last five years or so.'

'Why? What happened?' Paterson was curious.

'I don't know what sparked it. Scott would never say. But it was pretty bad. So much so that he ended up leaving home the first chance that he got. He stayed with various friends initially and then went to live in digs when he went to university. He couldn't wait to get away from his father.' She looked at both men in turn. 'So, does that answer your question?'

'Yes, it does. Thank you for your time and, again, I'm very sorry for your loss. I truly am.'

'Thank you.'

Mrs Meard stood.

'It's okay,' said Paterson. 'We'll show ourselves out. Do stay with your sister.'

'Where to now?' said Clocks as they stepped out into the rain.

'Now we keep our heads down and stay out of the way and hope that Temple takes the bait.'

CHAPTER FORTY-FOUR

Paterson gave a deep sigh and rubbed his eyes. Recovering from the physical wounds inflicted on him by the 'Childmaker' was one thing, but the psychological ones would take a lot longer. Perhaps they'd never heal. Clocks's call to come back to work had interfered with his recovery, and while he understood the reasons for it, he would have been happier with another month off.

His mobile phone rang. A glance at the screen showed an unknown number.

'Clocksy!'

Paterson put the phone on speaker. 'Paterson,' he said.

'Ah, the infamous Superintendent Ray Paterson,' said the voice on the other end.

'Temple, I take it?'

'Indeed.'

'You sound somewhat different from the last time we met.'

'Last time?'

'Yeah. When we came to your house. Three of us.' Paterson frowned at Clocks.

'Of course. I *was* someone different then, wasn't I?'

Clocks spun his finger around by the side of his head to indicate that the man was perhaps struggling from some sort of mental deficiency after all. Paterson nodded.

'Doesn't matter. You got my message then?'

'Very clever of you, Paterson. I see you've been talking to one of the chat room people.'

'Yep.'

'They are so, so stupid. They think they're clever. They think they know all about this kingdom's history. They know nothing.'

'Who gives a fuck, mate?' said Clocks. 'Get to the point.'

Paterson shook his head. 'You remember DI Clocks?'

The phone went silent. 'Vaguely. But I don't know why.'

'That's 'cos I was at yer 'ouse too, when you made out you 'ad a disability.'

'I don't know what you're talking about. I have no disability.'

'You fuckin' will 'ave when I get 'old of yer, son. Tell me where you are now an' I'll pop over an' deliver your disability to you right now.'

Temple chuckled. 'That's what I was calling for. I understand you want to talk to me. Correct?'

'Yep,' said Paterson. 'You're in a bit of trouble, fellah. Best we meet up and sort all of this out.'

'How do you propose we do that?'

'I was thinking we nick you and put you away for the rest of your life. Problem sorted.'

'I see. That doesn't sound too good for me, does it?'

'It's not supposed to,' said Paterson. 'It's supposed to stop you killing people.'

'I killed one. My father. Your boss.'

'Are you saying you had nothing to do with the other killings?'

'Not at all. It's true I was present at their demise. It's just that I never actually killed anyone else.'

'If you were there or knew anything about 'em,' said Clocks, 'then in the eyes of the law, you're guilty. You're involved up to yer mad little eyeballs.' Clocks mouthed at Paterson, *Ask 'im where 'e is.*

'Why'd you kill your father?' said Paterson.

Clocks rolled his eyes. *Where is he?* he mouthed again.

'He was no father. He was obsessed with his job. All he could think about was the police service. His whole life was wrapped up in it. He was an ignorant pig of a man, a sorry excuse for a father. Did you know he used to beat my mother?'

'Nope. I had no idea. But on the strength of that, you decided to Blood Eagle him?'

The phone went silent for a second. 'There was a lot more to it than that. An awful lot. But yes, it was so.'

'It was so,' Paterson repeated. 'Just like that.'

'Just like that. Oh, come on, Paterson. You and the Neanderthal aren't sorry to see him go, are you? He was always on your case. His two bravest warriors, and he wanted to crucify you both.'

'Yeah, but I don't think he meant it literally,' said Paterson. 'Besides, he was just a pain in the arse. Nothing more. Whatever your problems were with him, he didn't deserve that.'

'It is not for you to decide the punishment handed down to him. Only I decide.'

'Oi!' said Clocks. 'Stop bunnyin' on about yer old man. Who cares? Tell me where you are so I can get on with deliverin' yer disability. I'll give yers an extra disability as well for callin' me a Neanderthal. Come on. Out with it.'

'So, are we going to meet up then?' said Paterson.

'Of course. You threw down a challenge.'

'All yer little crew gonna be there too?' said Clocks.

'My Knights? Of course.'

'Fuckin' *Knights*. Whassamatter with you lot? You're a bunch of spoilt little rich kids with fuck all else to do but feel sorry for yourselves. So, you lot 'ave got the 'ump with Mummy and Daddy 'cos you didn't get enough kisses an' cuddles when you were toddlers. And now you think you're warriors of some sort. *Knights?* You knob.'

'For the record, yes. That's exactly why we are doing this, but you have no idea of the pain and suffering our *beloved* parents put us through. You cannot know unless you have felt it yourself.'

'Me mum used to shut me 'ead in a door if I'd been a bad boy. Is that not the same?'

'No, it is not.'

'Similar, though?'

'No. You jest at our expense, at our pain and suffering.'

'Oh, leave off! Pain and suffering. You don't 'ave a clue about pain and suffering, you fuckwit. You've all got something wrong in yer 'eads and should be takin' yer medicines. This is what 'appens when you don't. You end up killin' people. You're all very bad knights.'

'You will come to regret your harsh words, Mr Clocks.'

'Yeah? Well, everyone says that to me, knobber, but no one's ever made me regret anything so far. I don't think a snot-gobbling little prick like you and yer little gang of inbred toy soldiers are gonna be the ones to make me do it.'

'We shall see, Mr Clocks. We shall see.'

'When and where?' said Paterson.

'Just you two, Paterson. Nobody else.'

'Oh, absolutely. It'll be just us. You have my word.'

'Good. Midnight tonight. Where the Sawn Man came to his end.'

'That's a crime scene. Police on the door.'

'I hear you're resourceful men. I'm sure you can think of something.'

'Too right we can,' said Clocks. 'Make sure you all bring yer overnight bags with yer. You lot won't be goin' 'ome, matey boy.'

'Until midnight then, gentlemen. I bid you farewell.'

He hung up at the same moment Clocks bunched up his fists. 'Prick!' he said.

Paterson dropped the phone back in his pocket and looked at the clock that hung over his door. 'We've got a couple of hours.'

'For what?' said Clocks.

'To figure out if and how he's going to trap us.'

'I'll tell you what they'll do. They'll 'ide 'emselves behind a couple of packing crates and jump out when we're inside. That's all they're gonna plan.'

'You think so, do you?'

'Yep. They ain't clever, Ray. All they wanna do is kill us because we're onto 'em. We turn up, and they jump out waving axes an' swords an' shit. We pull out Mr and Mrs Glock Nineteen and shoot the fuckers. It's nighty-night bad people then back to the nick for tea an' toast.'

'Except we can't go back to the nick because we're wanted, aren't we?'

'Oh, yeah. So we are. I'd forgotten that. So in this particular case, we'll just shoot 'em an' skip the tea an' toast.'

'And I don't think it's a good idea for us to shoot anyone either. Seeing as how we're wanted for questioning in two murders, it won't look good if there are more bodies, will it?'

Clocks grimaced. 'I 'ate it when you're sensible. So, what's your plan?'

'Same as yours, really, but no guns.'

'Gotta tell yer, that's a shit plan, guv,' said Clocks as he followed him out.

CHAPTER FORTY-FIVE

Paterson checked his watch. Five to midnight. 'You ready, John?'

'Born ready. Let's get on with it. We've been standin' in these bushes for the best part of an hour now and I'm bored out of me skull.'

Paterson took another look at the building in which the Sawn Man met his grisly end. There was a piece of yellow tape strewn across the only entrance to the building with a solitary uniformed police officer milling about, never straying too far from the entrance. The crime scene was shut down for the evening. Normal service would resume during office hours.

'Any movement elsewhere?' Paterson said.

'Can't see anything. All quiet. We doin' this?'

'Something's not right.'

Clocks looked at him. 'What? What d'you mean, *not right*? What's up?'

'I dunno, mate. Something's not right with this. Can't you feel it?'

Clocks shrugged. 'I can't even feel me feet, it's so bleedin' cold out 'ere. I just 'ope they've put the 'eatin' on in there.'

'No. Something's wrong, Clocksy.'

'Okay. If you say so. So what do we do then? If they're in there, this may well be our best shot at getting 'em.'

'Hmm. I dunno.'

'It's simple, mate. We go or we don't. Trust yer gut.'

Paterson thought about it for a couple of seconds. 'We go.'

'Good man. You know it makes sense. I'll distract the uniform, you creep up and choke him off to bye-byes.'

Before Paterson could answer, Clocks was away moving through the undergrowth and coming out a hundred yards from where the uniformed officer stood. Paterson followed close behind but stayed in the shadows when Clocks broke cover.

'All right, mate?' Clocks shouted. 'Murder squad. Sorry to sod about, but we need to go over the scene again. I think forensics missed something.'

Clocks caught the PC's attention with his warrant card and drew him around so that his back was now facing Paterson.

'You're who?' said the PC. 'DI Clocks?'

'That's it, son.'

'Is this your case, then?'

'Yeah. Well, me an' me guv'nor. He'll be along in a minute.'

The PC looked down at his electronic tablet and checked the names against the persons authorised to enter list. 'Is that Superintendent Paterson?'

'That's the one. Nice fellah. You'll meet him soon.'

Paterson's right arm hooked around the PC's throat while he pushed the back of his head forward with his right.

'Ooh. 'Ere 'e is,' said Clocks.

The PC struggled furiously against Paterson's grip, but within a few seconds his body went limp. Paterson lowered him gently to the ground.

'Sorry, son,' he said. 'Needs must and all that.'

'Ready then?' said Clocks.

'Be careful, John. Don't go marching in there like you're the bloody cock of the walk. We don't know how many there are in there.'

'Lets' go find out, then.' Clocks turned and walked toward the entrance with his best cock-o-the-hoop strut. He grabbed at the yellow tape and pulled it away.

'John!' Paterson shouted. 'No!'

Clocks turned to look at him.

'Run!' shouted Paterson. He stood and ran past Clocks, who spun on his heels and followed him. A brilliant light cut through the dark of the building and out into the bushes. Someone shouted, 'Police! Stand still!'

Paterson and Clocks heard the roar of engines from somewhere in the distance. Behind them came the sounds of running feet. Lots of them. Shouts of 'Armed Police! Armed Police! Stop!' went up. Torches clipped to machine gun barrels cut swathes through the darkness as five armed police took off after them.

'Keep going, John' Paterson shouted back. Clocks said nothing as he ran.

'C'mon. This way. Move!' Paterson knew that, as fit as they were, the SCO19 officers wouldn't be able to keep pace with them, thanks to the weight they had to carry as part of their kit. His real worry was whether Clocks would be able to keep going for long enough.

They crashed on over the rubbish tip and headed for the building site. No shots were fired. A good sign, Paterson supposed. They ran until the shouts began to recede far enough behind them and then they slowed.

Clocks immediately bent double, hands on both thighs.

Paterson smiled. 'You all right?' His breathing was only slightly laboured, and there was only a thin film of sweat on his brow.

'F . . . f . . .' Clocks dropped to his knees and looked up to the sky.

Even in the dark, Paterson could see his friend was struggling. Clocks was sucking in huge gulps of air. 'Try to control your breathing, John. Slowly. Don't gulp it in.'

Clocks nodded, unable to speak.

'Don't get too comfortable, mate. We're gonna have to move in a minute. They'll still be coming for us.'

Clocks nodded again and struggled to stand up. Paterson took one arm and helped him stand. 'Bet you wish you'd come running with me now, eh? Three miles every day. Good for you.'

'F . . . fuck . . . off!' Clocks wheezed the words out and shook his head.

'Good man. You're getting your breath back. C'mon. We need to jog our way out of here.'

'The . . . car . . .'

'No chance. Uniforms all around it. C'mon. We move now and keep going until I say otherwise. Keep low. Keep quiet.' Paterson took off.

Clocks followed on but a lot slower than either of them would have liked.

The shouts drew closer as Paterson slid down a heap of rubbish, tearing his trousers on an old piece of metal sticking out of the pile. Clocks tumbled over and over and ended up flat on his back.

'Me . . . lungs . . .' Clocks gasped.

'Get up! Come on.' Paterson grabbed hold of Clocks's hand and hauled him to his feet. 'Got to move ourselves.'

'Fuck . . .' Clocks wobbled into a trot.

Paterson grabbed him by the collar. 'I said *move*, John. Come on, damn it!'

Clocks broke into an unsteady run.

'Into the building site,' said Paterson. He pulled Clocks by the arm and dragged him with him. They ducked down behind a wall.

'Keep it quiet, John. Control your breathing.'

'Can't . . . can't . . . I'm fucked.'

Paterson poked his head up a little way and looked over at the rubbish tip. A lone SCO19 was carefully sliding himself down the rubbish pile. Paterson waited. No one else was coming, so they must have split themselves up — this one was on his own. He had a radio though.

'John, I'm going over there, behind that doorway. Make a bit of noise. Not too much. I want him curious. To come and look. If he gets on the radio, we're finished. Understand?'

Clocks nodded. Paterson moved and hid behind the doorway.

The SCO19 officer moved carefully across the open ground toward where Clocks was hidden. He moved his machine gun from side to side, sweeping the area for movement.

He stopped and looked in Clocks's direction, staying in position for a few seconds before moving forward again. Clocks made a scratching noise on the small pile of bricks next to him. The gunman stopped again, listening. He moved forward, closing in on where Clocks was crouched down. Closer. He stepped over a low wall and stopped. The scratching noise again. This time the man moved quicker in the direction of the noise.

'Armed police!' he shouted. 'Whoever's there, show me your hands and step out. Slowly!' He waited. 'I said *armed police*! Step out and show me your hands. Do it!'

'All right, all right,' said Clocks. 'I'm here. No problem.'

The officers tone hardened. 'I said *out*. Do it!'

Clocks stood up and held up his hands. 'All right, mate. Take it easy. No need for guns. I'm not gonna give you any aggro.' He stepped forward. 'I'm knackered, fellah. Too old for this runnin' shit.'

'Where's the other one?' shouted the gunman.

'Ray? He's legged it, mate. He's been shot before. Didn't fancy it again.'

'Where is he?'

'I just told yer. 'E's on 'is toes, mate.'

'Which direction?'

'Like I'm gonna tell you.'

The officer thrust the machine gun forward. 'Which fucking direction, arsehole?'

'All right! Calm down. That way.' Clocks pointed behind him as the gunman carefully circled his way around him with the intention of putting his back to the wall to stop anyone jumping him from behind. Textbook.

With the gun trained on Clocks the gunman reached down onto his belt and pulled out a set of plasticuffs. 'Put these on. Do it!' He threw them at Clocks as he took a step nearer the wall.

'Fuck me, you're bossy, ain'tcha?' Clocks put one hand through the cuff but left it loose. 'Thinkin' about it, my guv'nor might 'ave gone that way.' He nodded to his left. The gunman frowned.

'No, I remember where he went . . .'

'Where the fuck is he?' the gunman shouted.

'Behind you.'

The gunman whirled around. Paterson was in close. His hand shot forward and hit the man in the throat. The gunman staggered backward, gun now dangling from its strap, his hands on his throat as it closed up. Paterson kicked the man's left leg to one side, breaking his balance. He followed up with a kick to the other side, bringing him to his knees. Paterson stepped behind him and dropped to one knee as he brought his arm up and around the man's throat. He held onto him as consciousness left him. Paterson laid him down gently. 'I'm sorry, mate. I really am.'

'Will he be all right, Ray? That's a double whammy to the ol' throat there.'

Paterson stood up. 'He'll be fine. The first one wasn't hard at all. A slight spasm that sent him into panic. He'll be fine in twenty minutes or so.'

'Good stuff. What's the plan now?'

'Put those plasticuffs on him, take his radio and in five minutes make a panicked shout for urgent assistance. Then we chuck the radio, and while his mates are following the GPS, we get back to the car and fuck off out of here. They'll be looking for either of our cars, not the borrowed one.'

'Now that's a plan, Ray,' said Clocks.

CHAPTER FORTY-SIX

Paterson lifted his face to the sky and let the rain tip-tap on his face as he figured out their next move. He and Clocks were soaked to the skin and feeling the cold bite into them. The car didn't have much of a heater, but Clocks was taking advantage of it, holding his hands in front of the air vent on the dashboard in between blowing onto his fingers.

Paterson just wanted to be outside. Standing in the rain was something he loved to do as a child, and whenever he had problems of any kind, the simple act of walking in the rain always gave him clarity. It was a habit that had stuck with him throughout his life.

He knew things were about as bad as they were going to get for them both and that at some point there would be a price to pay. Failing to surrender and going on the run was never going to go in their favour, but now he was tired. Tired of people, the job — always pointing the finger at him and Clocks, and always, always so desperate to bring them both down. It was true they rarely played things as they were expected to, but their results spoke for themselves. It had taken him a while and a few murder cases, but he was now fully on board with Clocks's way of seeing things, doing things. When he thought back to how he was when they first met, it was hard for him to believe they were once polar opposites. Two men from vastly different sides of the street had formed a bond so strong that they were now closer than brothers. He knew that if the chips were down, he would die for Clocks, and he didn't doubt that he would do the same for him.

'Ray, get in 'ere. Warm yerself up.'

'I'm all right, John. Just thinking.'

'What about?'

'How he set us up.'

'That was easy. He called the police.'

Paterson sighed. 'I know that, but how did he know we were wanted?'

'That's easy too.'

'Yeah, I know. Dr Rakes, yes?'

'Yep. Must be one of them.'

'Bitch.'

Paterson's burner phone rang.

'Paterson,' he said.

'Guv'nor. It's me, Monkey.'

'What's up, Monkey? Everything all right?'

'No, guv. No, it's not.'

'Talk to me.'

'I've just had a call from that Temple bloke.'

'And?'

'And he wants to meet with you and Clocksy.'

'He's just set us up, Monkey. We just managed to avoid capture. You think this could be another set up?'

'Yep. But not for arrest. I think this time he's serious.'

'Why?'

'He tells me he's got DS Rocket.'

Paterson froze.

'Guv?'

Clocks got out of the car.

'Guv! You there?' said Monkey.

'Yeah. Go on.'

'Said he wants to meet you and Clocksy to finish this, once and for all. Kept bangin' on about being brave knights and challenging you to a duel.'

Paterson shook his head. 'Fuck all that. Do you think he has her?'

'I can't get no answer from her phone, guv. I've got the troops out and about checking on her last known location.'

'Did he say anything else?'

'Only that you two better show up alone or Suzi will die. We're getting onto the night duty inspector now to rustle up his troops and have them go searching for her just in case he's lying.'

Clocks's phone pinged. He stood in front of Paterson and held his phone up to his face, showing him a picture.

Paterson held up a finger to him. 'Stand them down, Monkey.'

'Guv?' he said.

'He's got her.'

'How d'you know?'

'Clocksy's just been sent a photo of her. She's bound and gagged and looks like she's in a body of water of some kind.'

'Christ! Can you tell where she is?'

'No. Where does he want us to meet and at what time?'

'I'll text you the details, then we'll make our way over to back you up.'

'No, you won't,' said Paterson. 'Say nothing to no one. We'll deal with this ourselves.'

'Guv . . . ?'

'It'll be fine. Don't worry about it. He said he only wants us, didn't he?'

'Yeah.'

'So, that's how it's gonna be. Just us. You boys give it half an hour or so after the deadline and come then.'

'Yeah . . . I'm not happy about that, guv. Her life's at stake and so is yours. You're both being set up. That's all too big of a risk.'

'Looking at this picture, she may already be dead, and if she's not, she soon will be. John and me? We're both big boys. We can handle it. Look, I appreciate your concern. Get the troops together and wait outside in the cars.'

'Won't that be too late?'

'Yeah, it will be. But not for us.'

CHAPTER FORTY-SEVEN

Paterson recounted the conversation he'd just had with Monkey Harris to Clocks. He walked around in a small circle, something he always did when he was angry and frustrated.

'Right, so. 'Ow the fuck are we gonna play this? We've got no weapons and we're walkin' bang into another trap.'

Paterson swiped his hair back in a futile attempt to get the rain out of his eyes for a second. 'I know. I doubt this one will involve the police. He wants to end this. We can't ignore him, can we?'

'Wasn't suggestin' that, Ray. I was wonderin' how badly we're going to 'urt them.'

Paterson smiled. 'I think *very badly* is the order of the day, John.'

Clocks nodded. 'Two questions . . . Why did he ring Monkey and not you direct? And, 'ow did 'e know we'd got away?'

'Good questions. No idea. Unless he was watching us from somewhere.'

'Or someone on the inside fed 'im some info.'

'Possible. It's also possible he phoned the office to find out if we *had* been captured. Who knows? We haven't got time to ponder it either. C'mon.' Paterson opened the door of the car and slid into the seat. 'But we need a couple of things first.'

'Like what?'

'Like proof of life. Given that these fuckers are extraordinarily violent and madder than a box o' frogs, we need to know if she's still alive and in one piece.'

'And the other?'

'Give your mate Kevin a bell and see if he can get hold of a couple of guns for us. Tell him to meet us in Place Road, five minutes from here.'

Clocks fished his phone out of his pocket and dialled.

Paterson dialled the number that Temple had used to call him.

'Mr Paterson. There you are. You *did* escape! Well done!'

'If she's hurt, I'll destroy you. You understand me? I'll fucking destroy you and your little crew. Where are you, arsehole?'

'That's not the way to get what you want, is it? A simple hello would have been more polite.'

'Where are we doing this?'

'Patience, Mr Paterson. Patience. Why didn't you and Clocks answer your phones earlier?'

'What?'

'I called you both. No answer. Didn't you want to talk to me?'

Paterson looked at his phone, tapped the screen and scrolled. Two missed calls. That explained why Temple called the office and spoke to Monkey: no signal.

'Well, no matter. I have you now. Do you know the old derelict office block at the rear of Queen Elizabeth Street?'

'Yep.'

'That's where we'll be waiting. Four a.m.'

'Whereabouts?'

'Follow the light, Mr Paterson.' Temple hung up.

Clocks was off the phone.

'What did Kevin say?' said Paterson.

'That we're basically fucked. He's in the middle of Kent at some dodgy card game and he can't get guns to us anytime soon.'

Paterson looked at his watch. They had twenty minutes. 'Fucked we are, then. Let's just get on with it. You ready?'

Clocks banged out a drumroll on the dashboard. 'Born ready, matey. You know that.' He rammed the car into gear and spun the wheels as they shot off into the night. He barely slowed down as they approached a set of red traffic lights, overtook three cars on the inside and put two wheels on the pavement as he did so.

'John . . .' said Paterson.

'Shuddup! I'm concentratin'. Whaddyer want?'

'I was wondering. If you don't kill us before we get there with your dodgy driving, how do you want to play this?'

'Dunno. I s'pose we watch each other's back as usual and punch the granny out of anyone and everyone who looks or behaves like a bad guy. Usually works for us. So, I say we stick to what we know.'

Paterson watched the brightly lit shops shoot by as Clocks kept his foot down.

'Whassa time?' Clocks said.

'Thirteen minutes to deadline. We've got time.'

Clocks jammed on the brakes and slid the car to a halt outside an all-night convenience store.

'John! What the fuck?'

Clocks bailed out and ran around the front of the car. 'Gimme two minutes. I've 'ad meself a brainwave!' He disappeared inside the shop. True to his word, two minutes later, he came running out holding a carrier bag. He threw the bag into the back seat, but not before throwing a Snickers bar at Paterson. He then ripped open a Mars bar with his teeth as he screeched away from the kerb.

'What's going on?' said Paterson. 'You didn't stop to get sweets, surely?'

'Yep. I'm starvin' an' I ain't fightin' anyone on an empty stomach. Coupla cans of Coke in the back, if you fancy one.

Might make you gassy, though, an' you don't wanna end up fightin' an' fartin', do ya? That's embarrassing. Up to you, though.'

Paterson shook his head in bewilderment. 'No, you're all right. I'll pass. Just for the record, it just makes me burp, not fart.'

'Yeah, fair enough then. We don't want you killin' anyone with your dodgy burps do we? Tell you what . . . we can chuck 'em at that Temple geezer when we get there. He won't be expectin' that!'

Clocks swerved the car into a large puddle near the kerb and laughed out loud as a large wave of water engulfed an already drenched cyclist on his way to work. 'This is gonna be a good night, Ray. I can feel it in me willy.'

'You're off your fucking nut, Clocksy. I swear you're getting worse.'

'Ah, you love me, though.'

Paterson said nothing.

'You'll love me even more when I tell yer what else is in the bag.'

'What?'

Clocks glanced over at him with a grin.

'A couple of guns, mate. One for you. One for me.'

CHAPTER FORTY-EIGHT

Clocks pulled up outside the office block, killed the engine then leaned over to the back seat and grabbed hold of the carrier bag. He rummaged around and pulled out one of the guns.

Paterson looked at it. 'The fuck is this?'

'Your gun. It's a revolver. I got meself the automatic. Looks more badass.'

'Are you joking?'

'What d'you mean?'

'These are fucking plastic. You've bought two toy guns.'

'Oh, I'm sorry. Did you think I was just gonna pull up at some random shop in the middle of the night an' ask if they could sell me a coupla real guns? An' d'you think that even if they 'ad any under the counter, they'd 'ave just sold 'em to me, a total stranger?'

Paterson looked at the gun, held onto a piece of brightly coloured cardboard by a couple of plastic ties and bearing the slogan 'Cop Set'. 'I just thought . . . I dunno . . . You know lots of people dotted about all over London so, yeah, I figured the shop owner was someone you knew. Someone who owed you or something. Doing you a favour, perhaps.' He shook his head.

'We're not in Bermondsey now, Ray. And, for the record, I don't know everyone in London. We'll be all right. Trust me.'

Paterson looked at him. 'I do trust you, Clocksy, but . . . c'mon. You've done some daft things in your time . . . two toy guns, though? Jesus! If we end up getting killed, how will this look to the old bill that show up? They'll piss themselves laughing.'

'Well, that won't matter will it? We'll be fuckin' dead!'

'Is this gonna be our legacy then? I can see the headlines now. *Two top cops try and stop a bunch of homicidal maniacs with two plastic guns. Met definitely needs more funding.*'

'Yeah . . . that 'eadline's gonna need a bit more work. An' shut up moanin'. You're such a Negative Nancy. Look, 'ere's the plan . . . We tuck them in the back of our trousers and bowl in there, large as you like. When they start gettin' a bit rowdy, we whip the guns out an' start wavin' 'em about. We style it out. We start shoutin' an' 'ollerin' at 'em an' then they'll give up. It's an abandoned office buildin', so I can't see it being too well lit. An' while they're busy shittin' bricks at seein' two of the Met's finest wavin' guns at 'em, they won't be able to see they're plastic, will they?'

Paterson looked out of the car window toward the office building. 'Looks pretty well lit in there to me.'

'There you go with the negative stuff again.' Clocks tore the cardboard off his gun. 'All right then. Then they will know, won't they? We'll deal with that if it 'appens. But right now, this is all we got. You up for it?' He half opened the door and put one foot out while keeping his gaze on Paterson.

Paterson opened his door. 'Why not? The day can't get much sillier, can it? Surely to God.' He tore off the cardboard from around his own gun, stood up and tucked it in the back of his waistband.

'Don't forget, Ray. Coupla gangstas. You an' me. Badass all the way, mate.' He headed for the door.

CHAPTER FORTY-NINE

They took up position either side of the front entrance to the building. Clocks pushed open the door and waited for it to swing wide open. He poked his head cautiously inside then pulled it back out.

He shook his head. Clear. He stepped inside. Paterson followed, and the two men fanned out inside the musty old reception area. The room was large and empty; what little furniture had been left behind when the occupiers moved out had been stripped out by thieves. The room stank of stale urine. Ahead of them was a lit corridor.

Paterson nodded. They moved into the corridor and edged their way toward the end. Paterson could see a right turn ahead of them — another corridor, and that one was darker. No lights there.

At the junction, Paterson put his back to the wall and poked his head around the corner. It took him a few seconds for his eyes to adjust to the darkness ahead. He stepped forward and beckoned Clocks to follow.

They crept slowly along the passageway until they came to another right turn that took them into another darkened corridor. Looking into it, Paterson could see that at the end of this one was a double door, housing what he surmised was some sort of hall. There were lights on inside.

They moved forward, less cautious this time, until they took up position either side of the double doors. Clocks gingerly pushed the door open a crack and put his head inside for a few seconds before pulling himself back out, pursing his lips and making a raspberry sound before he started laughing.

'What? What is it?' said Paterson.

Clocks held his hand up. He got a grip but couldn't quite contain a smirk. 'You gotta 'ave a look at that, mate. Seriously. Go on.'

Paterson pushed the door open and put his head through the crack. 'Fuck me . . .'

'I know. Ain't it brilliant? You couldn't make this shit up if you tried.'

Paterson pushed the door open and stepped inside. Clocks followed. At the back of the hall, some thirty feet away, stood three figures, each a good six feet apart. In the middle stood Temple Anderson. On his head was a metal helmet; on his chest, a metal plate. In one hand he held the flag of St George and in the other, balanced over his shoulder, was a large sword.

Flanked either side of him stood a male and a female dressed similarly. The woman held a crossbow and the man a chain mace, an iron ball on the end of it studded with vicious-looking spikes.

'Fuck me blind!' Clocks shouted. 'What is wrong with you lot?'

'Tonight, it ends!' Temple shouted back in his best dramatic voice.

Clocks started giggling, triggering Paterson into joining him. For a good thirty seconds the two policemen had a hard time pulling themselves together, until finally, with their fits of giggles under control, they walked closer to the trio, wiping their eyes. All three raised their weapons.

'Look,' said Clocks, trying to suppress his laughter. 'Don't be fuckin' about, kids. Put yer silly little weapons down. Be'ave yerselves. Playtime's over.'

'Hold fast!' shouted Temple.

'Ah. The infamous Temple Anderson?' Paterson nodded to him. 'Thought you'd be a bit . . . bigger, to be honest. I've seen more muscle on a wet shrimp.'

Temple glared at Clocks.

'C'mon, kiddies,' said Clocks. 'I said *playtime's over*. Now. We've brought the special bus with us so we can get you all back to yer nice, warm padded rooms safe 'n' sound. Linda, I don't want you lickin' the windows. Understand?'

The woman started. 'What . . . ?'

Clocks chortled. 'You really think we didn't know? Jesus. We 'ad you pegged ages ago.' He looked at the second man. 'Who are you then, sonny?'

'You will soon find out,' said the man. His voice had a slight tremble.

''Course I'll find out, you two-bob fuckwit. Might 'ave to do it off yer fingerprints once I break yer neck, but . . . hey-ho.'

'You have one of my officers,' said Paterson.

'A prisoner of war,' said Temple.

Paterson cleared his throat. 'Son, there's no war except for the one that's raging inside your nut. You're just a bunch of fucked-up, spoilt little kids with mummy and daddy issues, but nothing being locked up for the rest of your sad little lives won't cure.' He turned to Clocks. 'What d'you reckon, Clocksy? How did that sound? More street?'

Clocks nodded. 'Yeah. Not bad, not bad. You lost it a bit at the end, but pretty badass overall, mate. Well done. You're gettin' better at this. Seven out of ten.'

'You dare to mock us?' Temple said. Paterson could see the young man going red in the face. It wouldn't take much to push him over the edge.

'We ain't mockin' yer, son,' said Clocks. 'You're doin' that to yerselves. Did any of you twats stop an' 'ave a look at yerself in the mirror before you come out tonight? Did yer?' Nobody answered. 'No, thought not. Now, do as yer told and drop yer weapons or I'll take that sword and ram it *right* up your arse end. You understand me, boy?' He glared at Temple.

'I want my officer back,' said Paterson. 'Now. Where is she? And she better be safe.'

It was Temple's turn to laugh. 'As we speak, the woman is suffering the death of a thousand cuts. *One thousand* cuts,' Temple smirked. 'Each one counted and verified.'

'What was that? What'd you say?' said Clocks, a scowl on his face. 'Did you say *cuts*? You better not 'ave said *cuts*.' The two policemen walked closer to the trio. The man and the woman raised their weapons. Paterson and Clocks stopped, four feet away from the group.

'Don't point that thing at me, love,' Clocks said to the woman. 'It looks bleedin' dangerous.'

'Stand back!' The man with the mace shouted. 'Get thee back!'

'*Get thee back*?' You soppy bastard. Or what? What you gonna do if we don't?'

'I will strike thee.'

Clocks tutted. 'Now you're being silly. Look at yer arms. You look too fuckin' skinny to wave that thing about for too long and if you manage to take a swing and miss me, which you will, I'll kick the living shit out of you. Don't be a prick. Put it down now before you piss me off. You an' all, love. Don't point pointy things at me.'

'Stand ready,' Temple commanded.

'Why don't you talk properly?' said Paterson. 'You sound like an idiot.'

'And you sound like a defeated man,' Temple retorted.

Paterson snorted. 'Defeated? You *are* an idiot if you think that.'

Paterson darted forward, pulled the toy gun out of his waistband and before Temple could react, shoved it an inch away from his nose. 'Drop the fucking weapon, boy! Do as you're fucking told!'

Clocks whipped out his toy gun and held it sideways on. He swung it around, pretending to give Paterson some armed cover while at the same disguising the fact that it was plastic. 'Stand still!' he shouted. 'Any of you fuckers move an' I'll shoot the bastard shit out of yer. Fourteen bullets. Seven each. Drop your fuckin' weapons now! Do it!'

The man and the woman didn't move, unsure of what to do.

Temple glared at Paterson, and for a second, Paterson really thought he might just ignore him. The sword clattered to the ground. 'Good boy,' said Paterson. 'Take that silly helmet off. You two as well.'

Though his stance was defiant, Temple Anderson complied. The silver helmet bounced around on the floor making a ringing sound as the metal met the concrete. Paterson butted him in the face knocking him backward.

The man and woman dropped their weapons quickly.

Paterson was on his man in an instant. He grabbed him by his hair and yanked his head up. 'Where the fuck *is* she?' he screamed into Temple's face. 'Fucking tell me now, you cunt!'

Temple Anderson shook his head, dazed. Paterson decided to take it as a sign of defiance. He butted him again, this time dropping him to the floor.

'Come on, then,' said Clocks. 'Take yer 'ats off.' Reluctantly, they did as they were told.

Paterson looked across at Linda Rakes. Temple was going nowhere. He strode across to her and watched her eyes widen. He grabbed her by the throat and pushed her back against the wall. The man who'd had the mace started to move, but Clocks gave him a look that indicated it was best if he stayed exactly where he was.

'I take it dinner's off, then?' Paterson said. 'No worries. Pity though. You seemed like a nice girl. Oh, well. Nothing's ever quite what it seems these days.'

He moved his face closer to hers. 'Just for my own peace of mind, it was you that told him we were wanted, right?'

She said nothing. 'Quite clever, really, those emails about meeting at "Temple". We were all wondering what the temple was, thinking it was a place, and it was all about meeting him, wasn't it? That pathetic little shit over there.'

Linda Rakes stood straight. 'Dare not to insult King Temple.'

Paterson sighed. 'Give it a rest, will you? He's no king. He's just another nutjob who's managed to recruit another couple of nutjobs to fuck up Mummy and Daddy for whatever reason. Which one did you kill, eh?'

She smiled.

Paterson squeezed her throat harder.

'*Poena*,' she squeaked.

'*Poena Cullei*. The man in the bag. Parricide. The death of a father. Okay, we'll find out why later. Right now, I want my officer back.' He squeezed harder. 'Where . . . is . . . she?'

Rakes said nothing.

'*Where is she, bitch?*'

Rakes gurgled as she tried to break Paterson's grip. He watched her face redden and smiled as her eyes bulged in their sockets. 'Was he telling the truth? *Is* she hurt?'

Rakes ignored him as she fought for air that wasn't coming. She gave three quick nods of her head. 'Last chance. Tell me where she is!'

'You're gonna 'ave to let go a bit, Ray,' said Clocks. 'I think she's finding it a little bit 'ard to speak.' Paterson released his grip slightly and the redness began to drain from her face.

'I don't . . .' she sputtered.

Paterson squeezed again and put his face even closer to hers. 'You think I'm playing? Do you? Five seconds!' He tightened his grip.

'Five.' Rakes's face turned a deep red again. She groaned and spat tiny flecks of spittle onto Paterson's hand as he squeezed her throat.

'Four.' Paterson felt her start to weaken as she began to lose consciousness. With a sudden desperate burst of energy, she began to fight back. Her hands, locked around Paterson's, began to scratch at his skin and she tried to bring her knee up to his groin. He was expecting it and had already turned himself away.

'Three.' Rakes's arms dropped by her side and her knees softened. Paterson kept the pressure on.

'Ray . . .' Clocks was getting agitated.

'Two.' Rakes's legs gave out. Paterson held her up against the wall.

'Ray!' Clocks moved forward.

'Leave her alone, heathen!' Anderson shouted.

Paterson released his grip and let Rakes drop to the ground.

'Jesus!' said Clocks as he went to her aid. Rakes desperately gulped in air and coughed several times. She began to massage her throat. Paterson turned and walked across to Anderson. As he went, he scowled at the lad who'd had the mace and pulled his fist back. His legs buckled as Paterson said, 'Boo!' and walked past him.

Anderson was up, swaying on his feet, blood streaming from his nose and mouth.

'Tell me where she is, Anderson.' A look of defiance froze on Anderson's face as Paterson, his forehead set into a deep scowl, grabbed his cheeks with one hand and pushed him backward, breaking his balance. Anderson tried to say something, but with his mouth squished into an 'O' shape he just made a strange, unintelligible sound. Paterson quickly dropped his hand and grabbed him by the throat. 'I swear to God I'll break every bone in your body, Anderson.' Before he could apply too much pressure, Anderson spat it out. 'She's in a sewer.'

Paterson glared at him. 'What? A *sewer*? Where?'

Temple Anderson shook his head. 'No.'

'No?' said Paterson. 'What d'you mean, *no*? You fucking idiot. Tell me where she is now or I swear I'll kill you and beat it out of them with your miserable carcass when you're dead.'

Anderson shook his head. Paterson squeezed tighter. Anderson struggled and, although not the fighter he imagined himself to be, somehow managed to land a punch on Paterson's chin, breaking the grip around his throat. As Paterson stepped backward, more surprised than hurt, Anderson darted sideways and held his fists up.

'Oh, no, no, no, no!' said Clocks. He left Rakes coughing on the floor and ran toward Anderson and Paterson. 'Ray! Don't!'

Paterson darted forward, blocked Anderson's clumsy punches and pushed him backward. Anderson staggered back a few steps then planted his feet. Paterson kept coming. Anderson flailed. Paterson pushed. Johnny Clocks stood by, watching this unfold. After Anderson's third attempt at hitting out, Paterson side-stepped, brought his arm up and around Anderson's throat and stepped forward, walking past him and breaking the man's balance. With Anderson in a throat lock, Paterson dragged him toward a dilapidated office.

Kicking the door open, he dragged Anderson inside and threw him into a swivel chair. Paterson called to Clocks. 'Keep an eye on the other two, John. Don't let them run.'

Clocks looked hesitant. 'What are you going to do?'

Paterson cocked his head. 'What'd you think I'm gonna to do? I wanna find out where Suzi is. Shouldn't be too long.'

'Ray . . .'

'It'll be fine. Trust me.'

'I . . .'

'Trust me! Go on. Keep your eye on the others.'

Clocks started to turn, then stopped.

'Go on,' said Paterson. 'And shut the door on your way out, mate.'

Reluctantly, Johnny Clocks did what Paterson said and returned to the other two.

Paterson took a quick look around the office and found what he needed on the desk behind Anderson.

'You won't find her,' said Anderson. 'You won't. I'm not saying anything.'

'No?' said Paterson. 'Okay. There are consequences to your actions. You understand?' I need you to clearly understand that this will go very badly for you.'

'She's probably dead already. The rain will have filled the sewer by now. She's been there for hours. If she hasn't already drowned, the sewer filth will have infected her system and she'll just die slowly. We win, heathen.'

Paterson picked up an old dust-covered fountain pen. He stood in front of Anderson and unscrewed the lid. He touched the tip of it with his thumb. In his head, he tried to push down the rage that was building inside him. 'You win, do you?' Paterson nodded slowly. 'Okay. Let me tell you how this game really ends. You will tell me exactly where she is in the next thirty seconds. If you don't, I will inflict so much pain on you you'll wish you'd stayed in your little university room, drinking your silly little half-per-cent beers, playing your silly little Dungeons 'n' Dragons game on your silly little PS5 or whatever the fuck it is you sad little wankers do when you get together. And if by any chance you manage to hold out longer than thirty seconds, I'll just kill you and move on to the next one. The only real question is, how much pain do you think you can endure?'

Paterson rammed the pen into Anderson's shoulder. Anderson screamed and recoiled in horror. Paterson looked at the second hand on his watch.

* * *

Clocks shook his head and looked at the other two. 'He's really, *really* not playin' around. Tell me where she is an' I'll get 'im to stop, but you better be quick. To tell yer the truth, I think 'e's got a few mental problems 'imself. He really fuckin' enjoys this sorta stuff, y'know?'

* * *

Twenty seconds. 'You think this is a game? You murdered three people, including your own father. I mean, come on!' Paterson levered the pen from side to side in Temple's shoulder. Temple's eyes widened and he screamed in agony as the pen scraped against his bone. 'Tell me. Tell me where to find her and I'll stop.'

* * *

Clocks winced at the scream. 'I told yer 'e's not fuckin' around, an' when he's finished with 'im, he'll come for you two. He is not an 'appy little bunny. Do either of you know where 'e's stashed 'er?'

Linda Rakes shook her head from side to side.

'You sure? He'll do you next, an' I'm not even jokin. S'up to you.'

* * *

Fifteen seconds. 'Tell me where she is!' Paterson yelled in Anderson's ear.

'Fuck off!' Anderson screamed back. Paterson yanked the pen out of Anderson's shoulder and backhanded him out of the chair, tumbling him to the floor. Blood seeped out of his shoulder wound and he let out a little whimper as he lay in the dust and dirt of the manky office.

Paterson flipped him onto his back and, bending on one knee, straddled him. He grabbed him by the hair and pulled his head toward him. From nowhere, the pen was suddenly less than two inches from Anderson's left eye.

'Where . . . is . . . she?' Anderson closed his eyes as if to block out Paterson's threat. He screamed again as Paterson raked the pen down his cheek opening up the flesh. Blood poured down his cheek. Paterson slashed it across his head and down the other cheek. He pressed it against Anderson's jugular. 'Last chance, boy.'

Ten seconds. 'I . . . said . . . fuc—' Paterson yanked him up off the ground and threw him across the desk. Anderson groaned as he crashed onto the floor. Paterson was on him again.

'Fuck you, you little prick! Tell me where she is — now!' He dragged him up again, pushed him toward the office door and shoved him hard. The wood splintered and the glass windowpane smashed, slicing Anderson's face as he stumbled head first into the main room.

Five seconds. Clocks turned at the sound of the door breaking and the glass tinkling on the ground. 'Christ!'

Anderson's battered, bloody body tumbled into a heap at Clocks's feet.

Paterson came out after him.

'Ray! Enough!'

Paterson kept coming.

Clocks stood in front of him and put his hand up. Paterson grabbed it and twisted it violently to the right, causing Clocks to spin away and lose his footing. He fell to the floor but jumped up as fast as he went down. 'Ray! Stop it!'

Paterson bent down to yank Anderson to his feet. He grabbed his collar just as the full weight of Johnny Clocks hit him broadside. The two men tumbled to the ground and were up on their feet in seconds, Clocks now between Anderson and Paterson. Paterson glared at him. Clocks held his fists up. 'Don't, Ray. Don't do this.' He stood his ground, defending Anderson.

'Get out of the way, John.'

'Not doin' it, mate. You've lost the plot a bit 'ere, ain'tcha? I know you've got the ragin' 'ump with 'im. Me too. But this ain't the way.'

'What's it to you what I do?'

'Every bleedin' thing. We'll both go down for murder, an' Lyndsey'll fuckin' kill me if I miss the weddin'. You know that. An' to be 'onest, I'm way more frightened of 'er than I am of you.'

Paterson stopped. 'We have to find Suzi, John.'

'I know, I know. We will. But ease up a bit.'

Paterson wiped his mouth with the back of his arm and moved again. 'I can't . . . *I won't* lose another officer.'

Clocks tensed himself. 'Calm down, Ray. Think it through. Ain't that what you tell me? *Think it through.* You're not thinkin', mate. You're ragin'.

Paterson pushed him in the chest. 'Move!'

Clocks kicked out and caught Paterson in the testicles. Paterson doubled over, hands on his balls.

'Ooh! Sorry, Ray. Force of 'abit, mate.'

Paterson couldn't speak for a full ten seconds. When he did, he wasn't happy. 'Fucking hell, Clocksy. That was out of order.' He leaned on a desk for support. 'I feel bloody sick.'

'I'm really sorry, but I know what you're capable of. I thought a swift kick in the boiled eggs would slow you down enough to think a bit. Sorry.'

A flash of lightning lit the room and a low rumble of thunder close behind.

'We're running out of time, John. Ooh, my balls.'

'I said I was sorry. I am. Let me try with 'im.'

Paterson nodded.

Anderson was flat on his back, breathing hard and bleeding profusely. 'Fucking . . . mad . . .'

Clocks bent down. 'Yes, 'e is. If you'd 'ave done yer 'omework or listened to yer old dad when he was no doubt slaggin' us off around the dinner table, you'd 'ave known that. Now . . . I've calmed him down for the time bein', but I promise you 'e won't stop for long. 'E won't fall for the kick-in-the-bollocks trick again, an' I can't stop 'im. I've seen 'im fight before, son, an' 'e'll go through me like a coupla vindaloos on a Friday night to get to you. An', being 'onest, if you don't cough 'er up, I'll fuckin' well just let 'im. Up to you.'

Anderson looked up at Clocks. He'd had enough. The evening hadn't quite turned out the way he'd planned. 'Mason Street . . . Ten minutes from here. Go . . . go to the end . . . the end of the road. There's a fence . . .' He groaned in pain and started to roll onto his side.

Clocks stopped him. 'And?'

'Go through the fence. There's an old storm drain entrance . . . hidden by weeds and stuff. It's unlocked. Climb down . . . turn left about a hundred metres in. She's there.'

'What? Metres? Do I sound French? What's metres in feet an' inches, then?'

'About a hundred and sixty-odd feet,' said Paterson.

Clocks looked up at Paterson. 'There you go. The gentle touch, mate. That's all it takes. Ask nicely.' He turned around and punched Anderson once in the face, knocking him spark out. 'Better put them to sleep as well.'

'Is he telling the truth?' Paterson said to Rakes. She nodded furiously.

'If he's not, and you're not, I swear I'll come back and bite your ugly face off.'

He spun her around and choked her out. He held onto her until she dropped. Only the other knight left.

"Oi! Oi! son.' Clocks pointed to the pool of urine he was now standing in. What's goin' on 'ere? I thought you was s'posed to be some sort of rufty-tufty Knight of the Realm. Ol' King Arthur's not gonna be pleased with you, is 'e? Pissin' yer pants like a scared little boy. Fuck me, Tin Man, you'll make yer armour all rusty.'

'Please . . .' the young man whimpered as Paterson hooked his arm around his throat.

'What's your name, son?'

'T. . .Toby. Toby Lavery.' Fifteen seconds later he was lying face down in his own pee.

'G'night, Toby.'

'Will they be out long?' said Clocks.

'Maybe half an hour, forty-five minutes or so.'

'Better find some way of securin' 'em then, just in case.'

CHAPTER FIFTY

Paterson slid the car to a halt at the end of Mason Street. Both men bailed out and ran out into the pelting rain, leaving the car doors wide open. On the way to their destination, Clocks had put in a call to Monkey Harris and told him to round up the rest of the team and call the paramedics to the scene.

Paterson found the hole in the fence and scrambled through it onto a rubbish-strewn patch of land. There was a couple of old tyres, empty KFC boxes, an old, rusty Asda trolley lying on its side and plenty of dog shit. Clocks followed behind, and together they found the storm drain. Paterson winced when he saw it — a large metal lid made of cast iron.

Paterson found the little hook that was used for inserting a lifting rod. With one finger he managed to lift it about a foot, his muscles straining to the max. Clocks darted forward and grabbed the lid, and with some effort they threw it to one side.

The first thing that hit them both was the smell. Paterson found the ladder rungs that protruded from the wall and was halfway down it as Clocks heaved. 'Jesus! That's fuckin' rank!'

'You got a torch?' said Paterson.

'No,' said Clocks. 'You?'

'No. Thought you might have picked up a couple of toy ones to go with the guns.' He swung himself into the hole.

'Worked didn't it?' said Clocks. 'Use yer phone. That's got a torch on it.'

'Good point. Now get your arse in here.' Paterson disappeared into the dark hole.

'I'm comin'. I'm comin'. Could just 'ave done without the smell, is all.'

He followed Paterson down the ladder until he landed in a good three feet of foul water. 'Great. That's another suit fucked up,' he moaned. 'Every bloody case we take on, I lose a suit. I'm goin' back to wearin' me soddin' jeans.' In the half-light that shone down the hole, he could see what looked like thick grease floating on the top of water. He dry heaved. 'Oh, this is eighteen carat. I'm standin' in water made entirely of piss, shit an' cookin' fat. Oh, I love my fuckin' job so much. I really do.' He dry heaved again. 'Gawd almighty.'

'Shut up, Clocksy!' Paterson's voice echoed along the tunnel. 'Suzi!' he shouted. He listened. Nothing. Just his own voice bouncing back off the stone walls. 'Suzi! It's me! Paterson.' No answer. 'Go that way,' he said to Clocks. 'I'll go this way.'

'Why? 'E said she was to the left.'

'And you believed him?'

'Good point. I'll go right.'

'John. Before you go, listen to me for a sec.'

'What?'

'Something's bothering me.'

'What?'

'It's this sewer.'

'*What*? For fuck's sake. Tell me.'

'If it's what I think it is, it could be a problem.'

'What d'you mean, *problem*?'

'I think it's what's known as a cross-connection drain.'

'What's that then? 'Ow is that a problem?'

'These old Victorian sewers were designed to take away all the foul water from houses and factories, but some of them also took away storm water. Doesn't happen nowadays because of the need to avoid cross-contamination and different regs, but back in the day it happened. We could be in for trouble.'

'So you keep sayin'. Now tell me how.'

'The storm outside. It's a bitch of a heavy one. Chances are there's a huge influx of water headed our way. If you hear a rumbling sound, get back up the ladder — quick.'

Clocks stared at him. 'And you tell me this *now*? Thanks a fuckin' bunch.'

'You're welcome.'

''Ow come you know all this?' said Clocks.

'I paid attention at school.'

'Of course you did, you fuckin' girly swot.'

Both men crouched down as they entered the sewer tunnel, with only their phone torches to light the way.

Paterson moved forward carefully, straining his eyes in the gloom, desperate to catch sight of Suzi Rocket. Twenty seconds in, an echoey yell of panic caught up with him.

'Oh, fuck! It's a rat!' Clocks shouted. 'A fuckin' rat! Kill it! Kill it! Kill it!' Paterson heard water splashing about and shook his head. He knew that Clocks would be freaking out on his own in the dark as it was. Add a swimming rat into the mix and that would tip him over the edge. He pressed on, leaving Clocks to sort himself out. Clocks's ranting grew more distant and less echoey as Paterson put more distance between them.

He stopped. Ahead of him he could just make out a dark shape jutting out of the water and in contact with the wall. He slowed down, unsure of what it was. He raised one fist in readiness, not knowing whether Temple and his Knights had laid a trap for him. There could be more of them, and they could be armed. He moved forward slowly, crouching even lower.

He felt his heart pound against his chest. Closer now, and the shape began to form. Not a trap. The light shimmered off the water and illuminated her face, lacerated with tiny cuts.

'Suzi! John, she's here!' he shouted. Suzi was slumped down in the water, her chin just touching the surface. In the distance, Clocks sploshed his way through the watery filth and back to them. Paterson pulled her upright, realising that she was naked with her hands tied behind her. 'Suzi! It's me — Paterson. Can you hear me?' She didn't answer. 'We need to get her out of here. Fast!' Paterson hauled her up. 'Grab her feet.'

Paterson wrapped his arms around her chest and Clocks lifted her feet up. As quickly as they could in the cramped space, they began to head back toward the ladder.

'Careful, Ray. There's rats down 'ere.'

'What? In a sewer? Who'd have thought?'

'Bastard things can swim an' all. Did you know that?'

'Everyone knows that.'

'I bloody didn't. I thought that was only Guinea pigs.'

Working together, splashing through the water and avoiding the swimming rats, they got Suzi back to the foot of the ladder. Rain was pouring in, the needle-shaped drops picked out by the shaft of bluish light that cut through the darkness.

'Jesus Christ Almighty!' said Paterson. 'He was serious.'

Suzi's body was covered in tiny cuts. Hundreds of them. Everywhere.

He bent over her and pressed his fingers against her jugular vein. 'Faint. Very faint.'

'So 'ow we gonna get 'er out?'

'Listen,' said Paterson. A low rumbling sound came from somewhere in the distance.

Clocks cocked his head.

'Hear it?' said Paterson.

'Yeah. Is that what I think it is?'

Paterson glanced around him at the walls and noticed the tidemark. 'I think so. The storm's flooded the system. We've got to get her out of here. C'mon!'

Paterson hauled her upright and struggled to get the dead weight of her over his shoulder. 'Get up the ladder, John. Go! Go!'

Clocks jumped onto the second rung and began to climb. The rumble of the water grew louder. 'Move it, John, move! C'mon!' He worked out that he needed to get her up six rungs before Clocks could make a decent grab for her.

Clocks clambered out into the rain, turned around and lay flat. 'C'mon, Ray. Get 'er up!'

The rumbling was closer now.

Paterson grunted as he pulled himself up the ladder, gravity pulling Suzi's weight down on his shoulder. He looked up at Clocks and re-evaluated. Suzi was out of it. She couldn't reach up or take Clocks's hand. It was ten steps to get her to where Clocks could get hold of her. He pulled himself up again, straining as he went.

'Nearly there, Ray. You can do it!' Clocks reached down into the shaft.

The torrent of water rounded a bend. Around fifteen seconds and it would take them. Paterson pulled them up higher.

'Couple more an' I can grab 'er.'

Paterson dug deep as he heard the water clearly now. Around ten seconds away. From behind Clocks came a familiar voice.

'I've gotcha, boss. Take her!' Monkey Harris had grabbed Clocks's belt and was holding on tight.

Clocks threw himself forward, further down the shaft, and snatched hold of Suzi's hand. 'Got er!' he shouted, and he wrenched her up toward him. 'Pull! Pull me up!'

Harris strained to drag them both out. He roared through gritted teeth as he managed to raise Clocks and Suzi by a foot. Still holding onto Clocks's belt, he made a grab for his jacket collar and heaved him out. Suzi's feet cleared the ceiling of the chamber.

Paterson, free of the dead weight, pulled himself upward just one step when the force of the water hit him like a steam train, knocking him sideways and tugging one foot off of the ladder. He groaned as he maintained a slippery, one-handed grip on the rung. He felt his grip weakening under the immense pressure of tens of thousands of gallons of water rushing past him, pushing at him, dragging him with it.

* * *

With a final heave from Harris, Clocks cleared the shaft and landed face down on the grass. Harris, on his feet, ran around him and grabbed Suzi's other hand. Together, they dragged her to safety. Clocks lay flat on his back, panting heavily. 'Fuck me . . . side . . . ways . . .' Then he remembered. 'Ray!' He rolled himself over and poked his head back down the shaft. 'Ray!' he shouted into the gloom.

Paterson was gone.

'Oh, shit! Ray! Ray! Monkey!'

Harris poked his head into the shaft next to Clocks. A torrent of water gushed past them. Clocks scrambled down the ladder.

'Guv, whatcha doing?' shouted Harris. 'He's gone.'

The water began to slow its pace.

'Bollocks to that! I'm goin' with 'im!' Gripping the ladder tight, Clocks climbed down into the raging water. He jumped the last few feet, but instead of landing on terra firma, he felt something moving under his feet. 'What the . . .'

He jumped back onto one of the rungs and with one arm, reached down into the water and felt hair. He grabbed it. With every muscle in his body straining, he pulled until Paterson's head broke the surface. 'Got 'im!' he shouted. Still holding Paterson's head out of the water, Clocks jumped off the ladder again and was immediately pushed against the wall by the force of the torrent. Paterson fell onto him. 'Fuck! Ray! C'mon, talk to me.' He spluttered and coughed. 'Talk to me!' Paterson stirred, coughing, too weak to move, his body trying to expel the water from his lungs.

With his back pushed into the wall and a half-conscious Paterson lying on his chest, all Clocks could do was wait it out. Two minutes later, the water slowed its pace to a manageable level. 'Ray! Ray! Wake up, you dozy fucker. I can't 'old on 'ere forever. You gotta get offa me. People will talk.'

With that, Paterson spluttered and coughed hard. He shook his head and stood himself up. He wiped the water from his face, spat several times and vomited.

'Jesus! I drank shit! Oh my God.' He spat and coughed again. 'A mouthful of shit!'

Clocks hauled himself up and dropped himself next to Paterson. 'Were you sittin' down under that water?' he said to him.

Paterson heaved again then spat some more. He coughed half a dozen times. 'Yeah. Water . . . was taking me . . . losing my . . . grip. The water took me off the ladder and I . . . and I dropped down. So, I'm underwater, I grabbed out, caught a rung, pulled myself forward and hooked my arm through it . . . and . . . held on. His breathing was laboured. He spat again. 'The water pressure wouldn't let me . . . stand up. Had to . . . wait it out. No choice.'

'So, what you're sayin' is, I didn't 'ave to 'ang upside down and put me shoulder out again?'

'No . . . sorry, mate. Thanks for coming to get me, though.'

'Oh, it was a pleasure, mate. Absolute pleasure. Think nothing of it.'

'Why did you jump on my head?'

'Because I didn't bloody know you were 'avin' a nice little sit down, did I?'

'No. I suppose not. What would you have done if I wasn't there?'

'Come and found you.'

'Really? You'd have chanced it in that maelstrom of water in the hope of saving me?'

'I dunno what *maelstrom* means, but if it means a bloody great load of water, then yeah, I would.'

'Even with all that shit floating about?'

'Yep. Even with shit floatin' about.'

'Even with the rats? There would have been a lot of rats.'

Clocks shuddered. 'Yep. Even with rats.'

Paterson smiled. 'I love you.'

'Fuck off, bender.'

Paterson laughed, coughed and then retched. 'John, I think I've swallowed some shit, mate.'

Clocks nodded. 'Yeah, I know. You did mention it a little while ago, funny enough. Don't forget the piss too. Must 'ave drank a couple of gallons of that. Still, ne'er mind. Bet it all tastes better than that organic plant crap you eat an' drink for yer dinner every day.' Clocks shuddered.

Clocks made his way out of the sewer, followed by a shaky Paterson. On the grass, Monkey Harris had done his best to cover Suzi Rocket with his jacket. Clocks pulled off his jacket and laid it over her legs.

'She alive?' he said to Harris.

'Yeah, but only just. Paramedics aren't too far away. Two minutes.'

'Keep an eye on 'er, Monkey.'

Clocks sat himself down on the grass. Paterson joined him. Flashing lights turned into Mason Street as people started to gather. Neighbours, intrigued and scared at the sight of so many police cars in their quiet little road, came scuttling out of their houses to see what the commotion was about. Gossip began to go back and forth. Some lifted their mobile phones to take video.

'Good job, Ray. We got 'er back,' said Clocks.

Exhausted, Paterson hung his head and spat on the grass. 'Yeah. Good job. Couldn't face losing another one. How bad is she, d'you know?'

'Nah. Bit 'ard to tell. She's absolutely smothered in cuts though. Bastards did a right number on 'er. Should think if she 'asn't bled out, she'll be ravaged with infections now, poor little cow. Can't see a tetanus jab bein' much 'elp to 'er.'

'Probably right. C'mon then.' Paterson pulled himself up of the grass.

'Where we goin'?'

'To get those three little pricks we left in the office block. And I've got a score to settle with the Anderson kid. I think he'll try and resist arrest again.'

Clocks got to his feet with some effort. 'Oh, leave off, Ray. He's already resisted it to the point of 'avin' a broken face, a stab wound in the shoulder *and* been chucked through a wooden door, treatin' 'imself to a few solid cuts to 'is face an' 'ands on the way through it.'

'Too much?'

'Yeah, I reckon so, mate. We've already gotta tell the wankers from Professional Standards that he threw a right wobbler an' started wavin' that big bastard sword about in a mad fit.'

'What about the other two? They witnessed it.'

'Witnessed what? All they heard was him shoutin'. All they saw was him 'eadbuttin' the glass and landin' on the deck. They don't know if 'e went for you and you defended yerself, do they? All they know is, the fucker lost, big time.'

'Will it work?'

'Dunno. Who cares?' He grinned.

Three other members of the team had arrived and were milling around, concerned for him and Clocks but more concerned for Suzi.

'Monkey!' Paterson waved Harris over.

'S'up, boss?'

'You know the old derelict office block just off of Queen Elizabeth Street?'

Harris nodded.

'Temple Anderson and two others are there having themselves an oxygen-deprived lie down. All under arrest for murder most foul. Take a couple with you and get them to the nick for me, please.'

'On my way.'

'Oh, and Monkey . . .'

'Yes, boss.'

'Take a paramedic with you. Turns out Anderson resisted arrest quite a bit more than he should have.'

Monkey Harris grinned. 'Yes, boss.'

CHAPTER FIFTY-ONE

'So, Alice came through for you, eh?' Wallace Young sat opposite Paterson and Clocks back in the café in Greenwich Park. He nursed a small cup of tea that had far too much milk in it for his liking. Clocks did mention it when he brought it back to the table, but it wasn't very high on Young's list of things to talk about.

'He did indeed. Bright young man, that,' said Paterson.

'Bloody weirdo if you ask me.' Clocks sat himself down, spilling some of his coffee as he did so and sending a stream of dark brown liquid toward the edge of the table and his trousers. 'Bollocks!' he said, before grabbing a fistful of serviettes off the table and mopping up the mess he'd made. 'What was I sayin'?'

'I believe you called Alice a "bloody weirdo",' said Young.

'Right an' all. D'you know what he gets up to in that place?'

Young nodded. 'Why? Is it a problem?'

'It's not a problem, Wol. Whichever what way you wrap it up, it's just bloody weird. I mean, grown men poncin' about in nappies and feedin' 'emselves off of a pregnant woman's thruppennies. Not right, mate. None of it.'

'Thruppennies?' Young had a slightly perplexed look on his face.

'Thruppenny bits. Tits.'

Young raised an eyebrow. 'I see.'

'I thought you were a Londoner?' said Clocks.

'I am. But I'm not one of the fucking common ones,' Young said in precise, clipped tones.

Clocks, sipping at his coffee, snorted and laughed at the same time, causing him to choke. As he coughed and went red in the face, Paterson patted him on the back until Clocks caught his breath again. He wiped away the tears on his cheeks with the heels of his hands.

'You okay?' said Paterson.

Clocks nodded. 'Yeah. Bloody tickled me, that did. I'm all right, I'm okay.'

'Did he ask you to one of his parties by any chance?' said Young.

'Yeah.' Clocks sniffed.

'What one?'

'Didn't say?'

'Do you like sadomasochism? That's on a Tuesday.'

Clocks shook his head.

'Nursery is on Wednesday — usually. Depends on the number of interested parties. You don't fancy being part of that, then?'

'No, I fuckin' well don't.' Clocks shuffled around in his seat.

'Do you like "sploshing"?'

Clocks wrinkled his nose. 'Come again. *Sploshin'?* What's that when it's at 'ome?'

Paterson had a grin on his face.

Young looked up to the ceiling for a second. 'Let's see. How to put it? It's a form of wet fetish.'

'A what? What's a wet fetish? Never 'eard of it.'

'Imagine you're sitting in a bath.'

'Yeah,' said Clocks.

'A bath full of baked beans.'

Clocks cocked his head slightly.

'And someone else joins you by emptying buckets full of beans over you. Or, you might be seated in a chair and another person rubs spaghetti over your body and genitals.'

Clocks looked at Young. 'Shut up! They don't? Spaghetti! That's not a thing, is it?' He turned to Paterson. 'Is it?'

'Yep,' said Paterson.

'*Really?* What for? What's the point of that, then?'

'It's a fetish. A kink. It turns some people on.'

Clocks looked back at Paterson. '*Really?* Is it 'ot or cold?'

'Does it matter?' Paterson tried not to laugh.

'Right, it does. Too 'ot and I could end up with burned bollocks. Too cold and it'll shrink me todger. If you're gonna do that, it's gotta be the right temperature, surely.'

'Quite right, Goldilocks,' said Young. 'So, you could go for sploshing as long as the temperature's just right?'

'No to sploshin' — at all!' Clocks sniffed indignantly and rubbed his nose.

'Zoophilia . . .' said Young. 'How about that?'

'What's that?'

'Sex with animals.'

'Oh, Jesus, Wol!'

'No? Not for you? Well, you won't like Fridays then.'

Paterson lost it and burst out laughing. Young joined him.

Clocks shook his head. 'Fuckin' weirdos,' he muttered to himself.

After a minute or so, the two men pulled themselves together and picked up their cups.

'So, why'd you drag us out 'ere again, Wol?' said Clocks. He drained his coffee.

'I have a proposition.'

'Oh, fuck,' said Clocks. 'It's not one of those sorts of parties at your place on a Saturday is it? Gawd knows what you'll 'ave in mind.'

'You're fine, John. Look, I've been thinking for some time now that I'd like to start up a business of my own, and I wondered if you two would be interested in joining me.'

'What sort of business, Wol?' said Paterson.

'It's a private investigations company.'

'What?' said Clocks. 'You're gonna be a PI? And you want us to do that too? Me an' 'im?'

Young nodded. 'Well, yes and no. By private investigators, I don't mean the sort that sit in cars all day spying on women having extramarital sex.'

'Really? That's a pity. I'd 'ave done that for nothing.'

Paterson shook his head. Part of him knew that Clocks was serious.

'I'm talking about a high-level business that operates globally. Over the years, I've built up strong relationships with ranking police officers and high-level business executives. In my discussions with them, it's apparent that there is a market for us, and with our combined experience, we would have a good head start. I'm talking about high-level fraud, kidnappings, murders — your speciality — drug cartel operations, that sort of thing.

'You've just caught a gang of killers, one of whom killed the commissioner of police. You've proved that you two weren't involved, and that nonsense about your being behind Chief Inspector Lambert's death is just that. Nonsense. That will go away. I don't think you realise just how much news of your methods has travelled. Many people outside of the UK have heard of you. Your kind of unorthodoxy makes you very attractive to a certain kind of client.

'You'd pretty much have free rein to travel wherever the work is. Worldwide. And, let's face it, there's nothing here for you in the police service, is there? You're watched pretty much twenty-four-seven and people are desperate to lock you two up. Seems to me like you have little to lose, and you've both talked about leaving the job often enough. Now's your chance. Think about it.' Young shuffled back in his seat and crossed his arms.

'Did you know we're suing the Met?' said Paterson, sidestepping the issue.

'I'd heard whispers, yes. Good for you, young man.' Young beamed a smile at him. 'Take the buggers for every penny you can. They've treated you both appallingly.'

'So, if we do agree,' said Clocks, 'will there be *any* spying on wayward women?'

'I'm sure it can be arranged, but I don't know how your wife-to-be will take to it.'

Clocks frowned. 'How's she gonna know?'

'I was going to ask her to join us too. And Alice.'

Clocks wobbled his head slightly. 'What? Lyndsey? Alice? Are you jokin'?'

'Not at all. Lyndsey is SCO19. Extremely calm under pressure, able to think clearly at all times, a weapons expert and can hold her own in a fight. She'd be perfect.'

'I'm not sure I'd wanna work with the missus all day. That won't end well,' said Clocks.

'Give it some thought, John. That's all I'm asking.'

'And Alice? Why 'im?'

'Already said. He's a genius with computers. Who better to help us gain access to people and places without their knowledge?'

Clocks nodded. 'Yep. I can see that.'

'I have vacancies for other field investigators. Anyone you fancy for the work?'

Paterson pondered for a couple of seconds. 'Yeah. Monkey Harris and Dusty Doneghan. They're good men. They'll be up for any grunt work, if that's what you're looking for.'

Young nodded. 'I also wanted to bring in a couple of others.'

The two looked at him, both intrigued.

'DC Jackie Hartnett is one. She'll start off in the office at first, and hopefully, when she's fully recovered, she can join you in the field.'

'I dunno about 'er workin' in an office at the moment, Wol. Poor little mare got stabbed in the throat didn't she? She's gonna be pretty shit at answerin' the phones.'

'And who's the other one?' said Paterson.

'Ah. Here's where it gets a bit tricky. Not sure you'll be too onboard with this one.'

Paterson's frown deepened. 'Go on.'

'Well, I tracked down the White Ghost. Remember him?'

Paterson's jaw dropped.

'Bumpy!' said Clocks.

'Ah,' said Young. 'You do remember him.'

Paterson nodded. 'Of course I do. Ex-military. Army sniper. Extremely formidable. Took out the African General and his wife. They were killing kids for magic rituals. How the hell did you track him down? I thought he'd slipped back to Africa.'

'I have my methods,' said Young. 'Besides, what sort of agency would I be fronting if I couldn't even find one man to recruit?'

'Point taken,' said Paterson.

'I remember 'im too,' said Clocks.

'Why'd you call him Bumpy?' said Young.

''Cos of all the people 'e bumped off.'

'He didn't like you too much, did he?' said Paterson.

Clocks shrugged. 'No one likes me. I don't care.'

'I seem to remember you once told me, John — and I quote — that he could "shoot the nut sack off of a fly at a thousand yards",' said Young. 'You remember that?'

'Sounds like the sort of thing I'd say. He *was* a bit tasty with a rifle, weren't 'e, Ray?'

'Bloody lethal,' Paterson nodded.

'Well, just so we're clear,' said Clocks. 'I ain't goin' on any surveillance jobs with 'im.'

'Why not?' said Young.

'Well, for starters 'e's an albino white man. The fucker practically glows in the dark 'e's so white. Bloody whiter than me, an' that's sayin' somethin'.'

'Are you sure, about him, Wol?' said Paterson. 'He's a stone-cold killer. No conscience at all. He told me once he doesn't see people, only targets, like a computer game.'

Young rubbed his chin. 'Believe me, I've thought it over and over. I've lain awake at nights thinking about it, but in the end it comes down to the fact that he's highly trained in so many other areas too — communications, escape and evasion, hand-to-hand combat, you name it. I believe he would be an asset.'

Paterson looked at Wallace Young carefully. He was very fond of the older man. He had always had their backs for them in the short time he'd known them. Stuck his neck out way too far sometimes. Argued with people higher up than him, pulled a few strokes when they needed bailing out of trouble and, of course, went to America with them when they chased after the criminal psychopath Albert Tanner. That little jaunt nearly cost Young his life. And here he was now, offering them a way out of their miserable lives, working for an organisation that didn't give a damn about their little idiosyncrasies.

'So, let me get this clear . . .' he said. 'Although this is an investigations agency, you're hiring one of the most formidable snipers in the world plus a highly weapons-trained SCO19 officer. It kinda sounds like you're expecting trouble.'

'I have to be honest. It's a distinct possibility. But who knows trouble better than you four?'

'Hmm. I'm not sure,' said Paterson. 'Sounds like we could be jumping out of the frying pan into a deep fat fryer.'

'What?' said Clocks. 'He's givin' us the chance to go traipsing off all over the world visiting exotic places, spyin' on people and flyin' business class everywhere?' He looked across at Young. 'It will be business class, yeah?'

Young nodded. 'There's a good possibility.'

Clocks looked back at Paterson. 'It's up to you, Ray. Do we really wanna be free agents, choosing what we do, staying in swanky 'otels and the like?'

Paterson sighed. 'Honestly? I'd like to . . .'

'Ah,' said Young. 'That's a no, then?'

Clocks's shoulders dropped.

Paterson looked at Young. 'Never say never, Wol. It's just that I don't know if I'm ready to leave just yet. There's a lot left to do in the Met.'

Young chortled. 'Seriously? You're the one who always brings up leaving the job. I thought you'd have bitten my arm off for a crack at something like this.'

'You're right. But while I was off on the sick I had time to think. Long and hard. Look, I know the job is done with me and John — and I can't speak for him — but I'm not done with the job. I don't know why. It's stupid, I know. But, I feel I . . . *we* have to prove ourselves still. I feel like there's this cloud always hanging over us all the time. That even people that we get along with are looking at us sometimes and wondering. Wondering if we are dodgy, if we are criminals, if we are killers. And I just feel that if we walk now, people will see it as us running. Running before the hammer drops. And I can't go forward thinking that's what people think of us — dodgy cops that did a runner before we got caught and put away.'

Young sighed deeply and nodded slowly. 'I get it. I can see your point. Don't agree with you, of course, and I'm sorry you feel that way, but I do get it. I do. John? I suspect I already know the answer, but what about you?'

Clocks had leaned back on a desk with his arms folded. 'Well, I love the idea meself. Gallivantin' about all over the world, meetin' new an' interestin' people, gettin' to rip the piss out of 'em an' then give 'em a good 'iding. Right up my alley, that is. But it's a no-brainer, mate. If 'e's stayin', I'm stayin'.'

Paterson gave him a weak smile. 'John—'

'Nope. I'm with you, mate. Besides, who else am I gonna work with? Who else is gonna put up with all my shit day after day? Who else is gonna keep an eye on you when you fuck up an' get yerself in a tight spot? Who else is gonna bring you your favourite whatthefuckacoffees an' take you to all the greasy spoons you like so much? I'll tell yer who — nobody. So, it's more puppy walkin' for me until you learn 'ow to be a real copper.'

'John . . . I don't know what—'

'Turn it in, Ray. Don't go gettin' all misty eyed an' girly on me, you big ol' tart. It is what it is. No big deal, is it?'

Paterson shook his head. 'I'm sorry—'

'I said *turn it in*. It's done. We crack on with pissin' off everyone in Bermondsey and the Metropolitan Police. I'm good with that.'

'I was going to say sorry to Wol,' said Paterson, 'but whatever.' He grinned at Clocks, who promptly gave him the finger.

'Gentlemen,' said Young, 'I understand. Thank you for listening to me and hearing me out. Just know that if you change your mind at any time, you two are in. No ifs, no buts. Just call me. Understood?'

Both men nodded.

'Where you off to now then, Wol?' said Paterson.

'I'm off to see John's better half and see if she wants to come and work with me. We always did get on well,' he said, with a sly grin on his face.

'Oi! You ol' bugger. Don't you go near 'er. Keep yer wrinkly ol' 'ands off of 'er, y'hear me? You're as bad as Ray.'

'I'll see you two soon,' said Young. 'John, is there anything you want me to say to Lyndsey when I get there?'

'Fuck off out of it, you ol' sod!' said Clocks.

'Take good care of yourselves, boys.' With that, Wallace Young left the building.

CHAPTER FIFTY-TWO

'Well, gentlemen, it seems as if you have had yet another productive few days.' Deputy Assistant Commissioner Sam Morne poured out a small glass of whisky for himself and a larger glass for Paterson and Clocks. He settled himself back into his chair and took stock of the two men opposite him. They looked weary and worn down, but he had come to know that these two would be up and running again. Soon. For now, they needed a boost.

'I have to say, you did an incredible job again. Four suspects in custody, all facing life sentences, and we'll be pushing for "life means life" at their trial.'

'They'll get off with a nut 'n' gut report, guv,' said Clocks.

Morne frowned at him. 'A psychiatric report? That's a possibility, I suppose. I'm told all four do have a history of mental health issues, but we're prepared for that as a possible defence. Should it go that way, then we're recommending that they be detained at Her Majesty's pleasure. Either way, we're looking to keep them inside for the rest of their natural lives.'

Paterson nodded and took a sip of his whisky. He grimaced and tapped at his chest as the drink burned his gullet. He coughed slightly. 'That's good enough for me,' he said. 'Sick bastards, all of them.'

'Indeed,' said Morne. 'How are you both? You look . . . tired.'

'That's 'cos we *are* tired,' Clocks said. He drained his glass and screwed his face up. 'Fuck me, guv. What you given us 'ere? Diesel? Good gawd. You coulda got the good stuff out for us.'

'That is good stuff, John — do you mind if I call you John?'

'I'd prefer you called me an ambulance. This is poison, mate. Poison.'

'That's actually a twenty-five-year-old single malt. I suspect you're not acquainted with the taste.'

'Twenny-five years? That's why it's 'orrible, then. It's gone off. Aint'cha got anything newer in yer drawer?'

Morne smiled. 'Ah. I see. You're winding me up aren't you? I've heard about this. That's what you do, isn't it? I get it.'

'Ain't winding you up, guv. This is rough.'

'I don't think he is, sir,' said Paterson. 'His whisky normally costs about seven pounds a bottle. Fifteen for three bottles at Christmas if Lidl's having a special.'

'Fuck right off,' said Clocks. He put his glass down on Morne's desk.

'It would have helped if you'd sipped it,' said Paterson.

'Would it? I don't think so.' Clocks shook his head. 'Nasty.'

'Moving on,' said Morne. 'I asked you here today to thank you, obviously, and also to let you know that I've written you both up for commendations. I'm putting you forward for Detective Investigation of the Year plus silver medal awards from the Royal Humane Society for your acts of bravery. You both put your lives at risk, and that is something that needs to be recognised. And the Police Federation want you to receive bravery awards. Personally, I think you should have a ton of them. I'll see what else is available.' He beamed at them.

'Is there a wage increase to go with all them gongs?' said Clocks.

Morne looked taken aback. 'What? A wage increase? No, I don't think so.'

'Then you can keep 'em, guv. If there's no extra dosh in it for us, then they're just bits of paper. Apart from the medals. They're probably zinc.'

'I don't understand.'

'What John's saying is thanks but no thanks,' said Paterson. 'We appreciate what you're doing, sir, but we really don't need awards. All we ask is that we can get on with our jobs without having to look over our shoulders every five minutes. If you can fix that, that's something we would be happy to accept.'

'I'm ahead of you, Ray. I'm calling a meeting with a number of heads of department in the coming week. A few people will be spoken to and made to understand the position. Things will be a little easier for you both. You have my word.'

'Thank you, sir. Much appreciated.'

'So . . . that aside, I understand you two have turned down Wallace Young's offer, yes?'

Both men tensed slightly

'It's all right. He told me himself. It's a shame for him but a plus for the Met. Are you sure?'

Paterson nodded. 'For now, yes. Things may change in the future. We'll see.'

'So,' said Morne. 'What have you found out about these so-called knights?'

Paterson cleared his throat. 'From what we can make of it so far is that they were all at uni together and they all had the same sort of interest in history. The methods of torture used back then fascinated them to the point where they became obsessed. Searching their properties, we found loads of books and articles on the subject. They all felt that the punishments we have today for crimes were a bit . . . weak. So, they decided to form their own little group to hand out punishments to those criminals who managed to walk free. In order to test themselves, to see what they were really capable of, they decided to rehearse on their respective parents. They'd all suffered abuse in one form or another from their families and none of them had any love or respect for their parents. Lavery hated his father with a passion.

'Which one was he again? Remind me.'

'The Sawn Man.'

'Indeed.'

'It's highly unusual for newbies to the murder scene to carry out such gross murders first go around, but this mob all had mental health issues and had been working themselves up for years. I think they'd done these killings so many times in their heads that when it came to *actually* doing it, it was nothing to them. Literally a dream come true.'

Morne shook his head.

'What about the woman, this "Rakes", wasn't it?'

'Yeah,' said Clocks. 'She's an odd ol' bod that one. Clever girl. Got all the right qualifications, doin' well for 'erself, but got 'erself hiked up with Anderson's kid. They became a couple. Turns out she was as batty as a box of frogs too. Daddy brought her up alone and, well . . . you can guess where that story goes. Used to lock 'er in a cupboard when she came 'ome from school until it was time for playtime in the evenin's. She reckons he used to chuck 'er dog in there with 'er and 'ol Rover didn't like that one little bit. Bit her a few times, she said.

'That's why she, and the other 'erberts, chucked 'im in a sack and sprinkled in an assortment of animals. Bit of the ol' revenge pie served up on the cold side. She was never at the other killin's though. Didn't 'ave the stomach for it.'

'Do you know how DS Rocket is doing, sir?' said Paterson.

'Yes. Latest report I have is that she is out of danger but still very sick. All manner of disease got in through those cuts, and I'm afraid she'll be in hospital for a while yet.' He shook his head. 'We're not sure yet if she will suffer permanent scarring. A few of the cuts on her face were quite deep.'

Paterson instinctively touched his own jaw, feeling the new scar tissue under his stubble.

'She'll be scarred alright,' said Clocks. He tapped the side of his temple. 'In the nut. That sort of shit stays for life.'

'Get her whatever she needs, sir. I know a good plastic surgeon,' said Paterson.

'D'you know 'ow many cuts she 'ad in the end, guv?' said Clocks.

'Er, yes. She was about ten shy of a thousand.'

'You owe me twenny quid, Ray. Told you they'd lose count an' fuck it up.'

Morne frowned. 'Yes. Right. Well, good to see you again.'

Paterson and Clocks stood, hands outstretched.

'Thank you, sir,' Paterson said. 'For believing in us. Means a lot.'

Handshakes over, they headed for the door.

'Ooh! Guv,' said Clocks.

'Yes?'

'Is Mr Stannard in his office, d'you know?'

'Yes, he is. I think. He should be. Why?'

'No reason,' said Clocks as he swanned out of the office and closed the door behind him.

'Have fun, John,' said Morne, quietly.

* * *

Assistant Commissioner Stannard stood by a large window holding a small glass jug and was in the process of watering a plant. He jumped when his office door flew open. 'What the—?' he sputtered, spilling water over his shirt and trousers.

'You all right then, Pete?' said Clocks. Clocks peered at his shirt. 'You've spilt some. You need to be a bit careful.'

'What the hell are you doing, Clocks? You don't come barging into my office! Who the hell do you think you are?' Stannard's face had turned a nice florid colour.

Clocks looked back at the door. 'Bargin' in? Door was open, guv. I'm sure it was. Anyway, don't you senior managers have an "open-door" policy these days?'

'Get out, Clocks! Get out now!'

'Don't be like that, sir,' said Paterson as he wandered into the office. 'It's been a nice day so far. Don't spoil it.'

'What's going on here?' Stannard's voice took on a grave tone. 'What do you two want?'

'We were just down the hallway there, with the big guv'nor,' said Clocks, 'and just thought we'd pop by to say a big thank you for tryin' to 'ave us nicked an' failin' so badly. Gave us both a good ol' laugh that did, Pete. Good effort on your part — but no banana, me ol' sunshine.' He grinned at Stannard, who did his best to stare Clocks down.

'Don't you dare call me, Pete, Clocks. You address me as "sir", you understand me?'

Clocks raised his eyebrows. 'Really? I thought we were all mates now and on first-name terms. Jesus. What's wrong with this lot of seniors, Ray? No open-door policy. No first-name terms. Ain't even offered us a cup of tea. All very uncivilised, innit?'

'I said what do you want?'

'Nuffin',' said Clocks. 'Can't two people drop in on friends an' gloat?'

Stannard drew in a deep breath. 'Out you go. Both of you. I haven't got time for your childish games.'

'Oh, well. Fuck it, then. If you're gonna be arsey about it, we'll leave.' Clocks put his hand on the door handle.

'Good . . . Wait! Before you leave, Clocks, I want to ask you something.'

'Do yer? Go on then. I've got nothing on for the time bein'. 'Ow can I 'elp you, Mr Stannard?'

'Perhaps you could enlighten me as to why I've been receiving phone calls from strange men at all hours of the day and night asking if I could *service* them?'

Clocks grinned and shrugged. 'I dunno. Nothin' to do with me, mate.'

'Is that so? I ask because my private telephone number was scrawled all over the walls of the gentlemen's toilet down the hall *and*, I'm told, in a few public toilets not far from these offices.'

'Oh, dear. That's unfortunate. Wonder 'ow that happened.'

'I wondered that myself. I don't suppose it had anything to do with you, did it?'

'Told yer. Nothin' to do with me. Best you launch an investigation into it. You lot love an' investigation, doncha? Should keep you 'appy for a while.'

'I have launched an investigation, Mr Clocks. Violating the privacy of a senior police officer carries consequences.'

'So does pissin' me off, Pete. Now, if we're done 'ere, I'm off to the café. All this excitement 'as got me juices flowin'. Grub time. Know what I mean?'

Paterson shook his head. 'Close the door, John.'

Stannard frowned.

'I thought now would be a good time to let you know we're not playing games anymore, sir,' said Paterson. 'We wanted to have a quick chat with you.'

'Then make a bloody appointment.' Stannard slammed the little watering jug down on his desk.

'You don't seem overly busy,' said Paterson. 'I'm sure you can spare us a minute or two.'

Stannard glared at Paterson. 'Get on with it then. Say what you've come to say, then go.' He sat himself down behind his desk.

'We just wanted you to know that we get it,' said Paterson. 'We get that you want the next rung on the ladder — Mr Morne's top job when he goes. But you need to understand that *we're* not going anywhere. We'll still be doing our job when Sam goes, so I just thought it might be an idea to give you the heads-up about our intention to stay and tell you not to keep wasting your time and resources on us. There's nothing else to say, really. Just get out of our way and stay out of it.'

'Or what?' said Stannard, as he sat himself up. 'Are you threatening me, Paterson?'

Paterson shrugged and looked him in the eye. 'Threatening you? No, sir. That would make us the people you think we are. I'm just asking that you leave us alone to do our job. That's all.'

'Sounds like a threat to me.'

'Because that's what you want to believe. You, Anderson, DCI Lambert — you all want to think that we're criminals and you desperately search for things to reinforce your belief. It's hard to let go of a false belief if it's held deeply enough, so you do what everyone does when that belief is challenged by incontrovertible truth. You'll double down on it.'

Stannard rolled his eyes. 'Save me the pseudo-psychology bullshit, Paterson.'

'It's not bullshit, sir. It's fact. The thing is, when someone believes something so badly, it distorts their view of the world. A lot of people have died for their beliefs. Do you understand me?'

Stannard looked shocked. His stomach lurched. Clocks grinned at him.

'Are you . . . saying . . . are you saying what I think you're saying?'

'All I'm saying is, sir . . . don't die for *your* beliefs.'

Clocks opened the door. 'We done, Ray?'

'We're done, John. Thank you for your time, Mr Stannard. See you soon, no doubt.' He walked out of the office.

As Clocks reached the door he lifted his right leg and let rip with an enormous fart. 'An there's yer goodbye kiss from us, mate.' He closed the door behind him and ran to catch up with a laughing Paterson.

CHAPTER FIFTY-THREE

The crowd inside the wedding circle grew larger and larger as guest after guest made their way through the woodlands, having made the short walk from the car park to where Clocks and Lyndsey were about to be married. The wedding planners Paterson had hired had done a truly spectacular job. Everything was exactly as Lyndsey had wished for: a large canvas canopy strung beneath the trees, thousands of tiny white lights wrapped around the branches and trunks, and trained white doves and small woodland animals wandering around, being greeted by some and shooed away by others.

A small group of musicians played new-age-type music on guitars and harps while a young Irish girl sang the most haunting of melodies.

There to greet the arrivals was a beaming Ray Paterson and a very edgy Johnny Clocks. Paterson greeted everyone with a warm smile, a friendly handshake and a peck on the cheek for the ladies. Clocks smiled, mostly through gritted teeth, as people congratulated him and made various cooing noises about how beautiful everything was, telling him how happy they were for him and that his wife-to-be, Lyndsey, was a beautiful girl and he was so lucky to have her. He nodded politely, hugged them, cheek-kissed them or shook hands and thanked them for coming. He was genuinely pleased to see some people — others, not so much. Especially Uncle Dennis.

'And you are?' said Paterson, as he shook the old man's hand.

'I'm Dennis,' the old man said. 'I'm 'is uncle.' He pointed a bony finger at Clocks.

'Uncle Dennis!' Paterson's eyes widened. 'Are you . . . '

The old man wagged his head from side to side. 'Has 'e been callin' me "Dirty Dennis" again, the nasty little fucker?'

Paterson eyed Clocks suspiciously. 'He has as a matter of fact.'

'Little bastard. What he don't bleedin' tell anyone is that it's all bullshit. When he was a nipper, his muvver asked me to pick him up from the park one day and he was there playin' with 'is little mates. A couple of 'em was girls. I 'ad a bag of sweeties in me pocket and I offered them around and the little fucker started tellin' everyone I was a perv just for giggles. I knew I shouldn't 'ave come.'

'Well, if that's all there is to it, Dennis, you're all right, mate. Go take a seat for me, please.'

Paterson watched the old man toddle off down the aisle.

'Here, John.'

Clocks stopped what he was doing. 'Whassup?'

'You really do have an uncle Dennis, then?'

Clocks shrugged. 'Yeah. Told you I did. Did he have any sweeties with 'im?'

'I don't honestly know. He didn't show me any.'

'Well, if 'e does, watch yerself. As far as 'e's concerned, you're just a little kid to 'im, don't forget. And don't bend over in front of him either. He'll be up you like a rat up a drainpipe despite 'is dodgy knees.'

The guests made their way to the venue to be met by the ushers, Monkey Harris and Ronnie Doneghan.

By 7.50 p.m. everyone was seated, and a low hum of excitement provided an almost Zen-like vibration to the sounds of the musicians and the woodland. Lyndsey was due at eight.

'How you feeling, mate?' said Paterson, when everyone was seated.

'Truth? Scared shitless.'

Paterson chuckled. 'Yeah. It's a bit daunting. You'll be fine.'

'I know. I'm just a bit worried.'

Paterson frowned. 'About what?'

'That I'll fuck it up.'

'What? The evening or her entire life?'

Clocks burst out laughing. 'Funny bastard, you are.'

'You'll be all right. Just listen to what's being said. Do as the celebrant tells you and everything will be fine.' He put his hand on Clocks's shoulder. 'It'll be fine.'

'I know. Thanks, Ray. You're a real brick, y'know that?'

Paterson smiled.

Clocks looked behind him at the guests. 'I don't know 'alf of these people 'ere.'

'Doesn't surprise me. I didn't know most of the people at mine either.'

'I can't believe we're gettin' married in a fuckin' forest either. I mean, what's that about?'

'Lots of people do this now. I think it's lovely.'

'Lovely? I wanted a town hall job an' a drink up at the local boozer. Fish 'n' chips, the lot. Instead, I've got dangly spiders in me hair and fuckin' owls 'ootin' at me. There's pigeons flyin' around me 'ead and some geezer playin' some sort of fuck-off-big guitar. And . . . and there's some Irish bird squawkin' on about somethin' in some language I do not understand.'

'I know it's not what you wanted, but then, as we know, you're a heathen. Lyndsey did this partly for you too, y'know.'

'Me?'

'Yeah. She knows you were raised by wolves and figured you and your family would be at home here.'

'Har-de-har,' Clocks said. 'Funny fucker.'

'Listen, John. Tell me there's no surprises coming our way tonight before you stand up there. No bat-shit-crazy women you've pissed off likely to come screaming down the aisle, is there?'

'I don't think so. My Aunt Trish was bat-shit crazy and I pissed her off more than once, but I think she's dead. She was Uncle Dennis's wife. She got the 'ump with me startin' all those rumours about 'im.'

'I meant girlfriends. No pissed-off, jilted old flames likely to pop up?'

'Nah. Doubt that very much. I know it's 'ard to believe, but I ain't been all that lucky with the ladies.'

'I wonder if that's got anything to do with you being a misogynistic pig?'

Clocks shrugged. 'Dunno. Might've 'ad summing to do with it, I s'pose. But you make it sound like that's a bad thing, Ray.'

'C'mon, Romeo. Better go take our seats. She'll be here soon.'

'Yeah. You got the rings?'

'Of course I've got the rings. This is me we're talking about. Not you. You'd forget to turn up if it wasn't for me.'

'True. C'mon, then. Sit me down before me legs give out.'

As they turned to walk to their seats, Paterson heard a car pull up and doors slam from the car park in the distance. He stopped and turned.

'Whassamatter?' said Clocks.

'Nothing,' said Paterson. 'Either someone's late or Lyndsey's early. Go and sit down. I'll wait here for a minute until I know what's going on.'

Clocks moved off as Paterson walked toward the sound of voices coming closer.

A few seconds later, a young man, suited and booted hurried through the clearing. Holding his hand and a step or two behind him, immaculately dressed in a lemon two-piece complete with a large floppy white hat, was a strikingly attractive young girl.

'Don't bloody pull me, innit!' she said. 'I'll go arse over tit in these shoes.'

Paterson grimaced at the sound of her voice. Pure Southeast London wrapped up in a patois so favoured by the young these days. He made a mental bet with himself she would use the word *like* at least ten times before she sat down.

'Good evening,' said Paterson.

'All right, mate?' said the young man.

Paterson had the sudden feeling he knew him. 'You just made it in time,' he said, smiling and holding his hand out to the young lady.

'Yeah,' said the young man. ''Er bloody fault. Takes 'er a good two hours to cake 'er face in make-up. Looks like that Donald Trump geezer.'

Paterson looked at her face. It looked all right to him. The make-up *was* a bit on the orange side, but not that bad. 'Mind your step,' he said to her. 'It's a bit tricky in places.'

'Fanks, luv.' She looked at him for the first time. 'Blimey! Like, is it you what's gettin' married, then?'

'No, no. Not me.' Paterson squinted at her. 'Why?'

'Good to know, that's all. A bit of 'ope for us all, like.'

Paterson grinned. The man didn't.

'Not started 'as it? We got lost as well. Fuckin' GPS ain't no good on me Audi.'

'You're okay. Couple of minutes before the bride arrives. C'mon.'

Everyone turned at the arrival of the noisy young couple, Clocks included, before turning back to give the celebrant a nervous smile.

'You friends or family?' asked Paterson.

'Family,' said the young man.

'Okay.' Paterson quickly skimmed the crowd for two empty seats. 'Over there.' He pointed off to the side. 'Two there. See them?'

'Yep. Cheers, geezer.'

'Point of interest,' said Paterson. 'Bride or groom's family?'

The young man smiled. 'Groom's, mate. That's me dad up there gettin' married.'

THE END

ALSO BY STEVE PARKER

DETECTIVE RAY PATERSON BOOKS

Book 1: THEIR LAST WORDS
Book 2: THE LOST CHILDREN
Book 3: THE BURNING MEN
Book 4: YOU CAN'T HIDE
Book 5: THEIR DYING BREATH
Book 6: CHILD BEHIND THE WALL
Book 7: HIS MOTHER'S BONES

Thank you for reading this book.

If you enjoyed it please leave feedback on Amazon or Goodreads, and if there is anything we missed or you have a question about, then please get in touch. We appreciate you choosing our book.

Founded in 2014 in Shoreditch, London, we at Joffe Books pride ourselves on our history of innovative publishing. We were thrilled to be shortlisted for Independent Publisher of the Year at the British Book Awards.

www.joffebooks.com

We're very grateful to eagle-eyed readers who take the time to contact us. Please send any errors you find to corrections@joffebooks.com. We'll get them fixed ASAP.